A Shivery Tale Of Urban Horror.
Like *Rosemary's Baby*—
Somewhere Beyond Reason...

"The book brings shudders. . . . The climax is surprising, and the kind any reader of a sinister book will relish."
—*Pittsburgh Post-Gazette*

"A solid suspense story that gradually builds to a horrifying climax . . . casts an eerie light in shadows that will make the reader look nervously over his shoulder."
—*Sidney Sheldon*

THE GLOW

A NOVEL BY

Brooks Stanwood

FAWCETT CREST • NEW YORK

THE GLOW is a work of fiction. The characters and events depicted here are totally products of the author's imagination and any resemblance of the fictional characters to real persons, living or dead, or real events is coincidental.

THE GLOW

Published by Fawcett Crest Books, a unit of CBS Publications, the Consumer Publishing Division of CBS Inc., by arrangement with McGraw-Hill Book Company

ISBN: 0-449-24333-8

This book contains the complete text of the original hardcover edition.

Printed in the United States of America

Fawcett Crest printing: September 1980

7   6   5   4   3   2   1

In memory of
M.K., A.W.K. and C.E.P.
with love that keeps growing

Before

I have
immortal longings in me.
—Shakespeare
Antony and Cleopatra

Vinnie Romano carefully tucked his pint of Fleischmann's into the barrel of leaves, then stuck his heavy bristle broom in on top of it, handle first, and, whistling what he thought was an aria, started toward his next section. He had been with the Parks Department for twelve years, after seven in Sanitation. His first four years in a small park in the Bay Ridge section of Brooklyn had been a drag. No one to talk to. Hard to goof off. But since then he had been in Central Park, and he loved it. Always action. Even with the cuts and layoffs (thank God for his seniority!) there was still not much to do and lots to look at.

As he neared the reservoir he stopped to watch two young kids neck with a passion that was almost frightening. They couldn't have been more than sixteen, and the boy almost had her sweater off. Vinnie didn't linger long for he had seen more and better before. Whistling on, he passed the huge black man with the diamond front tooth who dealt grass, coke, and uppers to the kids from some of those fancy private schools. It was still too early for the man's business, and he lounged on the park bench reading a copy of *Hustler*. A well-tailored young woman on a dove-gray horse cantered by, followed by an older man on a large bay. They both could ride. Vinnie couldn't keep count of how many people he had had to call ambulances for who had taken falls, some very bad. He told his wife, Angie, "Better to bet them than ride them. The fuckers are too high off the ground."

And then he saw them. His favorites. Of all the weird, dippy, bizarre people in the park, his favorites were the Pacemaker Pacers. He had named them himself and was proud of the tag. They ran every day, and all wore matching powder-blue jogging suits. Their number fluctuated. Sometimes there were as many as eight, but never fewer than three. There were four men and four women. And not one of them was under fifty-five.

Vinnie leaned against his broom as they glided by. It was probably their second lap, and they hadn't broken into a sweat. And that was with each lap at slightly under 1.6 miles. They really looked good today. Their skin glowed with a healthy flush, and they ran with a sprightly bounce.

As they moved away from him, mushroom puffs

of dry cinders kicked up by their Adidas running shoes hung for a moment in their wake. With legs pumping high and smooth they disappeared around the bend.

Part One

1

MARCH

"If you can't put them on without pain, dear, the *effect* just *won't* be there."

Jackie Lawrence gritted her teeth as the two salesmen, Darby and Syd, pulled and jammed her tiny figure into a pair of even tinier French jeans. She had read about the shop in *Women's Wear Daily* ("the Bible"), which was delivered daily to her office at Henri Bendel. Everyone thought her figure looked great, except Pete, who always found her pants baggy. So here she was at the Le Derriere Monde with two muscular but sweet (and totally safe) salesmen wrestling her into a pair of jeans that Tatum O'Neal would have had to reduce to get into.

"Positively Grecian," said Syd as he stepped back to assess the image.

"I'm having trouble breathing."

"It's a small price to pay, dear," said Darby.

"Positively sculpted," said Syd, now a few steps further back.

She had to admit that she noticed heads turning as she walked up Madison toward Seventy-ninth to catch the cross-town bus.

Pete once asked Jackie what three presents she would like most in the world if they suddenly became rich. She didn't remember if the first was a super house in the Berkshires or a designer collection every year for the rest of her life. But she knew that the third was definitely an eternal low number at the cold cuts counter at Zabar's.

This flashed through Jackie's mind as she waded into the crowd in Zabar's, the last stop on her way home. Zabar's was to the New York food freak what the Sandoz experimental drug lab was to an addict. Above the babble of voices and cash registers and slicing machines came a mistral aroma of cheeses, spices, coffees, charcuterie of bewildering ethnicity, and cold fish of every kind from Scottish salmon to kippered white fish. She inhaled deeply and slid her newly contoured self to the cold cuts department where she grabbed a ticket: 94. They were only up to customer 79, so Jackie struggled to the back of the store for a jar of cornichons and a pound of freshly ground coffee. By the time she made it back to cold cuts they had just hit the 90s.

Number 90 was a zaftig lady with an inordinate fondness for American Indian jewelry. "Sir," said the woman, "I'm buying Westphalian ham, not paper." She pointed an accusatory finger at the counterman. "Please don't put paper between each slice. Use it to line your parakeet's cage."

"Lady, this is wax paper, not tar paper. It doesn't weigh a thing."

"I'd like to hear you say that to Betty Furness."

"Lady, I'd say it to Sadat."

The West Side, Jackie smiled; it did have its moments.

Jackie's good humor faded as she entered their apartment. When they'd moved in two years ago, shortly before they were married, they'd been pleased. The bedroom was small, the kitchen even smaller, but the living room had potential. And it was cheap. They gave everything two coats of white paint. A paint chip of geological thickness revealed that some fool had painted the kitchen black once, and the black still crept through in spots.

The line being given out then by the decorating honchos was that all it took was a thousand dollars and a little imagination to create a stylish-looking apartment from scratch. What they hadn't said was that to pull it off you had to have either the instincts of a Billy Baldwin or a great space to work with. And what they hadn't had in mind was what real estate people called a "junior three"—and one with all the lightness and airiness of a cave. In recent months Jackie's disappointment had escalated to dissatisfaction, then dislike, and now loathing. The sooner they checked out of here, the happier she would be.

When Jackie heard Pete's key in the lock, she

had almost finished frying eggplant for a spaghetti sauce as feisty as her temper. The air was dense with smoke. She eased the last two pieces into the skillet as he came into the kitchen.

Pete was a shade under six feet but gave the impression of being taller because he stood so straight. He had lively brown eyes that seemed darker under a head of tight, black curls.

"I bet I can guess what we're having for dinner," he said, sniffing the air. "I think folks in the Village know, too."

"You loved this dish the last time I made it," said Jackie quickly.

"Hey, take it easy," Pete said, hugging her. "Now kiss me before I crack your spine and send the remains to Paul Bocuse."

Jackie tilted her head up and smiled. Pete always could get to her. Thank God! She had blond hair, gray-blue eyes, and classic features that had been the envy of her friends at school as soon as they were old enough to realize that some girls are prettier than others. At age thirteen, she had worried obsessively that she'd be short when she grew up. She turned out to barely top five feet, but everything else checked out fine. Now she reached up and ran her fingers through Pete's wiry hair and pulled his head toward her.

"You taste great," Pete said. "How about skipping dinner?"

"How about postponing it? I've already invested a half hour in it."

"My time-and-motion expert," he said, laughing.

"At least come sit down. We can just catch the seven o'clock news."

Jackie pulled the cooked eggplant from the pan and called after Pete as he headed for the living room.

"Anything happen in the great world of publishing today?"

"Not much. Aside from having my mind blown and being very depressed all day."

"What are you talking about?"

"Well, I stopped at the candy store downstairs and picked up the *Times*. As usual. Then I went down to wait for the train, which was late. As usual. Anyway, I started to look through the paper and when I got to the obit page, damn it if Sheldon Haber's face didn't jump out at me."

"Who's he?"

"You remember. You met him at the Doubleday party at ABA in San Francisco. The guy who thought you had great legs."

"Oh! The small, round man who was guzzling those martinis?"

"Right. Probably the best editor of serious fiction around. Dead. At the New School. Five minutes into a question-and-answer period after delivering a lecture on 'Pynchon and the New WASP Imagination.' Just keeled over. Thirty-nine!"

"That's terrible."

"Yeah. I had lunch with him last week. At the Italian Pavilion. They knew him better there than they knew the owner. He had three dry Bombay martinis. Tortellini in brodo. A bowl, not a cup. Vitello tonnato, with a side order of creamed spinach. And then some rum cake with a snifter of Remy Martin. He did that five days a week. Only sometimes the food was French. The most strenuous exercise he ever had was carrying bound galleys home in his attache case."

"It sounds like nobody pushed him."

"You're right. And it's got me thinking about myself. And you, too. Maybe it's being thirty. I don't mind getting older, but I don't want to deteriorate."

"You've been to too many Bergman movies."

"What I mean, babes, is that the better we take care of ourselves, the better everything else will be. Sheldon was an extreme case, but we drink too much, too. And we like good—meaning rich—food."

He took hold of her shoulders and turned her toward him. "You're beautiful. And I'm not half bad myself. But I want us to stay this way. I'm out of shape. And I don't like it. I could go on. But the bottom line is we have to watch ourselves. And exercise."

"Good idea. I've got a copy of that Royal Canadian exercise manual somewhere."

"Jackie, I'm not talking about touching your toes and waving your arms in the air five minutes a day. I'm serious. We should *really* do something. Like jogging. We can go over to Riverside Drive, run up to, say, Ninety-sixth Street, then loop back on the promenade. I figure that's about a mile and a half. Or we could run around the reservoir in Central Park."

"I'm beginning to be afraid you mean it."

"You're damned right."

Jackie assessed Pete silently.

"This calls for a drink," she said, jumping up. Then she remembered the new jeans. "Darling," she said, pirouetting in front of him, "don't you notice anything new and different around here?"

"Oh, wow," said Pete delightedly. "They're perfect. How could I have missed them?"

Jackie leaned down and gave him a long kiss. "Be right back," she said, straightening up and heading toward the kitchen.

"Get me a drink, too, will you, love?" Pete called after her. She poured Pete a Stolichnaya, then constructed a martini for herself. She and poor Sheldon Haber, hooked on that drink.

"Okay," she said, coming back into the living room. "I think you're going overboard. But I'll make you a deal. I'll start jogging with you. But I want something in return."

"What?"

"A new apartment."

"Oh sure. Let's start the process again. It'll make this dump look good after we see the rents being asked for other dumps."

"Come on. Show a little enthusiasm. You're like an old hound dog. As long as you know where to find your dish and a warm place to sleep, you're content."

"Don't forget Stolichnayas and a nice round tush to bump against occasionally," he said, cupping her fanny appreciatively.

"I mean it, Pete. This place is getting to me. We were talking the other day about building some more bookcases. Where are we going to put them? In the elevator? And look at these walls. Gray! Besides, I've had it with the West Side."

"Where's your loyalty?"

"My loyalty stops at Zabar's, and on off days it doesn't go that far. I want a place like Allan and Trish's."

"And I'd like to make sixty thousand a year like Allan. Remember, I'm an editor, not a banker."

"I'm not saying we have to live on Seventieth and Park. But I'd sure like to give it a try."

"I capitulate. This weekend it's apartment-hunting. *And* jogging."

"You nut, I love you," she said, sliding toward Pete. She put her head in his lap and pulled him down toward her. They kissed, their tongues tingling from the booze.

"Now," said Pete, "get up and get out of this gear."

Jackie pulled her shirt and bra off. Pete ran his hands over her breasts, gently pinching her nipples. As she bent down to step out of her pants, he pressed his face against the small of her back and took a bite.

"I feel very kinky tonight," he said into her back.

"I wouldn't want you any other way."

2

Jackie knew what she wanted, which in real estate parlance was an apartment in a "prewar drmn bldg, spacious, brite, 4½ rms." They had decided they would not insist on *hi clgs*, a *wbf*, *parq flrs*, *south expos*, a *vu*, or an *eat-in kit*, but that they must have a *drmn* (though not the kind decked out as a policeman), *lite* (Jackie had had it with dracaenas and philodendrons), and *2 BRs* (Pete wanted a study). They ruled out new, so-called luxury highrises, with their thin walls, cramped rooms, and lobbies filled with stained glass, fake stone grottoes, chandeliers, and plastic palms. They decided to first look in the East Seventies and Eighties, and they set an upper limit on the rent of eight hundred dollars, which they both knew meant that they would go to eight-fifty if sufficiently tempted.

The next morning, Jackie canceled her lunch

date with a rep from a Seventh Avenue fabric
house and, as soon as she had finished her Danish,
began following up listings on the real estate page
of the *Times*. She set up dates to see two apartments that noon on the East Side.

At the first, a garden apartment, daylight barely
penetrated two small windows at the front and a
French door at the rear, before which a snarling
German shepherd stood guard. She peered through
the prison-like grillwork at the packed dirt beyond,
and retreated. For "garden apartment," read, "basement with dog-run."

Apartment number two was a "sixer," and as
soon as she walked through the front door, Jackie
understood why it was priced so reasonably. It was
as if a crazed "small-is-beautiful" advocate had
been given his head. Walls made of plasterboard divided already minuscule rooms, giving the feeling
of a laboratory maze. "If you're not looking for
something that's large and ostentatious, this could
fill the bill," the agent said.

On the next day, a Saturday, Jackie bought an
early copy of Sunday's *Times* and checked out a
"large and airy 4½." The catch was that the 4½
rooms faced rows of other people's rooms only
yards away. In one of these rooms Jackie saw a fat
man in an undershirt, leisurely exploring his nose
while reading the *National Enquirer*. She quickly
turned away.

She registered their names with the best half-
dozen real estate agents in town and started spread-
ing the word to friends. Sunday was anticlimactic
because she already knew the real estate section by

heart. However, she persuaded Pete to walk from block to block through the high Seventies, canvassing supers and doormen. This proved to be a bust: The buildings they liked invariably were either coops or choice townhouses of the sort that had no turnover. After a few hours they gave up and went to the new Stella show at the Whitney.

In the weeks that followed, Jackie abandoned the absolute necessity of an East Side address. She flirted with the idea of Brooklyn Heights, but only briefly. No amount of double-talk could make it pass for Manhattan. To keep from losing her sense of humor, she pinned a list of real estate hyperbole on her bulletin board: "ideal," "magnificent," "choice," "fabulous," "unique," "unbelievable," "charming," and, for those under four feet tall, "cozy." Pete was ready to meet her anywhere on a half hour's notice, but she turned up no apartments worth this red-alert urgency.

The one positive development from that night of promises was that Pete had started jogging every day. Despite his verbal abuse, Jackie only occasionally ran with him. She had discovered that cigarets and jogging didn't mix, and it was much easier to put up with Pete's self-righteous needling than give up smoking. Besides, she hated the boredom of running.

One morning, minutes after Jackie arrived at her office, Pete called. "Larry's grandmother died," he said.

"I'm sorry to hear that."

"I'm sorry, too, but that's not the point. Turn to obits. Page thirty-three. Look at the address."

"Oh, I see what you mean. Her apartment. But we can't call Larry up now."

"I'm not saying we should call up Larry, dummy. Why don't you go by the building, and see if the doorman will show the apartment to you. It's rent controlled. And it's exactly where you want to be. East Sixty-eighth Street."

"You're a ghoul. And it's a great idea."

The experience was humiliating. The doorman refused to acknowledge that there was an apartment available and referred her to the rental agent. When she telephoned the agent, he acted outraged. Who did madam think she was? Didn't she realize there was a long waiting list for that apartment? He stopped just short of accusing her of knocking the old lady off.

They had been apartment-hunting now for one month, and the scorecard was a disaster. Apartments inspected—21. Apartments screened over the telephone—36. Real estate agents contacted and vigorously pursued—12. Apartments located—0.

At one real estate office Jackie was asked to fill out a questionnaire that was more prying than a membership application for the Racquet Club. Jackie told the real estate agent—a spry, elderly woman in a jump suit—that she saw no reason to answer such personal questions. The old lady smiled at her patronizingly. She explained that they had a fabulous apartment in a very exclusive building and the owners required more than the usual background on their prospective tenants. With a sigh, Jackie filled in the form. It took her almost fifteen minutes, and she had to call Pete twice, once for the date he graduated from college and then, again, for his blood type.

"Why do you need our blood types?" Jackie asked the woman.

"Accidents can happen. These people are very careful."

Two days later the woman telephoned Jackie to say the apartment had been rented to somebody else.

Soon after, she stopped checking the real estate listings and began to toy with the idea of covering the living room walls with fabric.

Yes, she thought, admit it. You've given up.

3

APRIL

At first his mouth tasted of pennies. He'd read about that cliche plenty of times, but damn it if it wasn't true. He took a swipe at his forehead, and a spray of perspiration flew off his fingers. His T-shirt clung to his back like wet newspaper. He could swear he tasted sweatsocks now, joining but not eliminating the pennies. His legs were numb. They almost seemed disconnected from his body except that they ached with a dull vengeance. His breath came in short, scratchy gasps.

It was almost 7:30 in the morning, still cool. Pete was three-quarters through his first attempt to complete one lap of the 1.6 mile course that girdled the reservoir in Central Park.

Just at the point when he had reached an almost sublime misery and was debating what part of his body hurt him the most—his chest, his legs, his feet, his left big toe; he had plastered a couple of Band-Aids on to a budding callous there and now the Band-Aids were pulling and sticking—when he was prepared to quit at any moment, he heard someone overtaking him. He glanced to the left as a figure came into his field of vision. Gray hair. Then two more people, another man and a woman. They all looked solidly into their mid-fifties. All three were dressed in matching powder-blue jogging suits, and they moved in synchronized, effortless strides. Their heads were held high and they were smiling.

Jesus Christ! They had passed him once before, just as he'd been starting out. The fires of hypochondria were quickly fueled. An image flashed before his eyes. Himself prostrate on the track. A cop bending over him, feeling his pulse. Nothing. The youngest cardiac of the year. *Daily News* centerfold material. Jackie, in tears, dialing Frank Campbell's. As if to confirm his worst fears, he suddenly felt a savage stitch in his right side. He really must be in rotten shape; he would call Dr. Howard as soon as he got to the office and go in for a full checkup. He had meant to do that last month, but he had been so pleased with his running that he had let it slide. Now he could see that his progress was an illusion. This was the first time he had pushed himself, and it was a disaster.

Finally the end was in sight. Up ahead the three middle-aged bluebirds were chatting animatedly. They looked cool and relaxed. With a rush of determination, Pete completed the lap and gratefully broke stride. His chest was heaving, and sweat washed down his face. He tugged off his jacket and threw it to the ground. His legs were rubbery, but he resisted the impulse to collapse and began to walk off his fatigue. He looked again at his watch. He had been running for sixteen minutes.

"Hey," someone shouted. Pete turned just in time to see a thin black man with an overgrown, copper-colored Afro grab his jacket and, wheeling around in one smooth motion, sprint uphill toward a thick clump of bushes. To his amazement, the two men in powder blue took off after the thief, and, before Pete could catch up, had recovered the jacket. The thief was gone. Pete puffed up to the men and, reaching for his jacket, thanked them.

"Think nothing of it, young man," one of them said. "I'm glad we could help. This sort of thing happens too often, I'm afraid."

He had thick gray hair cut in a trim crew cut and cheery blue eyes set off well by a ruddy tan. The other's hair was thinner, but if anything he looked healthier.

"I hope nothing's missing," the man added. They both looked like airline pilots with a Fort Lauderdale run.

"That's what I'm afraid of," said Pete, checking the second pocket. "Yep, he got my wallet. That means my credit cards and license. Hell. What a way to start the day."

By now they had been joined by the woman. The man with the crew cut quickly explained the situation.

"Can we help you?" asked the woman. "Do you

want us to come to the police station with you as witnesses? I think I could give them a very clear description of the man."

"No, but thanks anyway. I'll report this, of course, though I doubt it'll do any good. What I've got to do right away is phone the credit card people. Oh, damn it," Pete paused, and ran his hands over his pants pockets. "My keys. He got those, too. I've got to call my wife."

"I'll tell you what," the crew cut began. Then interrupting himself, he said, "By the way, I'm Arnold Jensen. This is my wife, Phoebe, and my neighbor, Victor Macrae. You're . . ."

Pete introduced himself. As they were shaking hands, Jensen said, "We live right near by, Mr. Lawrence. Come back to our place and make your telephone calls. It's the least we can do."

When Pete protested, Phoebe Jensen spoke for the first time. She was tall and elegant with lustrous gray hair—she must have been a beauty; she was handsome still—and her voice was surprisingly gentle for someone so commanding in appearance. "No, please, Mr. Lawrence, don't argue. We insist. Come."

And so he did. He was angry, but not at himself. He took the kinds of normal precautions any sensible citizen of New York did, but who could figure the brazenness of that sneak thief. He had been only twenty feet from the jacket when the man grabbed it. And here he was with this improbable trio. Powder blue! Well, that color-coordinated business seemed ridiculous, but they were being as nice as they could be. They were really putting themselves out for him and it would make things much easier. The next time any one from out of town gave him any crap about the callousness of New Yorkers, he'd tell them about these people.

4

Jackie was the assistant buyer for less expensive dresses at Bendel's. The office she shared with Tyrone LeBlanc, the assistant buyer for accessories, was squirreled away on the fourth floor behind the boutique next to the ladies' room. It was just large enough for two desks, three chairs, and one filing cabinet, and its walls were dense with newspaper ads and pages torn from *Women's Wear Daily, Vogue,* and *Bazaar.* Jackie edged past Tyrone, who seemed to have succeeded in snaring a date with the man who was on the other end of the telephone. She dumped her purse onto her desk and sat down to sort through the collection of telephone messages on her spike. She had been out on Seventh Avenue since early morning and was tired. Pete had called. And Trish. And a couple of manufacturers, one of whom she'd been avoiding. And a real estate agent about an apartment at 301 East Ninety-seventh Street. Tyrone had scribbled, "She says you must see." That agent had a long wait in store for her. East Ninety-seventy Street off Second Avenue, indeed! She heard Tyrone winding up his conversation and swiveled her chair around to say hello.

"Hey, baby," he said. "You know, sometimes I think there might be something to being straight." Tyrone LeBlanc (né Theodore Carver White) was very black and wore a beautifully tailored brilliant orange shirt, open at the neck, with a small white rosebud tucked into the top buttonhole of his wheat-colored linen jacket.

"Tyrone, you've been having your lunch in the Ramble again. What happened? Strike out?"

"Now don't sass me, woman," he said, waving another pink slip in her direction. "I just five minutes ago took a delightful message from that beautiful hunk of man you have. He said for you to meet him tonight at La Grenouille at seven-thirty."

"All right, joker. You failed the audition. What did he say?"

"I kid you not. That's what he said. And he also said, don't try to get back to him, he's tied up for the afternoon." He paused. "Tied up. What a delicious idea." He gave a mock shiver and continued. "The Frog Pond'll set him back at least a hundred, if, that is, you drink Ripple. You must be doing something right, baby."

5

Pete was already seated when Jackie was led into the restaurant. The maître d' rolled officiously on ahead of her. Pete had chosen La Grenouille because Jackie, in star-struck moments, referred to it with awe. It was a favorite of all those people with names like Bunny and Swifty and Muffy, whose every move *Women's Wear Daily* chronicled faithfully. He didn't give a damn about the doings of that set, but they knew where to find some of the best French food in town—at a price, of course.

It was a light and airy room filled with huge vases abrim with spring flowers. A smattering of tables were occupied by early diners. The maître d' pulled back their table, and Jackie slipped down beside Pete on the banquette. She looked smashing in a slate-blue Calvin Klein blouse that looked as if it had been dyed to match her eyes. She was going to flip when he gave her the news. He still couldn't believe it himself.

Jackie squeezed his hand and brushed his cheek with her lips. Then, before he could speak, she said, "All right, love, explain. Why are we here? Have you gone crazy or did you just win first prize at the lottery?"

"A little of both. A great thing happened to me today."

"You fell and hit your head."

"No, my wallet containing almost a hundred bucks and all my credit cards was stolen."

"You're getting funnier by the second."

"No, I mean it. Oh, wait a minute. Here's a little something for us."

A waiter approached their table carrying a bottle of champagne wedged firmly in a silver bucket. He reached over to a serving tray for two iced glasses, then held the bottle up, label side toward them.

"Roederer Cristal, 1964. Perfect," said Pete. He nodded his approval, and the waiter filled their glasses.

"To us," said Pete, checking the date on his watch, "and to April seventeenth." Then, starting at the beginning, he told her about the freaky thing that had happened to him in the park and about how two of the runners in baby blue had asked him back to their apartment to make whatever calls he needed to.

"I thought I'd get hold of you and you could bring the keys up so I could change."

"Yes, Tyrone told me you called. Go on, go on."

Pete paused for a moment and then laughed.

"Oh, shit. I can't string this out any longer. I've found it."

"Found what? What are you talking about?"

"An apartment. *The* apartment. Jackie, this is it."

"You've got to be kidding."

"No, I mean it. Listen, after I tried to reach you and didn't, Arnold Jensen—that's one of the men who chased the guy who took my jacket, the other one's named Victor Macrae—said not to worry, they'd lend me some taxi money to get home and didn't our superintendent have a spare set of keys. We had a cup of tea, one of those herb teas, some kind of crazy mix of camomile, sassafras, and God knows what else. Jensen called it 'Phoebe's Brew,' and teased his wife about it."

"Get on with it, Pete," Jackie implored. "I can't stand it."

"Well, I was just about to leave when I said something about what a terrific place they had and how you would give your eye teeth to have an apartment like that. And this is what really gets me, I just *happened* to say that. What if I hadn't? And Phoebe asked right away, were we looking for an apartment, because they had one available. Seems they own the building. With Macrae and some of the other people who live there, I think. Jensen's an anthropologist. Still lectures occasionally at Columbia. Macrae's a chemist, though I got the feeling he no longer works. Early retirement, I guess.

"Anyway, it seems they always rent a few of the apartments out. To young people, they said, because they like having them around. The couple in the apartment they had in mind had been transferred to Tacoma, and they were about to put it on the market. They asked me if I wanted to see it, and, Jackie, it blew my mind. It's perfect."

"Oh, my God. What's it like? Tell me."

"First, let me get the waiter. We need some more champagne." Pete signaled, and when their glasses were filled again, continued. "It's a four-and-a-half, I guess you'd call it. It's got a really large living room, L-shaped, with, dig this, a working fireplace set in a marvelous old carved-marble mantelpiece. There are two terrific bay windows in the room, too. All the windows, by the way, have built-in shutters. The originals it looked like, not new ones. There are two bedrooms—we can use the smaller one as a study. Hurray! The master bedroom has a fireplace, too. And yes, it works. It already has one whole wall of bookshelves. And the kitchen you won't believe. It must be at least fifteen feet square, and it looks like they've recently redone it. Built-in dishwasher, butcher-block counters, lots of working space, and a fabulous floor. Quarry tiles, polyurethaned, easy as hell to take care of."

"Stop. You're right. I don't believe it. Are you sure you're not making this whole thing up?"

"There's more. The ceilings are probably eleven feet high, maybe higher. There are closets all over the place, and the whole thing looks over a great garden, southern exposure. I could go on. But you haven't heard anything yet. The rent's only six-fifty."

"Come off it!"

"Oh. I forgot one thing. Utilities are included.

And even though you didn't ask, I'll tell you. The address is Twelve East Eighty-third Street. Which, in case you can't calculate fast enough, means it's between Fifth and Madison."

"When can I see it?" Jackie's face was flushed and her voice was hoarse with excitement.

"Tonight, after dinner. They're having a party in the garden, and they asked us to come over and meet everybody."

"Oh, Pete."

He leaned over and kissed her, then raised his glass again.

"To jogging," he said.

"And to sneak thieves," Jackie replied, touching her glass to Pete's.

6

As the taxi turned off Madison onto Eighty-third Street, Pete said, "Now shut your eyes. I'll tell you when you can open them." Seconds later the cab drew to a stop. "Okay, honey, you're on."

"Oh, Pete, it's beautiful," said Jackie.

She opened the cab door and slid out. Before her was an elegant four-story apartment building with a soft brick facade. The trim, shutters, and front door were painted a cream color. The front door was paneled, with small panes of old glass lining the sides. A garage, its glossy oak door set flush to the outer wall, was to the left. In the windows on the first floor were flowerboxes filled with ivy. It had the look of a handsome, old house in Belgravia, and it was clear that whoever owned it loved it.

Jackie shivered expectantly. Pete moved next to

her and squeezed her. "I'm on target so far, aren't I?" he said.

"Oh, Pete, you've walked into my head. It's perfect."

"Wait. This is just a taste. The apartment's even better."

They opened the low iron gate leading to the building and stepped up to the door. A neatly lettered note was taped next to the row of doorbells: "Jackie and Pete: Please ring the bell marked Macrae." They pushed the button indicated and heard the buzzer sound distantly somewhere at the rear of the building. Jackie fluffed her hair out with her fingers and peered through the glass panes at the side of the door.

"Someone's coming," she said.

Before Pete had a chance to see who it was, the door swung open. A wiry, middle-aged man in an open-necked plaid shirt reached out and gripped Pete's hand.

"Good evening, Pete," he said. He turned to Jackie. "I am Victor Macrae. And you must be Jackie." He cupped her right hand in both of his and smiled at her with an intensity that Jackie found difficult to return. Then, breaking the mood, he gestured expansively toward the interior. "Welcome to Number Twelve. We're having a celebration in the garden. Our first of the spring season. We're delighted you could join us."

The lobby was small and tasteful. A low black glove-leather sofa stood against one wall. Behind it was a large smoked-glass mirror. On the wall opposite the sofa, a cut glass bowl containing a striking arrangement of wild cattails mixed with dried bittersweet rested on a dark mahogany lowboy. Jackie noticed a small sign next to the bowl: "Thank you for not smoking," someone had lettered in stylish calligraphy. From the ceiling hung a delicate pewter chandelier that cast a spiderweb shadow against the far wall. The marble floor shone.

"Here we are," Macrae was saying. "This door leads to the garden. All the tenants are welcome to use it as much as they please. A spot of sun and air can be such a tonic. But," he chuckled, "I'm getting ahead of myself. We don't know yet whether you will agree to share our habitat with us. Now let me introduce you to the other . . . Twelvers, we like to call ourselves."

As they started down the steps into the garden, the people seated around the table below broke off their conversations and turned with interest toward Jackie and Pete. The men rose to greet them. Candlelight from hurricane lamps danced on their faces. Along one wall several kerosene torches flickered, and at the rear the gray and ruby coals of a large charcoal grill cast a warm light on the dark figure stacking dishes and utensils onto a trolley cart next to the grill.

One of the women pushed back her chair and stood.

"Pete, good evening," she said, "and, my dear Jackie. I am Phoebe Jensen. We've been brought together in a true New York fashion." The others laughed. "It is our great pleasure to welcome you here. Victor, will you do the honors?"

Macrae led Jackie and Pete over to the group at the table. He cleared his throat. "Ladies and gentlemen, this is Pete and Jackie Lawrence. Jackie and Pete, I'd like to introduce you first to Eileen Cole." A thin bird-like woman smiled and nodded good evening. "And, Arnold Jensen. Pete, you and Arnold have already met, of course. My wife, Miriam." Miriam Macrae was round-faced with perfectly synchronized steel-gray spit curls marching in close order across her forehead. The man next to her took over.

"I'm Ben Goodman, and this is my wife, Sylvia," he said, resting his arm on the shoulders of the woman next to him. The Goodmans could have been twins. Both were short and chunky with healthy, ruddy complexions. Ben was almost completely bald except for a gray fringe that capped the back of his head. Sylvia, who had a broad, captivating smile, wore her vividly dyed red hair in a net snood à la Veronica Lake. It was, to put it mildly, striking.

"Next we have Richard Kelly . . ."

Kelly, a very tall man who stood ramrod straight, grabbed Pete's hand in a vise-like grip. His deep black eyes locked on Pete. He smiled as if it didn't come naturally.

". . . and last but not least, Dave Barnett and his lovely wife, Kim."

The Barnetts both looked like Central Casting's idea for late-twenties-to-early-thirties Olympic material. Dave stood just over six feet tall, and you could see there wasn't an ounce of fat on him. Though Kim was still seated, you could tell that she, too, had a great figure. Her honey blond hair shone in the candlelight. The Barnetts simply glowed with good health. They almost looked too healthy.

"Dave here is our excuse for tonight's celebration. He came in sixty-seventh in last Saturday's mini-marathon in Central Park. Sixty-seventh! Out of a field of close to five hundred. And after only four months' training. I don't know if you follow this sort of thing, but don't be misled by the phrase 'mini.' The course was ten miles. Pete, maybe you can appreciate what a run of ten miles demands of a person. And, let me tell you, we're proud of him. Now what can we offer you? Would you like something to drink? Or better yet, let Buddy rustle up a couple of steaks for you. What do you say, Buddy?" Goodman asked the slight but muscular black man who walked over from the grill. Without waiting for a response, he continued. "Pete and Jackie Lawrence, meet Buddy Johnson. And vice versa. Buddy is our superintendent and very much a part of our family. He and his wife, Lil, have an apartment here. She's inside preparing dessert. You'll meet her in a moment. And you must try her Savannah fruit compote. Now, how about some of that steak?"

"We'd love to, but we just finished dinner."

"Are you sure you won't change your minds?" piped up Eileen Cole. "I promise you these steaks are the best you'll ever taste. Just as lean as lean can be, and no noxious hormones pumped into them."

"Oh, Eileen, you always have to get in your two

cents' worth," said Goodman with a laugh. "Eileen is our resident food expert," he explained. "For years she was the head nutritionist for CCNY and she's tops in her field. As a matter of fact, this beef was raised especially for us by one of the suppliers she used to deal with. Organic feed only. You wouldn't believe the difference that makes. But I can see you wouldn't be able to do it justice this evening. So, another time. Now enough of this food talk. I'll bet," he said, smiling at Jackie, "that what *you* want to do—though you're too polite to say so—is see the apartment. Am I right or am I not?"

"You read my mind, Mr. Goodman."

"Please. It's Ben. First names only around here. Now run along with Phoebe and Arnold. They'll give you the grand tour."

After the Jensens had disappeared inside with Jackie, Pete pulled up a canvas deck chair next to Dave Barnett and his wife. He offered Dave his congratulations, and they began to talk about running. Dave invited Pete to meet him at the reservoir the next day.

"I don't think I'm in your league."

Understatement of the century, thought Pete. He hoped Macrae, who had witnessed his stumbling performance that morning, hadn't overheard.

Dave said he was with IT&T. In public relations. Kim was a fabric designer currently involved in cataloging the Cooper-Hewitt Museum's collection of two hundred years of American fabric.

Pete noticed that Kim was very relaxed. No, that wasn't right. Serene. That was it! It was not a word he had much occasion to apply to people he en-

countered. As he listened to her, he became aware
that she'd hardly moved a muscle since he'd joined
them. Her hands were folded loosely in her lap, her
shoulders still. It seemed very natural. He glanced
at Dave, who lolled low in his chair, legs stretched
out, crossed at the ankles. Not exactly the picture
of a tense young executive. It must have something
to do with all that exercise.

Pete had just begun to explain why the paperback rights to Mario Puzo's new novel had been
sold for over two million dollars, when Jackie returned.

"Darling, I love it! It's . . . oh, my God, I don't
even know where to begin. You weren't exagger-
ating. Phoebe and Arnold say we can have it as of
the first. I don't care if we have to forfeit our security where we are now. I can't wait to get out of
that place. And just as I thought we never would."

Pete, standing at her side now, put his arm
around her shoulders and gave her a hug. "Didn't I
tell you?"

The others watched, smiling.

"We're so happy to see that you share Pete's re-
gard for the apartment," said Macrae. "We dis-
cussed it this afternoon, and we agreed that you'd
make a most welcome addition. We didn't doubt
for a moment, Pete, that Jackie would be just as
charming and attractive as she is. You know,
maybe we're a bit old-fashioned. But we all feel
very strongly the need to have people we care for
under our roof. Not, mind you, that we spend that
much time in each other's company. A party such
as this evening's is a rarity. Of course, we couldn't

let the occasion of Dave's accomplishment go unnoticed. But, most importantly, here you are, and you fit in beautifully."

"Well, I'm delighted," said Jackie, hurriedly deflecting Macrae's tribute. She reached into her shoulder bag and rummaged in it for a moment. "Darn it. No matches. Who's got a light?" she asked, holding up a cigaret.

Macrae scowled. The faces of the other middle-aged residents hardened. Phoebe glanced quickly at Arnold, then spoke. "My dear, we have no hard and fast rules here, but we do take our physical well-being seriously. We don't allow smoking in the communal areas of our building. Perhaps you noticed our sign in the lobby? Of course, what you do in your own apartment is your own affair."

"Oh, I'm sorry. I didn't realize," said Jackie, jamming the cigaret back into her bag. She was startled. The reaction of the others had been so swift, and so disproportionate. She fell silent.

"Don't worry, Jackie. We're all liberal Democrats. And we even laugh at off-color jokes," said Ben Goodman with a smile, breaking the tension. "And I'd like to have the pleasure of showing you an added wonder of this dwelling that I think not even Pete is aware of. If you please, come with me."

Pete and Jackie exchanged goodbyes with the group and followed Ben into the building. It was funny, thought Jackie as she climbed the stairs, but all eight of the older tenants seemed to be the same age. All of them somewhere in their middle fifties.

And every one of them Jack La Lanne lookalikes. She felt healthier already just being around them.

By the second floor, Pete and Jackie were panting as they tried to keep up with Ben Goodman, who resembled a mountain goat more than a middle-aged man. He took the steps two at a time, all the while chatting over his shoulder.

"I don't want to tell you what this costs. Thank God for the monopolistic practices of Arnold Jensen's father. And for Arnold Jensen. I designed the setup, but frankly I never thought I'd see it realized in a private dwelling. We've had it now for over seven years, and I can tell you it's hard to remember what things were like before it."

Goodman waited at the top landing while Pete and Jackie stumbled up.

"I guess doing these stairs every day makes them a little easier for me. You'll get used to it in no time."

He waited until they were alongside him and then threw open the door and turned on the lights.

All Jackie could say was, "Wow." Pete just stared.

There in front of them was a twenty-yard, gleaming tile pool, its amethyst waters twinkling under a glass ceiling.

"This is as fine an indoor pool as can be built. We keep it at a constant seventy-two, which is both refreshing and invigorating. In the summer the ceiling can be pulled back. We're all such exercise nuts that we use it daily all year round. Though I run with the rest of the group, I believe more in swimming as both a conditioner and a cardiovascular aid."

He led them around the pool to a shining steel contraption that seemed to be a prop from *Star Wars*. It looked both expensive and complicated.

"Here's our latest goody. This is the top-of-the-line Nautilus Exercise machine. It'll take me several evenings to walk you through all its facets, but let me just say that it's fantastic."

The tour continued. Ben quickly ticked off the Jacuzzi, professional scale, treadmill, exercise bicycle, rowing machine, and (Jackie had to pinch herself, it was too much like the set for a James Bond movie) a sauna.

"If you belong to the Y, quit it immediately and buy yourselves new sneakers."

Jackie and Pete stood there, Pete's mouth slightly agape, Jackie's eyes blinking.

"You'll get to meet Jerry and Francie McDonald when you move in. They're our other young couple. He works for CBS as an associate producer in the sports department. He's out of town covering a tennis match, and he took Francie along for a bit of a vacation. You'll see a lot of them up here. They both swim like seals. Unfortunately, Jerry has to travel a lot and falls a bit out of condition from being on the road. But Victor has a friend at ABC, and he's working behind the scenes to get Jerry a better job, without traveling. Well, I guess that's it."

As they followed Ben out, Jackie whispered to Pete, "Maybe if you get me to stop smoking, Victor will get you a job as president of Random House."

"Shh, you nut."

"I'll be quiet but I just don't believe all of this. It's too good to be happening to us."

"That's just your orphan mentality. I always told you we were lucky. It's just starting a little late, that's all."

7

MAY

The move into the new apartment went
smoothly. Partly because Jackie threw out a lot of
stuff before the move, but mainly because they
didn't have that much to begin with.

Jackie spent her lunches, weekends, and spare
moments haunting Design Research, Conran's,
Bloomingdale's, and scores of fabric and antique
stores. Occasionally she took along her best friend,
Trish, also a shopping junkie.

When Pete wasn't immersed in editing, he was
jogging. When not reading a manuscript, he was either swimming in the pool or using the Nautilus.
And Jackie had to admit that he was looking better. She hated the sniffing sound he made whenever
she lit a cigaret, but, thank God, he didn't prose-
lytize.

The others in the building had given up on her jogging when she stopped at Baskin-Robbins for a cone the third time in a row after dropping out with only a half mile completed. Pete was now up to two miles and she was into Peppermint Fudge. But weren't women supposed to be softer than men? The older folks in the house were nuts. No two ways about it. And Pete and the other two young couples were just as crazy. They were all gulping down vitamins for all they were worth. But they were nice crazy. And she loved their new apartment. Life was very good.

8

"Fifty-one . . . agh . . . fifty-two . . . eegh . . . fifty-three . . ." Pete was in the bedroom doing sit-ups. His face was contorted from the exertion and his voice, as he counted out loud, strangled

Jackie leaned into the bedroom.

"Stop that a second, will you, love, and help me with the table? Trish and Allan will be here in fifteen minutes."

"Yeah . . . be there . . . right away . . . I'm going to do . . . eighty. If it kills . . . me. Don't make me lose . . . fifty-nine yugh . . . sixty . . . track."

"Can't you quit for tonight?"

"Just be . . . sixty-one . . . eegh . . . sixty-two . . . a minute."

"Boy, a lot of help you are. I'll do it myself."

She retreated to the kitchen, cursing Pete under

her breath. She felt a rush of pleasure as she caught sight again of the black parsons table they had ordered for their dining area. It had been delivered only a few days earlier. It filled out the corner of their living room perfectly and, surrounded by six Breuer cane chairs, made a handsome and simple dining room. Jackie placed a large glass bowl of tulips in the center of the table. Perfect. This would be the first time they'd entertained since they moved in. She wanted everything to be right. Pete continued to groan in the bedroom as she set the table with place mats, silver, wine glasses, and candles, and two small crystal ashtrays for herself and Allan. She walked past the bedroom into the bathroom, peeling her jersey over her shoulders as she went.

"I'm going to take a shower. Don't forget to get out the ice."

"Almost . . . there . . . seventy-six . . . agh . . . you don't know what a . . . seventy-seven . . . high this is."

"Such a high that you've never been so boring."

When the doorbell rang and Trish and Allan stepped into the apartment, Jackie watched Allan's face expectantly. Trish, of course, had had a hand in the decorating, but Allan had been in London on business until a few days earlier and was seeing it for the first time.

"My God, this is unbelievable," said Allan. "How'd you find it?"

"Pete's genius as an apartment-hunter," said Jackie.

"We got lucky," said Pete. "Come on, we'll show you around."

Allan, though only thirty-two, looked every inch the banker. From his slight paunch to his well-tailored vest and his prematurely thinning hair, he radiated trustworthiness and unflappable calm.

Trish, a full three inches taller than Allan, was the kind of plain woman who nonetheless made men turn and notice her. Her figure was good, but it was her canny sense of herself and her artful way with makeup and clothes that made her extremely attractive. Her stylishness was lost on the students of the Montessori nursery school where she taught four mornings a week.

As they walked their friends from room to room, Jackie and Pete opened closet doors, demonstrated the articulation of shutters, pointed to details on the mantel, the hardwood floors, the view from their windows. Jackie couldn't wait to show it off to everyone they knew. They could easily throw a cocktail party for sixty people.

Back in the living room, Pete mixed drinks all around.

"And there's the garden . . ." he said.

"It's great. Everyone in the building has a key to it, and they really seem to have meant it when they told us to use it any time we wanted. Pete and I took some white wine down there after dinner last night, and it was heavenly."

"And remember the pool and gym I told you about on the roof? Wait till you see it. Come to think of it, I haven't spoken with Ben about this— he used to head up athletics at Brandeis and he seems to be in charge of that kind of stuff around here—but I bet they wouldn't mind our bringing up friends." He nodded smilingly at Allan's girth. "What do you say? You want to meet me after work tomorrow for twenty laps?"

Allan laughed good-naturedly.

"You've got a point, buddy. But, thank you, no. I firmly believe that exercise does more harm than help. I'm fat and happy, and I intend to stay that way." He took off his jacket and sat down. "And for the moment, I'm bushed. I've still got a case of jet lag."

"How was London?" asked Jackie.

Last October she'd met Pete in England after the annual book fair in Frankfurt. They'd spent five days driving through Devon and then five more in London camping out in the spare bedroom of a friend's flat in Chelsea. Soggy. And glorious. If they ever left New York City, which Jackie could not imagine their doing, it would be for London. Allan expanded on the pleasures of breakfast at the Connaught, then settled down with Pete to a discussion of the British economy, which he knew cold. He was a foreign exchange officer with Citibank.

Jackie led Trish into the bedroom to show her some fabric she'd just picked out. She spread a large swatch of it on the bed. It was a lemony-yellow chintz with a bold, swirling pattern of white, pink, and pale purple flowers.

"It's a Clarence House knock-off, and it sure beats paying thirty-four dollars a yard. *Wholesale.* I'm shooting the works on it. Bedspread. Curtains. I'm going to get two small overstuffed armchairs and cover them, too. We can put our feet up in front of the fire and pretend we're in an English country house. Now, come with me into the kitchen and talk. I've still got a couple of things to do."

As they passed the living room, Pete was speculating on how the English managed to live on the paltry salaries they made. Jackie interrupted to ask Pete which wine he'd chosen for the evening.

"The Beaujolais we got the other day, but don't put out a glass for me. I'll have water instead. With lots of ice."

"You what?"

"You heard right. New rule. When I have a drink before dinner, no wine with the meal. Doesn't that make sense?"

"Maybe for you. Certainly not for me. But that's all the more wine for the rest of us." Her voice was tight with annoyance.

She uncorked the Beaujolais and placed it on the counter to breathe. Ice water! Next it would be Tiger's Milk. She mixed the vinaigrette for the salad, rinsed her hands, opened the refrigerator door. Now for the mousse. She dipped the bottom of the mold in hot water, quickly inverted it, waited anxiously for the mousse to release itself. Ah, beautiful. She lighted the candles and called, "All right, gang. Dinner's served."

When the others were seated, she brought out the mousse and sat down. "That looks gorgeous," said Trish. "I don't know how you have the time to do it."

Pete frowned. "That's not what you said you were serving."

"Salmon mousse? It's one of your favorites. You love it."

"Correction. I used to love it. All that cream. What are you trying to do, sabotage me?"

"Pipe down, you can save your beautiful body for the main course. Beef paillard. Didn't I tell you, Trish? He's becoming impossible."

"I see what you mean."

Since Pete wasn't eating his first course, he held forth on his latest raison d'être: the inner runner.

"Does he go on like this all the time?" asked Trish sotto voce.

"It's like living with Jim Fixx."

After they had finished dinner and were settled again in the living room, Allan pulled a flat, rust and black Art Deco tin from his pocket. He took out some cigaret papers from another pocket and opened the tin.

"Now, my friends," he said, as he began to roll a joint, "you are about to experience something unique. Macao mauve. Straight from that exotic port with a short stopover in San Blas. Grown from seeds that have been blasting Oriental minds for centuries. Until you've smoked this, you haven't smoked anything."

"According to Allan, there's a legend behind every joint he rolls," said Trish.

"Everybody set?" asked Allan. He paused while Pete dropped a record on the turntable. The sound of the Beach Boys roared through the room. "Gather round me, then. I don't want us to waste a drop of this."

He struck a match, held it to the joint, and inhaled with a groan of satisfaction. He turned to Jackie. "You're next, princess. Waste not, want not." Closing her eyes, the better to concentrate, Jackie took several short, staccato puffs.

Pete started to hum, "Don't Bogart that joint."

"Oh, Allan, you kid us not," Jackie said, handing the joint to Trish. Trish drew deeply on it and passed it to Pete.

There was a sudden, short rap on the front door. "Oh, shit," hissed Pete, handing the joint back to Allan before taking a hit. "Put it out. Quick."

He jumped up, opened one of the windows, and waved his arms futilely in the smoky air. "Just a minute," he shouted, then, lowering the stereo to a murmur, he opened the door.

It was Ben Goodman. He smiled apologetically. "I'm awfully sorry to intrude on your party, but it's Sylvia. She's got one of her sinus migraines. That beat, whatever it was you were playing, sounds like hammers in her head. We wouldn't bother you otherwise."

Ben sniffed the air a few times, looking pointedly at Pete, then smiled again.

"That's all right, Ben. I understand. Please apologize to Sylvia for us. We'll keep the sound low from now on."

Paranoia time, thought Jackie. Ben's a secret narc. There goes our apartment.

"By the way, Pete, you're running with us tomorrow morning at six, yes?" asked Ben.

"Sure thing," Pete replied.

After the door had closed behind Ben, Allan

turned in amazement to Pete. "Did I hear that guy right? Christ, he doesn't look like he could make it around the block!"

"You'd be surprised," said Pete.

"You know, Pete," said Jackie thoughtfully, "Allan's right. Ben doesn't look so good. He seems a little worn around the edges, like maybe he has some kind of low-grade infection. Come to think of it, they've all looked a bit punk lately."

"Listen, all of you should be in the kind of shape Ben and the others are in," Pete answered defensively.

There was an awkward pause. Pete's tone had been abrupt.

"Well," said Allan brightly, "let's get back to more important things."

Pete looked at his watch. "It's getting late. Let's call it quits for tonight. Tomorrow's a workday, and I've got to get up early."

Jackie, who'd been fluffing out pillows on the couch, whirled and faced Pete. "My God, I can't believe it. It's not even ten-thirty!"

"Are you really serious about getting up and running at the crack of dawn?" asked Allan.

"You're damned right."

"I'm afraid so," said Jackie disgustedly.

"Well," said Allan, shaking his head and laughing, "I guess we know when to take a hint. Trish, let's push on." He turned to Jackie. "I tell you what. I'll leave the rest of this joint with you. Maybe you can even get the old bozo here to lower his guard and join you."

"Thanks, Allan," said Jackie, giving him a hug. "I am sorry about our Bruce Jenner."

"Forget it. It doesn't matter."

After Allan and Trish had left, Jackie said, "You were a real winner tonight, darling. A real piece of work."

"Oh, come off it, Jackie. Don't you think *you're* acting a little stupidly?"

"No, I do not!" she yelled, losing her temper. "Since when do you treat our friends that way? Get your priorities straight. I don't want to talk to you. Go get your beauty sleep."

Pete closed the bedroom door behind him. Jackie cleared tables of dishes and glasses, stacked the dishwasher, straightened out the kitchen. Then she went into the living room and opened the shutters. She hated waking in the morning to a dark apartment. She leaned her forehead against one of the window panes, rubbing with one hand the knotted muscles in her neck and shoulders. She saw candlelight in the garden below, and spotted figures seated at the table. They must have had dinner outdoors again. It was a lovely evening for it. Ben Goodman's balding head made him easy to pick out. And there were Miriam and Victor Macrae next to him. And Sylvia Goodman. If Sylvia had such a rotten headache, what was she doing outside, Jackie wondered idly. Well, it was none of her business. She poured herself a large brandy, hesitated for a moment, then lighted the joint that Allan had left her. She sat down and closed her eyes. A pleasurable tingling sensation slowly filtered through her body. She inhaled a second time. The tensions that had built up inside her seemed to be flowing out through her toes. Pete was right. She'd been uptight and bitchy. His perseverance in all these new exercise routines amazed her. Why couldn't she just go along with it? She would apologize to him. Now. She loathed being on the outs with him, even one minute more than was necessary. She took a short swallow of brandy and carefully opened the bedroom door. Pete was asleep, his body curled around one of the pillows. She sat down beside him and ran her fingers along his shoulders and down one arm. He stirred in his sleep. God, she wanted him. She bent and kissed his cheek. "Pete?" she whispered. It was no use. She would have to wait until tomorrow to make it up to him.

Later, lying in bed before falling asleep, she thought about Ben's knock on the door. Funny how everyone had had a chance for a nice big toke except for Pete. Maybe Ben was more than a trainer. Maybe he was Pete's guardian angel of health. It had to be the grass that made this seem so amusing. She laughed to herself and then quickly fell into a deep, dreamless sleep.

9

JUNE

There's a confidence that you sometimes feel
when you're on your third martini, a sense of the
rightness of things, a feeling that maybe life is really pretty good. Pete had it, and the beauty of it was
that he was stone cold sober. He had a wife who
was beautiful and whom he loved very much. He
loved his work. He couldn't think of anything he'd
rather do more. He was even living in a place he
loved. And last, but certainly not least, he felt
good. No. Not good. Great.

He had been a semi-jock in high school. A decent competitor in the two-hundred breaststroke. A
good third baseman with too little bat. Not a bad
boxer, but with a light jaw. He'd been in shape
then, but that was twelve years ago. Now he was
running every day. At least three miles. He spent

thirty minutes doing calisthenics and working out on the Nautilus, and then, before dinner, he did laps in the pool. He felt lean and hard and more alive than at any other time in his life. Everything was perfect.

A few days earlier, a handsomely lettered invitation had been slipped under their door. It was for a party at the Jensens' officially welcoming them to the building. Now here they were. He and Jackie had been talking with Jerry and Francie McDonald since they had arrived. Out of the corner of his eye, Pete saw Phoebe making her rounds with a pink concoction that looked suspiciously like Pepto Bismol. Jackie had not touched her glass, which confirmed its non-alcoholic content. He heard Jackie mention Tanglewood, and tuned back into the conversation. She and Jerry McDonald were arguing about the best location for a weekend house. Jackie was coming on strong for the Berkshires.

Jerry looked the way a sports producer should. Tall and muscular, with broad shoulders and an overdeveloped neck. Francie was slightly shorter than her husband and looked in marvelous shape. She was a hair stylist for Cinandre. She stood next to Jerry, one arm looped possessively around his waist, as if she expected someone to make a pass at him. If she had Jackie in mind, she could have relaxed. Jerry was not Jackie's type. Jackie disliked team sports, and Jerry seemed a team player par excellence. Sincere, hearty, uncomplicated.

"We love our place in Seaview," said Jerry. "This will be the second summer we've rented there. It's terrific. We just take it easy. No cars. No rushing around. We have volleyball games on Saturday and Sunday, and I always run on the beach. At least six miles. Have you ever tried running on sand? It really works the leg muscles."

"Ben was saying the other day," Pete chimed in, "that the resistance you get from running on the beach makes it equal as a leg conditioner to a much greater distance on asphalt."

"He's absolutely right," added Francie. "I can hardly do two miles on the Island, but I can run two and a half laps around the reservoir without pushing myself."

All I need is a jockstrap and a can of Miller's, thought Jackie, and I'd fit right in. How can they stand to talk about running all the time?

"What I can't take about Fire Island and the Hamptons," she said, trying to get them off the subject, "is that you bump into the very people you've been trying to avoid all week. It's New York City all over again. Writers. Advertising types. Agents. Shrinks. The whole scene. And everybody's busy being au courant. The latest chic bestseller tucked into their beachbags. It's so trendy that it's suffocating."

"Oh, my dears," said Phoebe, sweeping up, pitcher in hand. "I hate to interrupt your conversation, but, Pete, it looks like you need a refill. We want to keep our guests of honor happy."

Pete obligingly held out his glass. She filled it to the brim, then topped off the McDonalds' glasses and turned to Jackie. "What about you, dear?"

"I've just had a refill," she lied.

As soon as Phoebe was out of earshot, Jackie

poked Pete in the ribs. "How can you? This stuff could drive a person to Blue Nun."

"I kind of like it. Besides, it's probably loaded with things that are good for you."

He heard a commotion at the front door and glanced away. Arnold Jensen caught his eye and swept his arm upward in a beckoning gesture.

"Hey, it looks like Arnold wants to see us. Come on, darling."

Someone new was standing next to Arnold. Pete had never seen her before, but she was a knockout. She had thick, wavy chestnut hair held back by a blue headband. Even though she was wearing a loose-fitting royal blue and gold warm-up suit, he could see she had a dynamite body. Long legs and a tight little ass. The Goodmans and Miriam Macrae were crowded close to her, and there was a lot of hugging and kissing.

"Come here, friends," said Arnold, reaching out for Jackie's hand. "I want you to meet my favorite niece in the whole world. My sister's daughter, Allison Ramsey. Allison, meet Pete and Jackie Lawrence. Allison lives just around the corner, but we think of her as part of our own special little group here. She's heard so much about you that she's been dying to meet you. Be flattered, my friends. She's a young lady with a very heavy social schedule."

Allison turned first to Jackie and shook her hand warmly. Pete watched her closely, fascinated. Now he saw the resemblance to Arnold, the same vivid blue eyes and high cheekbones. How old was she, he wondered. Thirty-four? Thirty-five? Allison took his hand. Soft, but firm. Was he imagining things or

ad she given his hand an extra squeeze? Momen-
arily flustered, he said the first thing that popped
nto his head, conscious that his voice was too loud.
'Well, it looks like you've just been running."

"Yes and no," said Allison.

"Just a minute," interrupted Arnold. "I know
you two runners are going to want to exchange phi-
osophies and pointers, but before you get into it,
et me steal Jackie away. She should be spared your
unbridled enthusiasm. You know, my dear," he
continued, putting his arm around Jackie, "the very
first day I met your husband, he was kind enough
o allow me to introduce him to my . . . booty
from Belize, though, of course, the country wasn't
called Belize when I went there. I am extraordinar-
ily fortunate to be its custodian. It is a gift from the
gods."

Arnold swept his arm slowly from one side of the
room to the other. Walls, shelves, and tables were
filled with clay and stone sculptures, masks, carv-
ings, and oddly shaped implements, many still carrying traces of brilliant coloring. Most of the male
figures were young and vibrant. A few, in stark
contrast, were in reclining positions, their bodies
wasted and shriveled. The expressions on the faces
of them all were inward-gazing, mysterious.

"These are my treasures."

Arnold's voice trembled with emotion just as it
had on the day that he had first led Pete through
the apartment, from object to object.

"Jackie, it's a unique collection," interjected Pete,
catching the change in the older man's tone.

"Yes," said Arnold, "it is probably the only such

collection in the civilized world. The tribe who fashioned these stunning objects lived, essentially, in the Stone Age. Tragically, a few years after I made contact with them, the entire tribe succumbed to an attack of influenza brought to them unwittingly by a group of missionaries. The missionaries regarded their statuary and artifacts as idolatry and dutifully destroyed what remained of the tribe's artistic history. Then they proceeded to inter the entire village under a cross, hoping to send them to an afterworld they could never even have imagined. Apart from one or two isolated pieces, my collection represents all that the world knows of them."

"How fascinating," said Jackie politely. "I'd love to have you tell me more about them."

"One day I will, my dear Jackie," said Arnold. "But let me show you the collection first. The Museum of Primitive Art has been after me for the last decade to donate it. They've made handsome offers. Just last year they even obtained an option to buy the townhouse next to the museum. They were ready to name it the Arnold and Phoebe Jensen Wing. But," he smiled, "maybe it's selfish, but we can't imagine parting with a single piece."

Pete, who already felt twinges of guilt for what was going through his mind about Allison, interrupted. "Let's *all* take a look at the collection."

"Pete, there are very few people I could say this of," said Arnold quickly, "but my niece knows my treasures as well as I. You'd do me a great favor if you'd keep her company, while I show off to your wife."

He turned to Jackie. "I saw you looking at that

little figure on the shelf near where you and the McDonalds were standing." He pointed to a ceramic statue of a muscular man standing on one foot. "It's one of my pets. It is, believe it or not, a fertility charm. Let's begin with it." He pressed Jackie forward.

Allison turned to Pete, giving him her full attention. "My uncle tells me you're in publishing," she said. "I have a friend who works for a company called Wiley. She edits chemistry or physics texts, I think. Her name is Christine Waits. Do you know her?"

"Well, no. You see the kind of publishing I do . . ." and Pete trailed into a long expatiation on hardcover fiction (his love), agents (his bane), writers' advances (becoming way too high), paperback advances (beyond insanity), and so on. Allison, her eyes homing in on Pete's like a heat-sensing missile, devoured it all.

"Where were we?" said Pete, holding her stare for a moment and losing track of the point he was making. "You were saying earlier that you ran today. Did you just come from the reservoir?"

"You mean because I'm dressed this way?" said Allison with a laugh, looking down at her warm-up suit. "Actually, it's become my uniform for any time of day. I finished my laps a while ago and then I showered and changed into a fresh suit before coming over here. I can't stand the feel of my body when it's all hot and sweaty, can you? And there's nothing that feels better than a hot, tingling shower after a lot of exercise. Last week I found a marvelous new bath oil, too. It makes your skin so silky. Maybe you should try it. What do you think?" Allison held up one of her hands to Pete.

Pete took her hand gingerly. It was smooth and pale and perfectly manicured. "It smells nice," he murmured. "Do you always run at the reservoir?" he added, in an effort to be matter-of-fact.

"Where else?"

"Me, too. How much do you do a day?"

"It depends. On weekends, only about three laps. There are just too many pickup artists around."

"Hey, that's almost five miles!"

"That's nothing. On weekdays, I do between eight and ten miles."

"You're way too good for me."

"I doubt it," said Allison, smiling encouragingly. "It's just a matter of working your way up to it. Do you run with the gang from here?"

"Most days. The timing's good. They get me out between six and seven and we're back home in under an hour. While we're showering, Phoebe makes breakfast for us. I used to be a bacon-and-eggs man with plenty of buttered toast and two cups of coffee. But now I realize it was that kind of start to the day that produced an astronomical number of coronaries thirty and forty years ago. Phoebe puts together a drink in her blender that has everything in it from kelp to carrots. Then we all have a special granola mix with herb tea on the side. They've also got me into the habit of taking a handful of vitamin supplements. I don't know if it's the vitamins or the exercise, but I've never felt better."

"Does Jackie run with you?"

"No, I've tried, but Jackie feels that a person should only run when he or she's in danger."

They both laughed.

"She won't even have breakfast with us. She thinks vitamins are for kids and Phoebe's brew is for masochists."

They laughed again.

"Well, I'm not as early a riser as these folks," said Allison. "A pity. I'd love to have some company."

Allison paused and looked at Pete expectantly. Christ, thought Pete, does she always come on this strong? He checked quickly to see where Jackie was. She and Arnold were on the far side of the room. He decided to take the bait.

"How about my joining you then?"

"What a marvelous idea!" answered Allison.

She seemed so surprised at the suggestion that it occurred to Pete that perhaps he'd been wrong. Perhaps she had not been leading him on. He forged ahead before he had time to fully weigh the dangers of what he was proposing.

"Let's make a date then. For tomorrow. When do you usually run?"

"I get on the track at eight sharp."

"So late?"

"I suppose that does seem late to most people, but my office doesn't open until ten. I work for a foundation. Fund-raising." She laughed. "Most of the people whose money we're after aren't prepared to answer their phones until then."

"We can't swing it, then."

"Oh?"

"I'm flexible, but not that flexible," said Pete, keeping his disappointment from his voice.

"Darling girl," said Victor Macrae, walking up to them. "I haven't had a chance to say hello yet. Pete here has had you cornered ever since you arrived."

Allison roared as if Victor were Henny Youngman. Pete hung on the edge of their conversation for a few minutes. Damn the little bitch. He was convinced now that she was a tease. She had manipulated him from the start. She'd known all along that their schedules were too different for him to be able to run with her. Anger mixed with desire, and he became aware that he was perspiring so much that his shirt was clinging to his back. He'd better get the hell away from her. He spotted the Barnetts standing with the Goodmans, and seized the excuse to break away gracefully from Allison and Victor. Just before he reached the others, Jackie, still in Arnold's tow, grabbed his wrist and pulled him sharply toward her.

"Did Farrah Fawcett-Minor make a play for you?" she whispered.

"Don't be silly, love," he said quickly. "Let's say a quick hello to Dave and Kim and the Goodmans, then run along."

The more he saw of the Barnetts, the more he liked them. They were both warm, low-keyed . . . nice. He asked Kim what the new show at the Cooper-Hewitt was, only half listening to her reply, then questioned Dave about an upcoming marathon in Central Park that he was slated to run in.

Someone mentioned the handsome calligraphy

on the evening's party invitations. Sylvia, it turned out, was the person who'd lettered the invitations as well as the no-smoking sign in the lobby. She shrugged her shoulders deprecatingly.

"If Sylvia won't toot her own horn, I will," said Ben. "Not only is she excellent at calligraphy, she's also a graphologist. And first-rate. So good, in fact, that she's testified at trials. I've always said she'd make a better counterfeiter than a housewife."

"*This* housewife is starving," said Jackie.

"We've got to cut out now," said Pete. "I promised Jackie we'd have sushi at the Nippon."

They headed for the foyer to say goodbye to the others. Jackie was immediately set upon by Eileen Cole, who was carrying a tray of crudités grouped around a bowl of pale-green sauce.

"You must try some," Eileen said. "The dip is my own inspiration. Bean sprouts and pea pods blended in the Cuisinart for half a minute."

Victor and Allison were standing where Pete had left them. Pete watched Jackie trying to extricate herself from Eileen, then stepped up to Victor and clapped him on the shoulder.

"Well, we're off," he boomed with the artificial good cheer he reserved for book salesmen and young children. He turned to Allison. "And it was a special pleasure to meet you."

Allison tilted her head upward and almost brushed his cheek with her lips, then whispered in his ear. "Let's compromise. I'll meet you at seven-thirty in front of the Guggenheim. Tomorrow."

10

Jackie stirred and shifted from her back to her side, pushing the pillow tighter under her cheek. She cracked her eyes half open. The light seeping under the shades was dark gray. She must have an hour to go before she had to get up. As she began to drift back to the dream she had just left, she moved closer to Pete's side of the bed. Ah, Pete. But he wasn't there. She turned abruptly in his direction. Of course. He was already up. He wore a T-shirt and running shorts and was seated on the edge of the bed, tying his shoes.

"Do you have to run *every* morning?" she murmured.

Pete grunted noncommittally.

"Come here," she whispered.

He came into her arms and slid his body over hers. She took one of his hands.

"Feel me. I want you."

"Oh, honey. I want you, too. Tonight, I promise."

He reached his tongue into her mouth and eagerly ran his hand down her body. The T-shirt she had slept in had ridden up over her breasts.

"Why are you so tough on me?" asked Jackie. "You don't know what you're doing to me. You stinker," she added good-humoredly. She released him and silently watched him drop his keys into a pocket. She was happy to be where she was: <u>in</u> bed. Except that she wanted Pete with her.

"Run fast," she said drowsily, yielding again to sleep. "Maybe there'll be time when you get back. Say hi to everyone."

"Hi to everyone?" he echoed.

"Arnold and Phoebe and Victor and Ben . . ."

"Oh, yeah. I will if I see them."

"What do you mean?" she said, really awake for the first time. "Who *are* you running with?"

"Allison."

"That's the second time this week! Not to mention last week!"

"What's it matter who I run with? It's the running that counts," he said, closing the bedroom door behind him.

11

The sun, just touching the horizon, threw a soft, shimmering cone of light over the surface of the reservoir. The wind was gusty but gentle, and there was a slight chop to the water. It was the following day, and a gorgeous morning. However, the forecast predicted temperatures in the low nineties by mid-afternoon. The Yankees were scheduled to play Kansas City, and though the fans would suffer, it was unlikely that the heat would keep them from the game. The Yankees were only a half game from taking the lead in their division. Nor were the temperatures likely to blunt a demonstration promised by angry welfare mothers against Jimmy Carter, who was flying into New York that afternoon to receive a humanitarian award at the Waldorf.

Early morning newscasters had been rehashing these and other upcoming events of the day for a good two hours, but the concerns of those on the reservoir track were more immediate. Pete and Allison had just completed their second lap, running side by side. If Allison slowed her stride and if Pete pressed hard, they were able to keep pace together. Two hundred yards into the third lap, Pete pulled up short.

"I can't hack another round," he gasped. "I'll sit this one out."

As Pete collapsed onto the grass, Allison gave him a thumbs up and quickened her stride. Her long, slender legs moved gracefully. Soon she disappeared around the bend.

In the short time they had been jogging together, Pete had learned that she had grown up in Philadelphia (on the Main Line), the elder of two sisters and, so she said, the heart and soul of her rich daddy's life. Her mother, Arnold Jensen's sister, had died when she was a teenager. After two years of college in Switzerland (finishing school, she amended), she had come to New York, married, and two years later divorced her husband, a broker, when she discovered him in bed with one of his partners. A male. She was enthusiastic about her work and apparently was good at it. She was one of three fund-raisers assigned to corporate gifts. Her job was to see that the companies in her charge not only maintained but increased their annual donations. Although she was vague about it, Pete suspected that she shared her East Hampton weekend house with a young executive from one of these companies.

Twelve minutes later, Allison pulled up in front of Pete.

"Hi," she said, sitting down beside him.

She pulled off her sweatband and shook out her hair. Her cheeks were pink. "Don't be discouraged. In two weeks, you've improved tremendously. Do you realize that we ran that second lap in about . . . thirteen minutes, which means you're running a mile in slightly over eight minutes?"

"I can't believe I'll ever get down to six minutes. That's what Dave Barnett does."

"Just give it time. Why are you so pooped today?"

"Jackie and I were out with friends," said Pete. "Stayed up too late." While he spoke, he rubbed his shoulders absentmindedly. Now he winced. "Oh, shit. I don't want to believe this, but I think I've pulled a muscle." He tilted his head back and twisted it around full circle, then hunched his shoulders up. "Ah, that's better." He laughed. "Did I do this this morning? I don't remember it. Oh, damn. There it goes again."

"Wait a second. Relax and don't move," said Allison. "I'll give you a massage. I know about these things. Pulled muscles. I've had them plenty of times." She kneeled down behind him and placed her hands on his shoulders. "Now take a deep breath. Breathe out. Slowly. Let the tension flow out. That's it." Pete shut his eyes and leaned back toward Allison. Slowly she kneaded his shoulders. Then she applied more pressure. "How's that? Not too much, I hope."

"Oh, no. That's wonderful. Keep it up. You're an

angel." Pete half-turned his head and smiled. Now Allison pressed hard against Pete, pushing down with firm and sure strokes.

"Perfect," sighed Pete.

Two cops paused on the walk that circled close to the reservoir. This was their turf, and they had seen it all. The fatties. The oldies. The crazies. The serious ones. And those out to score. Jogging sure beat dog-walking for pickups.

"Look at that," said one, directing his partner's attention to Allison. "It's got a great ass. And tits. Christ! What odds will you lay he'll be in her pants in fifteen minutes?"

"No bet," laughed his partner. "Lucky bastard!"

Nor would a bet have been taken by Jackie, who sat, half hidden by a tree, on a rise above Pete and Allison holding the *New York Times* in front of her as a screen. She could not believe she was where she was, or doing what she was. Spying! And she could not believe what she was witnessing. It was devastating. The sexual electricity between Pete and Allison was so clear and so strong that she shuddered and then began to weep.

12

Jackie and Tyrone LeBlanc rushed through the claustrophobic maze of tunnels and platforms at the Union Square subway station like divers struggling to the surface for air. A raucous Hispanic song blared from the speaker system of an underground record store. The smells of donuts, chuchufritos, potato knishes, and sausages blended together, fogging the air with a dense ethnic smog.

Tyrone brushed against a short, squat woman carrying an infant in one arm, holding fast to a squalling toddler with the other. The woman glared at Tyrone and screamed at him in Spanish. Tyrone stuck out his tongue. A woman paused to stare, her face blank, then moved on.

"Come on, let's go," said Jackie, grabbing Tyrone's hand. They pushed through the turnstiles and ran up the steps into the open air.

"Where have you brought me?" said Tyrone, with exaggerated delivery, as though he were being thrust into the dirtiest cage at the Central Park Zoo monkey house. "Why am I here?"

"I need a friend is why. And you're it."

"You *are* serious about this shape-up jazz, aren't you?"

"You bet your black tush I'm serious," said Jackie.

Again she saw, in her mind's eye, Allison kneel behind Pete and begin to rub his shoulders, his neck, his back . . . his body. Pete rocked toward Allison, his eyes shutting. The joys of instant replay, thought Jackie bitterly, remembering all the times Pete had yelled at her to "watch this" as some poor schnook running down the field in the Monday night football game got hit from five directions, shown again and again in painful slow motion. She could not shake herself free of the scene that she had witnessed the day before. Over and over it intruded itself into her consciousness: Allison leaned forward, Pete leaned back. The motion was smooth and synchronized like a kid's game of row your boat. Only there was nothing innocent about it. It seemed unreal. Yet inevitable. She felt her eyes begin to tear, and blinked rapidly. Tyrone was a best buddy, but there was a limit to his need to know. She pointed across the square northward.

"Paragon's that way. But, first, Brownie's for lunch."

Brownie's Restaurant was a mecca for natural food faddists from all over the city. How many times had she heard their very own Eileen Cole complain how far away it was from Twelve East Eighty-third Street.

They waited silently for the light to change. Union Square was shabby and depressing. Traffic streamed around the small park in the middle of the square. Behind them, on Fourteenth Street, bargain hunters picked their way through bins of mismatched underwear and cheap stuffed animals shoved onto the street at them from discount stores. To the east stood the decaying mass of the old S. Klein department store. Out of business for years, but still there, like a sunken ship in Pearl Harbor. Its windows boarded over, paint flaking off its sides in leprous patches, it stood forlorn. The words "A square deal to all," lettered in dark blue, were still legible on one of its walls. Several stolid office buildings poked above the tree line to the north and west, and on the side streets off the square some needle trade unions still had headquarters. Occasionally they held rallies in the square, perhaps hoping to catch the fervor of the past, when the words "Union Square" were a promise to New York's immigrant workers. Nowadays the crowds were small, and it always seemed to be raining.

The traffic stopped, and Jackie and Tyrone edged their way between the converging trucks and cars, into and through the tattered park, and out the other side past street vendors hawking their wares. Peaches and mangoes. (Unripe.) Wool knit caps. (Never mind that it was June.) Real leather belts. (The hides of God knows what poor, derelict animals.) And the newest street product—rolling papers in twelve different flavors from licorice to guacamole.

On Sixteenth Street, they paused before Brownie's rustic wooden exterior and then pushed their way inside. A counter stretched the length of the narrow room. Middle-aged waitresses in striped uniforms fussed attentively around their customers, first names flying back and forth across the counter as "family" ordered their "usuals." Behind the waitresses, a pair of fast-moving kitchen helpers chopped and squeezed and pureed their way through a stockpile of vegetables. Tyrone wavered at the sight of the mounds of shredded carrots, beets, cucumbers, lettuce. "How about some Chinese instead?" he asked, his eyes mock-pleading. Jackie urged him in, but midway through their salads, she suspected he was right. The nutritional value of the food did not make up for its blandness. Later, after she tipped over a shaker of sea salt onto the plate of the man sitting to the other side of her, she *knew* Tyrone was right. Ignoring her apologies, the man made an elaborate show of brushing away the grains of salt from his plate with his napkin, then glared at her for good measure. Jackie had forgotten the enforced intimacy of countertop meals.

Paragon came as a relief. It was a cavernous, no-frills sporting goods store with a businesslike atmosphere. And what a business. The whole country seemed to have gone berserk over flexing their muscles and running their feet flat. They were pounding along the banks of the Charles River, the Potomac, and Lake Michigan, and, in the middle of the country, where a pretty body of water might not be so handy, a nice manmade trail would do just fine. They were running solo, in pairs, and in groups. Just the other day, Jackie had seen a mother and father jogging while they pushed their baby in its carriage ahead of them. And it didn't seem to matter to anyone how miserable the weather was. When the thermometer was flirting with the hundred-degree mark and every other sensible person was sitting hard by an air conditioner, there'd always be some poor fool sweating his way through his daily quota of miles. The word had gone out—to everyone, it seemed. The gurus said running was like a second childhood, play rediscovered. Running like playing? That was nuts. Running was work. No matter. Jackie was about to join their ranks.

"Let's make this fast," she said to Tyrone. "Or I may change my mind."

"That's *your* problem, honey," said Tyrone. "I already see lots of goodies to keep me busy. Starting there." He pointed across the store to a rack of mustard-colored hunting jackets inundated with pockets, flaps, buckles. "Call me if you want a brutally honest reaction to how you look in one of those nasty warm-up suits. You wouldn't catch me in one of those baggy old things. My poor little sexy fanny would feel positively lost."

Jackie looked around the store for help. She would need some assistance choosing sneakers. Only, she knew, they weren't called sneakers and they bore no resemblance to the worn pair of Keds moldering in a corner of her closet.

Ten minutes later the salesman had her persuaded that she had just the right pair of running shoes, a little flex here, a little cushioning there, enough support and not too snug a fit. She chose the color: a deep mauve stripe against white; raspberry sherbet mixed with vanilla. Next, a warm-up suit, also in mauve. Then a couple of sweatbands in blue, a handful of white T-shirts, and, lastly, running shorts. She had tried on and rejected a couple of pairs and was just checking out the fit of another in the store's only mirror when Tyrone caught up with her.

"Forget those," he said. "They're too butch."

Three try-ons later she passed his test and her own, and they hustled on back uptown.

She was ready to beat Allison at her own game.

Balancing her Paragon paraphernalia in one arm and a large D'Agostino shopping bag in the other, Jackie struggled through the front door of the apartment and on into the kitchen. She put the groceries on the counter and went into the living room. Pete was stretched out on the couch reading a manuscript. He looked up and smiled. "Hi, baby. What's for supper? I'm starved."

Jackie dumped the things from Paragon on his stomach.

"Running shorts and Pumas, that's what. I give up. I'm getting on the treadmill. I took a look at myself, and I didn't like what I saw. Maybe our sex life isn't as good these days because *I* don't look or feel as good as I should."

She smiled tentatively, trying to make a joke out of it, but her eyes gave her away.

Pete swept the manuscript pages and sports equipment aside and jumped up and hugged her. "Oh, honey, you always look good to me. I love you so much. And I'm so proud of you. I can't wait to start running with you. You'll see. It's fantastic."

"What are we waiting for?" said Jackie, laughing. "How about right now? But go easy on me. I may give out after five minutes."

"Don't worry. I remember what it's like starting. Come on, let's go. But, first . . ."

He pulled her body tight against his, his tongue probing her mouth, while from behind his hand moved firmly down the curve of her back. Caught in the vise of his embrace, Jackie felt herself melting with happiness and relief. She had made her move in time. It was not too late.

13

The phone rang three times before it was picked up.

"Hello."

"You were marvelous, my dear, and more importantly, effective."

"Thank you, Uncle Arnold."

"It is *we* who should thank *you*, Allison."

"Do you think she's really motivated enough now to begin?"

"She began today. Nothing spurs the body more than the heart."

"Who said that, Uncle?"

"Arnold Jensen," he replied laughingly, and then he hung up.

Part Two

14

JULY

Jackie hung on the edge of the pool, panting. She had just completed twenty laps, and her arms, legs, her whole body ached from the exertion. But it was a pleasurable sensation. She had been running now with Pete every morning for a month, and the changes that already had occurred in her body astonished and thrilled her. She was more limber. Her legs were stronger. And she had more stamina. Pete, she knew, cut back his pace for her, but she was beginning to be able to keep up with him. She had begun, too, to think of her body as a piece of machinery, and she marveled at the synchronization of its parts—muscles, joints, bones, tissues.

As a kid, she'd been a tomboy. She'd climbed trees, shinnied up ropes, raced her bicycle through the streets of her neighborhood. During high school, she'd skated, played tennis, swum, ridden horseback. These things had come so easily to her, however—she had a naturally lean and athletic body and was well-coordinated—that she had taken that part of her life for granted. Then in college and later in New York she had drifted away from it. Until now, she hadn't realized how lazy she had become. She could count on one hand the number of times in the past year she had done anything more strenuous than a fast trot from Bendel's to Saks to shop during her lunch hour.

But that was past. Now she felt incredibly in tune with herself. Healthier. More alive. Of course, cutting back on cigarets—it was hard to believe that she was down to four a day—had helped. And without trying to, she found herself drinking less. Martinis suddenly tasted harsh. And if someone had told her a month ago that she, too, would be quaffing "Phoebe's brew" in the mornings with the rest of the group, she'd never have believed it.

She hoisted herself out of the pool and drew a towel over her shoulders as she looked around the gym. What an extraordinary luxury it was to have a facility like this where they lived. How many places were there like it in the whole of New York? Yet, after her initial excitement when they moved in, she had all but ignored its existence. Sure, Pete had come up here every evening after he got home from the office. He swam and worked out on the Nautilus and on the rowing machine. He always asked her to join him, but it was always inconvenient. She was either in the midst of cooking dinner or on the phone talking to Trish. What a fool she'd been.

Ironically, here was another thing for which she had Allison to thank. If it hadn't been for those few terrible moments she had spent cowering behind the *New York Times* and staring in horror at Pete and Allison, she never would have started exercising in the first place.

In the far corner of the gym, Pete was trying out a new maneuver on the Nautilus under Dave Barnett's supervision. The Barnetts were early-evening regulars. Jackie had thought Dave had been in great shape when they'd first met him, but seeing him here now, dressed only in a tank suit, he looked to her like a professional athlete. Not one of those beefy pro-football players who hawk beer and jockey shorts on TV, but a world-class gymnast at the top of his form. His stomach was as tight as a washboard, and even at a distance you could sense his strength and vitality.

Kim Barnett was swimming laps, and the sound she made blocked out Dave's instructions. Jackie stretched out lazily on her back. Above her was a peerless deep blue sky. Whenever the weather was good, Buddy was under orders to have the glass roof pulled open. It was early, probably not yet seven, and a little late-afternoon sun still spotlighted a corner of the pool.

"Hello," called a new voice. Jackie sat up. Ben was standing in the doorway. "How's everybody doing?" he asked.

"Just great," shouted Dave. "Pete's coming along beautifully on this, and Kim's working on a half mile, arms only. She ought to be through any minute."

"Fantastic! Jackie, how're *you* doing?"

"Great, now that I'm sitting down."

"Well, sweetheart, I'll admit it. I'd begun to despair of ever seeing you up here. Or on the track for that matter. How long has it been since you started working out?"

"About a month."

"And you look three months the better for it. Keep it up." Ben studied Jackie thoughtfully for a moment and then continued. "You know, I think you're ready for the Nautilus. Do you want to give it a shot?"

"If you think *it* can cope with *me*."

Ben laughed. "It's the other way around, actually. Before you start training regularly, you'll have to see your doctor for a complete physical as well as a stress test to measure your cardiovascular capacity. To see if you can handle the equipment. I'll have to have an okay from him on your overall fitness. In writing. Agreed?"

Jackie nodded.

"Good. We can't take any chances. Arnold's insurance premiums are staggering as it is without someone's collapsing up here. And, while you're at it, I'd appreciate it if you'd have the doctor make a copy for you of the results of his examination. Just for the insurance records. Now, how about your meeting me up here tomorrow about this time, and we'll start setting up a program for you."

"Fine," said Jackie.

Ben closed the door softly behind him. Jackie got up and walked over to Pete and Dave.

"What's this stuff about a doctor's okay for the

Nautilus?" asked Jackie. "And in writing! Is he kidding? If my mother were alive, he'd want a note from her, too."

"Kidding he is not," said Dave. "Do you realize that these machines are the same ones used by the pros? The Cosmos, the Knicks, they've all got them. And, believe me, no one should take on one of these things without a medical go-ahead. I'm up here half an hour each day on this little baby," he ruefully patted the saddle seat of the Nautilus, "and it's one hell of a workout. At least once a week Ben comes up and measures and charts my progress. Kim's, too. Hey, Kim," he broke off, turning to his wife, who had just pulled herself out of the pool. "Great going!"

"I had to get a checkup and doctor's approval, too, Jackie," said Pete.

"You never told me that."

"Well, maybe I forgot. Big deal. Would I tell you if I got my eyes tested to renew my driver's license?"

Kim approached them, smiling. She was not at all out of breath, though she had been swimming steadily for at least twenty minutes. She was encased in a racing suit made of one of the new synthetics and it revealed as much of her body as if she were naked. She was sleek and lithe—gorgeous, thought Jackie admiringly. Jackie wondered how old she was. Probably close to her own age. *She* should look so good. Well, maybe she would. In time.

"How about taking a sauna with us?" asked

Dave. "I turned it on about ten minutes ago. The temperature should be just right now."

"You mean we can just lie in there and do *nothing?*" asked Jackie feigning disbelief.

"That's the general idea. There's a stack of towels over there." Dave gestured toward a small closet next to the sauna.

The sauna was fitted with places for four people to lie down or sit. The walls were of well-seasoned cedar. Dave ladled some water from an oak bucket onto the hot coals, which hissed in response.

All four immediately stretched out flat, retreating to the privacy of their own thoughts. Jackie thought of Sallie Lasher, head buyer for the "Savvy" shop. Jackie was her number one assistant. Located on the fourth floor of Bendel's, it was one of the few places in the store where price tags ran under a hundred dollars, and its name was brilliantly appropriate: If you didn't have the loot to buy top fashions, you sure as hell had to have the smarts. Sallie was the presiding genius of the floor, but, just today, Jackie had heard that she was being wooed seriously by Lord & Taylor. Jackie adored Sallie and would miss her, but clearly this could be her big break. She forced her mind away from the seductive charms of blossoming career scenarios and asked the Barnetts how long they had lived in New York.

"Two years this September," answered Kim. "We love it. We plan to stay indefinitely. I guess you'd have to call us born-again New Yorkers."

"Good line. You could call us that, too. Where are you from originally?"

"I'm from outside of Detroit. Dave grew up in Kansas City. We met in Ann Arbor."

"College sweethearts?"

"That's us. What about you two?"

"Nothing so romantic. We met through work. My roommate here edited one of those make-your-self-over books. For men. Advice on what length their socks should be and whether to part their hair on the right or the left. You might have heard of it. It was called *The Now Man*."

"For Christ's sake, Jackie, can't you forget that fucking book?"

"We all know it was early in your career, dear. Pete sees himself now as a bionic editor: the soul of Max Perkins; the integrity of Alfred Knopf; the humor of Bennett Cerf."

"And the sexual prowess of T. S. Eliot," Pete added.

"But back to how we met. This book—I don't dare repeat the title again," Jackie glanced at Pete and continued. "The marketing people at Pete's publishing house decided to do a promotional tie-in with Saks, where I was working then. I was the bright young flunky charged with seeing that all the pieces of the show were in the right place at the right time. Pete had to take me out to lunch. He felt I was quite beneath him. I don't think I enjoyed myself any more than he did. Remember, darling? I wouldn't say we disliked each other, but we were . . . indifferent. We bumped into each other again about a year later at a party in Soho, and everything came together. Fast. But enough of us. How long have you been here?"

"Since November," said Dave. "When Richard Kelly first brought us over here, we couldn't believe our luck."

"*Our* Richard Kelly?" interrupted Pete. "Fourth floor rear?"

"Oh, didn't you know? He's a partner in a real estate agency. It's called 'York Properties,' I think. Kim and I almost didn't come over and look at the place, we were so ticked off at Kelly. He made us fill out an impossibly long application form that asked for the most personal information I've ever seen. Including medical data. Some stuff I didn't give them, but—"

"Wait a second," said Jackie. "That sounds like the same damn form I filled out at one place. Though I didn't see Kelly anywhere. Just some old woman in a get-up that looked like a space uniform for the aged. But I guess we shouldn't gripe. That is, *you* shouldn't gripe. It got you your apartment. We came across ours by accident."

"No. By theft," said Pete. He went on to describe how he'd met the Macraes and Jensens and how much they loved their apartment, and then the next thing Jackie knew she was asking Dave and Kim to come by for a drink on Saturday night. Her invitation rapidly developed into a plan to follow drinks with the new Truffaut movie and a late Chinese dinner.

Pete and Dave returned to their favorite subject of the moment: the Nautilus. After a few minutes, Dave interrupted himself: "Just so you two don't get too discouraged. I have a confession to make. Before Kimmie and I moved in here, we were in miserable condition. We didn't take care of ourselves at all. Oh, sure, sometimes I'd play squash with a college roommate, or Kim and I would rent bikes on a Sunday, but that was it. We didn't eat elaborate meals, just good old American cooking. Lots of it. And, let me tell you, even in the provinces we know about martinis."

"Viva the provinces," laughed Jackie.

"I used to sock away two at night before dinner. Regularly and very dry. And Kim," Dave bowed toward her, "kept up with me."

"Tell them what happened the other day," said Kim.

"Oh, yes, I was annoyed as hell, but, thinking back on it, it was pretty funny. Kim and I still like our occasional martinis, so every now and then we sneak one. Well, damn it, Lil—you know, Buddy the super's wife—she cleans for us once a week . . ."

"She also cleans for the McDonalds," interrupted Kim. "You should see if she has any extra time for you. She's very good. And cheap."

"Anyway, Lil found our bottle of Tanqueray, and she gave us a real dressing-down for it. On top of that, she told Victor about it, and he called me up on the phone. I felt like I was eight years old again. Of course, he's right. Gin is poison to the system."

"I've never felt better in my life, thanks to them, but they really are crazed on the subject of physical fitness, aren't they?" said Jackie.

"Speaking of fitness, they don't seem so fit lately, do they?" said Kim. "Ben and Victor, all of them. I noticed it again just now when Ben was up. He looked sort of pale and tired."

"A few weeks ago, Victor mentioned a bug making the rounds," said Dave. "One of those summer viruses. They see so much of each other, I bet they just pass something like that back and forth. But I'm sure they'll be okay soon. They really know how to cope. Listen to this. Last February, Kim had an awful siege. We didn't realize it, but she had pneumonia."

"One day I would be feeling fine, then the next day, I would be flat on my back," said Kim. "I couldn't breathe, my body would ache, and my temperature would be way up. It went on that way for weeks. I had gone to see our doctor, but he wasn't able to get rid of it. Then Arnold insisted we see his doctor. I was feeling terrible, so the doctor came to see me. Imagine, a doctor making a house call! For the first week, the doctor came by every evening on his way home from the office to see how I was doing. He refused to use antibiotics. He's a great believer in holistic medicine. And between the vitamins he prescribed—in massive amounts—and Miriam and Phoebe's teas and soups, I was up on my feet again in days. Even though I was completely recovered, they urged Dave and me to change our eating habits. Permanently. We followed up on their ideas, including the vitamins, and we felt better immediately. But, hold it," said Kim, interrupting herself. "I think you should check the time, Dave." She turned to Jackie and Pete. "We're due at the St. Regis at eight-fifteen," she explained. "Our oldest and closest friends are in town from

Ann Arbor for a week. We're having dinner with them tonight."

Dave opened the door and went into the gym, letting a cool blast of outside air into the sauna. The draft made Jackie realize how close to dehydration she was.

"I can only take about a minute more of this," she said to Pete.

Moments later, Dave was back. "It's seven-thirty. We've got to go, but I want to tell you something first. It may sound corny to you, but, you know, I love them all. I truly do. Apart from working out together, we actually don't see that much of them. But I know I can count on them. Always." Dave paused, and his voice softened as he continued. "I was an orphan, and Kim lost her mom and dad when she was very young and, for both of us, they're almost like the parents we never had. They're, well . . . they're very special people to us. But," he added briskly, "enough with the sentiment. This place is baking my brains. Kimmie, let's get the show on the road." He stood and pulled Kim to her feet. "See you Saturday at seven."

"Pete!" Jackie said, when they had gone. "Did you hear what Dave said?"

"Huh?" said Pete lazily. "Yeah, I heard. Kim's parents died when she was young. And Dave was an orphan. And Dave thinks of the gang as his parents. So what?"

"It's strange, that's what. Technically, we're all orphans. All four of us. None of our parents are alive."

"What's so strange? People grow old and die.

Sometimes people don't grow old and still they die. Like my mother and father. A head-on crash when they were only in their forties. That isn't fair. But it happened. Your parents, they were in their seventies when they passed away. Nothing more natural than that. Too bad you were born so late and didn't have more time with them."

"I still say it's peculiar. Four people our age without parents. And the two of us don't really have any other close relatives either. I must remember to ask Kim if it's the same with them. But I see your point, I guess. That's life."

"And this'll be death, if we don't get out now," said Pete, leaning toward Jackie.

"Don't try to kiss me. Our lips will singe."

15

Damn that Sony, thought Jackie, hurrying out of bed. The alarm hadn't gone off. It was already eleven-twenty, and she'd have to hustle to meet Pete by twelve-thirty. She'd taken the day off—the last few weeks had been so slow that Sallie Lasher had almost insisted on it—and Pete had promised her a lunch at a restaurant of her choice. Jackie had selected Coup de Fusil. This was one of the city's citadels for *cuisine minceur*, the new style of French cooking that contrived delectable yet light and delicate dishes from natural ingredients cooked without cream or flour and with only a hint of butter. It was a great place to "diet" without sacrificing any of the pleasures of fine food.

Jackie had run with Pete earlier in the morning and, after showering, had climbed back into bed for the luxury of more sleep, though sleeping until almost noon hadn't been part of her plan. Now, with an eye on the clock, she sped through her skin-cleansing routine and, in her mind, through her choice of what she might wear. Finally dressed and with ten minutes to make it to the restaurant, she opened the front door, stepped into the hall, and almost got knocked flat by a couch. She jumped back into the open doorway. A large, muscular bearded man, sweating profusely, struggled down the corridor past her, one end of a long beige couch hefted onto his shoulders, calling out directions to his partner behind.

"Lower it, Sal. I said *lower* it, shmuck, not raise it."

"Who you calling shmuck, asshole?" came a voice from the back.

The bearded mover noticed Jackie. "We got a lady here, pisshead. Knock it off," he said, winking at Jackie.

Wait a second, thought Jackie. Was someone moving out? What was going on? She hadn't heard a sound from inside. As soon as the movers were past, she hurried to the stairway and peered upward. Phoebe looked down at her, her expression startled.

"Dearie," Phoebe said. "What on earth are you doing home at this hour? Is something wrong?"

"I have the day off. What's going on?"

"Oh, didn't you know? The Barnetts are relocating." she replied.

"That's impossible! We just saw them two days ago, and they didn't say a word about moving."

"I think Dave was trying to get the company to change its mind, but you know how IT&T is. They ship people around all the time. Very inhumane, I've always thought. Still that's the penalty people pay for their nice salaries. My, you look well today. That's a lovely top you have on."

"Thank you," said Jackie impatiently. "Where are Kim and Dave?"

"Now? They've left already."

"*Left?*" said Jackie, staring wordlessly at the movers now heading up the stairs to the Barnetts' apartment for another load.

"Oh, I see what you mean," said Phoebe. "The furniture. They're not taking it with them."

Dave didn't think they'd be gone for more than six months, Phoebe explained. She and Arnold wished they could hold the apartment for them, but they really couldn't afford to let it sit empty. And, of course, they didn't allow sublets. She and Arnold had agreed that the least they could do for the Barnetts was to take care of putting their furniture in storage. Especially because Kim had wanted to go along with Dave right away to see if the apartment the company had lined up was up to snuff.

"Poor lambs," sighed Phoebe, "they only got word of Dave's new assignment yesterday."

"Where've they gone?"

"Somewhere warm. Let me think. I'm positive it began with an 's'. It was either San Antonio or San Diego. No, not San Diego. Somewhere in South America."

Jackie turned and walked back to lock the apartment door, her mind reeling.

"Now I remember," Phoebe called out. "It's Santo Domingo. Yes, that's it."

16

As soon as Jackie sat down next to Pete at Coup de Fusil, she told him about the Barnetts. The news did not surprise or disturb him. That was the way the big multinationals operated. Especially IT&T. Did she remember the book he had read last year? *The Sovereign State of ITT*. Those guys were as hard as Marine drill instructors. But Dave knew what the score was. Santo Domingo? Why not? Hell, they'd probably love it. Beaches. Great weather. Year-round tan. And it wasn't as if they were being sent there forever.

Jackie found it difficult to buy Pete's breezy explanations. The last time they'd seen Kim and Dave they'd made a date to see a movie together. This Saturday, for God's sake. If *she* had been Kim, she certainly would have said something. Pete accused her of examining the issue too closely and refused to discuss the subject further. They'd hear from the Barnetts soon enough.

Jackie was irked by Pete's peremptoriness, but after lunch, as she began walking slowly uptown on Madison Avenue, her thoughts shifted from the Barnetts to the attractions in the shop windows. Midsummer sales were going full tilt. She found a lovely violet silk blouse at a new boutique and a terrific pair of sandals at an Italian shoe store she'd never noticed before. Home again, she gave herself a manicure, then lay down on the bed with the latest Ira Levin thriller, which had just hit number one on the bestseller list.

Later, when Pete arrived home from the office, he was lovingly attentive, making up for his earlier short-temperedness. He insisted on putting fresh and deliciously cool sheets on the bed, then ordered her back into it. They made love with leisurely delight. Afterward he poured them glasses of chilled Orvieto. The wine sparked their appetite, and they got out a takeout menu from an excellent small Szechuan restaurant they'd discovered in the neighborhood. Just as Pete was leaving to pick up their order, the doorbell rang. Jackie recognized Phoebe's voice. Moments later, Pete returned to the bedroom balancing two large plastic containers.

"What's that?"

"Present from Phoebe. Supper. For us."

"What!"

"She says she always cooks in quantity. Part of her heritage from growing up in a big family. She made this this afternoon, and she wanted to share it with us."

"What is it?"

"You'll laugh. Chicken soup, though hopefully not the Grossinger's type. No little lily pads of fat floating on top, I trust. If there's anything on top of this, it'll be wheat germ. And to go with the soup—lentil salad."

"That *is* sweet of Phoebe. What do you think? Should we skip Chinese?"

"Are you kidding?"

"My sentiments exactly."

Jackie and Pete dined royally on hot-and-sour soup, followed by sesame noodles and double-sauteed pork. Later they made love again. It was, thought Jackie, the best it had been in weeks.

The next morning, Jackie woke feeling marvelous, but she immediately thought of the Barnetts. She was still bothered by their sudden and unannounced departure. After a cup of strong black coffee, she telephoned Phoebe. She complimented her on her cooking and asked for the Barnetts' forwarding address. Phoebe seemed surprised by the question. The Barnetts hadn't left an address. They'd said they would send it as soon as they were settled. Phoebe kept switching the conversation back to all the vitamins and other good things that were in her soup. Jackie finally short-circuited Phoebe's nutrition rap by promising to try Phoebe's bean-sprout casserole later in the week. The one that was served over seaweed instead of noodles.

"That does sound original," said Jackie, her stomach doing cartwheels at the thought of it.

After saying goodbye—at last!—to Phoebe, Jackie sat silently considering the problem of the Barnetts for a few more minutes, then she dialed IT&T. They had to know how to reach them. She was transferred four times before being connected with a "Quincy Clark, Personnel," who informed her with stuffy finality that it was not company policy to give out information regarding employees. Then she remembered the Barnetts' friends at the St. Regis. Hadn't Kim said they were their closest friends? When she reached the hotel's front desk, the manager was incredulous. If madame did not know the names of the people she was trying to reach, what could he do for her? Surely she did not expect him to remember which of their hundreds of guests were from Ann Arbor, Michigan, and no, he certainly would not review for her the guest register for the past week. Jackie began to feel foolish. Probably they would have a letter from the Barnetts within the week. Just as Pete had said.

That night, in front of their door, they found an empty carton from the Chinese restaurant they'd ordered food from the evening before. A note was stapled to it.

> Jackie and Pete—
>   Spicy is good. But MSG is not.
> Please eat wisely. We care for you.
>   Phoebe

17

The next morning, Jackie received a telephone call at her office from Design Research. Some bookshelves they had bought were ready for delivery, and would someone be at the apartment to accept them? Jackie arranged for Buddy to let the delivery men in and left for home earlier than usual.

She struggled briefly with the cardboard surrounding one of the units before giving up on the idea of surprising Pete by setting them up herself. The cartons were a packer's triumph. Houdini couldn't have gotten out with an ax. She definitely needed help.

She was in the bedroom changing into her running shorts when she heard Pete open the door. After Pete changed, they tackled the cartons, one bracing, the other pulling. Then they carried the cases into the study and lined them up flush against the wall opposite the built-in shelves. They were Italian, molded white plastic, and they were perfect.

Pete was as pleased as Jackie.

"You done good, kid," he said. "Now, let's get going. Come on and give me a hand."

"With what?"

"The books, what else?"

"Oh, come on, Pete," groaned Jackie. "'Let's run first. We can do the books tonight."

"Why wait? It'll only take five minutes."

An hour later, lathered with sweat from hefting cartons of books from the front hall closet where they'd been stored to the study and onto the shelves, they had filled every inch of new shelf space. At least a half dozen unopened cartons still remained in the closet. Now that Pete had been re-minded of them, he insisted they find some other place to store them. Immediately. He was an anal retentive with an oak leaf cluster. He hated disarray. The unopened cartons were a personal affront. Why not check out the basement? Buddy kept the barbe-cue equipment there. There must be a storeroom where the books would be safely out of the way, he reasoned.

The stairs leading down were dimly etched by a single bulb hung from the ceiling. The wattage was no more than that of a refrigerator light. Shadow enveloped the area at the bottom of the stairs. When they reached the bottom, Pete searched in the gloom for the basement's master switch. Just at the moment when Jackie was thinking how grateful she was not to be down in this creepy place alone, Pete announced that he would run upstairs and get a flashlight: "Should have thought of that in the first place. It'll only take a second." He was gone before she could answer.

How could she admit to him that she was scared? In the basement of their own building? She knew that the basement was safe. Victor Macrae had made a big point of the building's security the first time she and Pete had seen Number Twelve. No one had ever even tried to break into it. It was probably the only place in the entire borough aside from the Police Academy to enjoy that honor. Even so, her mind was intent on running a frightening loop of nonstop muggers and rapists.

Then, as she waited for Pete, she started focusing on sounds, and that made things worse. She heard her heart thumping, and the sound of her own breathing roared in her ears. The stairs creaked, and she jumped. Then she realized she had made the noise herself, rocking back and forth on the balls of her feet. She stood absolutely still, holding her breath and listening like a deer in hunting season. Nothing. She was alone. And she was being absurd. There was no need to worry.

She began to relax. And then she heard it. The sharp retort of a lock snapping open. She shrank back against the staircase, freezing into a half-crouch. She knew she should get out of there, run, but she couldn't move. Suddenly, almost directly in front of her, a door opened. Instinctively, she threw one arm up against her eyes. A glaring light flooded the basement. It was blinding. Cold and white. The man silhouetted in the funnel of light hurriedly closed the door behind him, instantly plunging the basement into blackness again. Flares of color played against Jackie's retinas.

The man stepped forward, and now Jackie saw that it was Arnold Jensen.

"Why, Jackie," he said, his voice brittle. "What are you doing here?"

"Oh, thank God it's you," said Jackie, sinking down onto one of the steps. Her muscles were like jelly. She could have laughed or cried with equal ease. She held her head in her hands, unwilling and unable to utter another word for a long moment.

"Is something wrong?" asked Arnold, bending over her solicitously.

Jackie shook her head no and then, looking up at Arnold, felt a delayed rush of relief.

"What a scare you gave me," she said. As she started to explain, they heard footsteps above them. Pete stood at the top of the staircase, beaming his flashlight down on them.

"I'm afraid I gave poor Jackie something of a shock," said Arnold. "I was down here working and, of course, she didn't expect me. . . . But what are *you* doing here?" The tone of his voice demanded an answer.

"We have some books upstairs, in cartons, and no place to keep them," said Pete. "I figured there had to be storerooms in the basement, and that you wouldn't mind our stashing them. Like maybe here." Pete shone the flashlight on the door that Arnold had just come through.

"No, no. That's my laboratory. My equipment's very delicate. I have humidity and temperature controls, and I never introduce any foreign objects in there. But I may have another spot for you. How many cartons do you have all together?"

"About a half dozen."

"That's nothing. We have room enough for them. Come on, I'll give you a hand." Arnold urged Jackie and Pete up the stairs ahead of him, continuing to speak as he followed. "We keep everything under lock and key down here, though. Just to play it safe. When you want to get at the books again, tell Buddy, and he'll let you in."

Jackie glanced back at Arnold as he rose out of the shadows behind them. Even in light as dim as this, she could see that he looked wonderful. There was something special about him. His cheeks were ruddy and glowing, and the whiteness of his teeth was striking as he smiled at her.

He went up the steps quickly, taking the top three in one easy motion. Upstairs, he effortlessly lifted two of the book cartons and started back toward the basement.

18

The following Wednesday, Jackie received a letter from Kim Barnett. The stationery read "Hotel Excelsior, Santo Domingo." Kim's handwriting was spidery, and Jackie had difficulty making it out:

Dear Jackie,

Just a note to tell you we wish we'd had a chance to say goodbye to you two. We phoned you a couple of times after we got the news. Then time ran out and we literally had to race to catch our plane.

We've only been here three days and already I love it. (Just came in from a dip in the pool—this is the life!) The company's found two apartment possibilities for us. Both terrific. We haven't decided which to take. As soon as we know where we'll be living, we'll let you know.

Sorry about Saturday night. We were really look-

ing forward to Mel Brooks' new movie. Me especially. You know what a fan I am.

Stay in touch.

Always,
Kim

P.S. *Kiss Pete for me. And keep jogging.*

Pete refrained from saying "I told you so" when Jackie showed him the letter. He scanned it quickly, then crumpled it and threw it in the wastebasket. Jackie retrieved it and smoothed it open again.

"What're you saving that for?" asked Pete.

"You're not the only pack rat in this house," said Jackie, avoiding his question. She folded the letter and put it in her pocket.

"Now don't you feel better? All that worrying for nothing. They're fine."

Pete bent over his briefcase, pulling out manuscripts and contracts. Jackie watched him, debating whether to tell him that something nagged at her about the letter, something she couldn't put her finger on. But he would laugh at her if she couldn't say what it was.

Jackie went into the kitchen to wash and cut vegetables. Kim did seem excited and happy. Certainly they wouldn't have trouble finding an apartment they liked. But it was odd that Kim had mentioned the Brooks movie. Jackie could have sworn she and Dave had said they'd already seen it. And she *knew* that the movie they had planned to see together was the new Truffaut. Kim must be very absentminded.

19

The Barnetts slipped from Jackie's mind in the weeks that immediately followed. Labor Day was fast approaching. The air turned slightly cooler, and there was a hint of the changing season in the lush, drooping foliage on the trees in Central Park. The greens were almost too green.

Jackie was exercising with a passion equal to Pete's now. And it was paying off. Her body felt alive. Sex was good. And sleep deep and easy. Together they rose at five-thirty, drank a high-protein whole-milk concoction that Jackie prepared the night before (following Phoebe's instructions), and swallowed their vitamins. Jackie, too, had become an eager convert to the brand Phoebe recommended. In appearance the pills resembled all the other multivitamins on the market—they were pale pink bullets, manufactured somewhere in New Jersey by a lab with two names, and they stank of yeast—but they seemed to pack a little extra punch. Phoebe was able to buy them at a special discount at a midtown pharmacy that she'd used for years. She was coy about naming the place.

By six they were ready to run, which they generally did with the Twelvers. The Jensens were always on hand, as were Victor Macrae and Ben Goodman. Sylvia Goodman seldom joined in. She had an obsession with canasta that she indulged with daily card parties, and she was reluctant to give up the extra hour of sleep that she believed kept her at her quick-witted card-playing best. Miriam Macrae lately had developed a foot complaint. Scrappy little Eileen Cole sometimes appeared, Richard Kelly almost never. That, in Jackie's view, was just as well. Whenever she remembered that his agency had turned down their application for an apartment, she became angry. It just showed how off he was. Everyone else loved them. Jerry McDonald's job producing the sports segment of the eleven o'clock evening news kept Francie and him on a different schedule altogether.

One day, when they were jogging slowly up Fifth Avenue toward the entrance to the reservoir track, Pete had pointed to Arnold's running suit and quipped, "Who's your tailor?" Arnold had looked puzzled. Pete placed his hand lightly on Arnold's powder-blue shoulder.

"We're regulars now, aren't we? Don't we qualify for the uniform?"

Phoebe, who was on Arnold's other side, leaned earnestly toward Pete. "No, you don't, Pete," she said. "You have to be over fifty. We need this," she tugged at the blue fabric on her chest, "to put sunshine and blue skies into our lives. You don't have to worry about that. *You* have your youth. Count your blessings. It's God's greatest gift."

Jackie, overhearing the exchange, marveled at the intensity of Phoebe's response. For a couple who had traveled as much as they, who were as well off, whose looks, whose very bone structure and bearing spoke of generations of good fortune, for two people who might easily have grown bored and blasé in the certainty that life would offer them, as it always had, only the best, they were surprisingly involved, engaged, even vulnerable, living, it seemed, on some yet-to-be-clarified thin edge. The nakedness of their emotions charmed and irritated Jackie, and constantly startled her.

After running fifteen or twenty minutes, Pete and Jackie would wave goodbye to the others, return to their apartment, shuck off their T-shirts and shorts (usually a grab bag of color combinations, but never including powder blue), shower, and leave for their offices by eight, Pete by subway, Jackie by bicycle through the park.

As the care and feeding of her body became increasingly important to her, Jackie's preoccupation with her career faded. In a surprise move, Sallie Lasher had turned down Lord & Taylor's job offer, but by then Jackie no longer cared. She still daydreamed of breakthroughs. But not in her career. Instead, her hopes were focused firmly on the running track or in the pool. At work, only Tyrone was aware of her new priorities. He dubbed her "Jockie."

At the end of the workday at five o'clock sharp, she would rush home to resume what she now thought of as her real life. She and Pete would work out in the gym for a minimum of an hour, usually under Ben's supervision. After that they sometimes would make a second trip to the reservoir track. At least one evening a week they would join the others in the garden for organically raised beef grilled to perfection by Buddy. Phoebe regularly prepared "special treats" and slipped them into their refrigerator to surprise them: walnut and carrot loaves, alfalfa puddings—unfamiliar but not unpleasant to the taste and loaded with nutrients. They always tried to be in bed by ten o'clock. If someone had told Jackie six months ago that she'd be living a life of healthful asceticism, she'd have ordered a martini for herself and a double for the other person to jar him or her back to reality.

20

Jackie completed her stretching exercises, just as Pete came into view. On the mornings they didn't run with the Twelvers, they had a special routine. Since Pete was ahead of her in endurance, he ran the first lap around the reservoir alone, while she warmed up before joining him. Then they would run a single lap together.

Now, as Pete drew even with her, she quickly got into stride with him. For the first two hundred yards or so they chatted back and forth, Jackie firing off questions: where to put the new lamp; what's wrong with running on the balls of your feet; did Pete want pasta for dinner that night. She had read that you should be able to carry on a conversation while jogging, but she hadn't yet been able to pull it off. This morning was no exception. After a few minutes, she realized that they'd both fallen silent. Just as well. She barely had enough breath to propel herself forward.

A sharp pain pinwheeled somewhere in the middle of her chest, and she began to concentrate on her body with the intensity of a demolition expert defusing a land mine. She picked up a clicking sound in her left knee joint, and the lower part of her legs ached with each step. Good God, were these the terrible shin splints she'd heard other joggers complain of? Even the term "shin splint" sounded painful.

Frantically Jackie willed herself to think of something else, anything else, and as the tall apartment tower on Central Park West that she used to mark the halfway point rose into view above the trees, she became aware that she'd been drifting around inside her head happily stringing together disconnected thoughts for several minutes, and that now she felt pretty good. They were running on the bridle path that circled below the reservoir track. Even though it was two-tenths of a mile longer than the reservoir's mile and six-tenths, Jackie preferred not being able to see at a glance how much farther she had to go. She also liked the muted light that splattered through the canopy of leaves over the path and the occasional horse and rider that would pop into view.

She looked around with curiosity, ready to be distracted. On the far side of the path an overweight woman with steel-gray hair churned along slowly, breaststroking through the humid air with richly padded arms and shoulders. Ahead a tall man pulled a scruffy Bedlington terrier along on its leash. It had rained the night before, and nuggets of mud stuck to the dog's coat. Her eyes slid back to Pete, running to her right. She loved the way he seemed to glide forward, his stride almost inevitable in its effortlessness. He held his head high, the expression on his face calm and determined. And he looked marvelous. Jackie felt the pleased possessiveness of a starlet for her first Rolls. He was gorgeous, and he was hers.

The next thing she knew they were nearing the finish line. So soon! She was almost sorry the run was coming to an end. It was becoming much easier to do. No doubt of it. As they crossed the line, she began to slow down, but Pete didn't even hint at stopping. He just casually said over his shoulder, "Come on, you can go a little farther."

"Oh, no I can't," said Jackie with the quickness of a knee jerk. But she kept on moving.

"Don't be silly. Of course you can."

"But I've never gone more than one lap."

"Tell you what," said Pete. "We'll stop as soon as you say. Promise. You set the pace."

Jackie saw Pete check his watch for the time, and then he dropped behind her. At first she thought, I can't believe what I'm doing, this is unreal, and then she let her mind go blank. After a while, she heard Pete speaking to her again.

"Another fourteen tenths of a mile, and we're home free," he said.

"Are you trying to be funny?" she said, managing a giggle.

And then, before she knew it, they didn't need to count in tenths of a mile any longer. They had run over half a lap. Part of her, the lazy side, wanted to tell Pete, enough, stop, I've gone far enough. But something kept her from saying it. She was tired. More tired than she could remember being in a long time. But she knew that she had a lot more left in her. And that made her feel good. Very good.

All at once Pete pulled quickly ahead of her. The bastard was sprinting. He's not going to leave me behind, thought Jackie. She reached deep down and came alongside him. He turned to her, smiling broadly. "I just wanted to see if you had it in you," he said, and love for her was so palpable in his voice and in his eyes that, right then, Jackie would have done anything for him that he asked, even keep up this crazy speed. But he let her off the hook.

"Take the lead again," he said, falling behind her once more.

Jackie cut back, but only by a little, to a good, hard tempo that called on every muscle in her body, and the joy of it was that now she felt completely ready for it. She felt an enormous rush of exhilaration. She was on the verge of a breakthrough, and she knew it. She was going to go the distance, double in one stroke the length she was capable of running, and just the thought of it sent her up on a high. Not that she was marathon material yet. It would be a long, long time before she'd be ready even for a 10K (didn't that sound good!), but now, for the first time, she thought she had an idea, a real idea, what all the excitement was about. She felt marvelous. As if she could go on forever. As if, she corrected herself, her *legs*

could. They seemed to have a life all their own.
And then before she had time to fully appreciate
and savor the moment, she was crossing the finish
line. She'd done it. And she felt terrific. Then Pete
was beside her, grinning like a madman.

"Up to that tree and back," he said, pointing to a
large, gnarled plane tree that sloped over the path
some two hundred feet ahead of them. As he
reached over to hug her around the shoulders,
Jackie grabbed his hand and gave it a quick
squeeze, and then they were off, sprinting now for
all they were worth, and back again in moments.
Pete stopped a few paces ahead of Jackie and, turning, opened his arms wide and enveloped her. They
held each other close.

"You're great," said Pete, stepping back. "Just
great. You know, not only did you run twice as far
as you've ever run before—excuse me, more than
twice as far!—but you ran it in unbelievable time.
Not to keep you in suspense, but," Pete glanced
down at the stopwatch in his palm, "you—we—ran
those two laps in just under twenty-eight minutes,
which means you're now running a mile in under
eight minutes. You're something. You cook like
Julia Child, run like Francie Larreau, and screw
like—"

"This better be good."

"Would you accept Dame May Whitty?"

"Absolutely. Now let's walk rapidly home and
shower and—"

"Let's run."

As they walked out of the park and then past the

Metropolitan, Jackie thought back on all the truly happy moments she'd had in her life and realized that, strange as it might seem to anyone else, this was one of them.

Jackie, you nut, listen to yourself. But she knew the words were true.

21

Early one morning toward the end of the month, Jackie received a call from Trish Anderson. Was she free for lunch? Jackie hesitated. Her day was jammed with overlapping appointments, but Trish sounded anxious to see her and so she agreed. They decided to meet at the Tavern-on-the-Green at 12:30.

Jackie was only ten minutes late. She chained her bike to a tree on the edge of the parking lot and entered the first of the restaurant's extravagant rooms, which followed one upon another like a string of glistening soap bubbles, each gaudier and wittier than the last. The first of these rooms was all brass and polished oak and dominated by a pair of aggressive, life-sized antlered bucks frozen in plaster of Paris. In the next, a vast greenhouse of a room was hung with giant multicolored chandeliers and framed by the branches of ancient trees growing just outside the floor-to-ceiling windows.

Jackie spotted Trish seated at a table against a glass wall. She caught her eye, waved, and walked quickly to the table, leaning down to kiss her on both cheeks. Jackie was wearing a flowered cotton skirt and an olive-green tank top, and her cheeks were still flushed from pedaling through the park.

"You look fantastic," said Trish. "There must be something to all this exercising."

"You're looking good, too."

Trish smiled. "Yes, but it isn't from exercising. Sit down."

As soon as Jackie was seated a waiter appeared at Trish's side and opened a bottle of Sancerre.

"I'm not drinking these days," said Jackie. "But I can bend a little."

Jackie took a sip. The wine was chilled just right. She rummaged in her handbag and pulled out a cigaret.

"Thank God, you're still doing something excessive," said Trish.

"I've managed to cut down to two a day, but you should hear the guff I have to take from Pete for those. Hey, it's great to see you again!"

"You're not kidding. How long's it been?"

Trish's question sent Jackie back to the last time the four had been together. Early one hot Saturday morning at the beginning of August—good God, that made it three weeks ago—they'd piled into the Andersons' car and beat the crowds out to Jones Beach. They'd stretched out on the sand and swum, had a lunch of fruit and cheeses washed down with ice-cold Pouilly-Fumé, and early in the afternoon, as other cars were still inching toward the beach, had breezed back into the city in less than an hour. A glorious day. Jackie felt a wave of deep affection for her friend, and considerable guilt. She wished her exercising weren't so all-consuming, so she could see more of Trish.

In answer to Trish's questions, she described what she and Pete had been doing. At first she exaggerated the wonders of their new life, wanting her friend to understand why they were so caught up with it and forgive them their recent unsociability. But then she realized there was no need to exaggerate. She passionately believed in the life she was describing. Her excitement was genuine. She told Trish about her running breakthrough and about their exercising goals, their protein-centered diet, their increased strength, their changed sleeping patterns.

"We've done everything short of joining a Vic Tanny monastery," she said laughingly.

Her greatest enthusiasm she reserved for their neighbors at Twelve East Eighty-third: "I know this will sound a little like a Jerry Lewis telethon, but what's wonderful is having somebody really care about you. Pete feels it especially. You know, he lost his parents when he was only twelve and he got shipped off to a maiden aunt in Pittsburgh. God knows, she must have tried, but she didn't know the first thing about kids, and he was lonely as hell. These people, particularly the Jensens, are so warm, so nice. It's wild, but I almost feel that suddenly, at the ripe old age of twenty-nine, I've got parents again. Can you understand?"

Trish nodded thoughtfully, then, after a moment of quiet, asked if the empty apartment in their building had been rented yet. Jackie, slightly taken aback, said no. Come to think of it, she wondered, why hadn't the Jensens found new tenants for the Barnetts' place? They'd seemed so eager to rent it at first. Trish said she had some friends who might be interested. She would let Jackie know.

Trish signaled the waiter. When their glasses were again full, she clicked hers against Jackie's. "There are two reasons for the wine." She paused to take a swallow. "First, I'm pregnant."

"Wow! Congratulations!" said Jackie, grinning with total pleasure. She quickly kissed Trish. "Why didn't you stop me from babbling on about Pete and me? That's fantastic. When are you due?"

"March eighteenth's the date Doctor McCarry has given me. And that's the other reason for the wine. The baby's due date is tied to something the four of us have been talking about doing for ages, and we'd better do it soon. Before I need a forklift to get around. Do you know what I'm talking about?"

"I haven't a clue."

"Think."

"I am thinking. Give me a hint."

"Two syllables. First one rhymes with—" Trish shook her head from side to side, demonstrating.

"No?"

"Start at the beginning of the alphabet," said Trish.

"Bo?"

"Right. Second syllable rhymes with—" She placed her hands antler-like on her head.

"Deer?"

"No."

"I got it!" said Jackie. "Moose. Coose. *Bocuse!*"

"Right. Our eating tour of Burgundy!" said Trish.

They both laughed heartily. A couple of nearby diners stared at them.

"Well, how long've we been talking about it?" continued Trish. "What do you say? Can you and Pete break away?"

"When?"

"October."

"Why so soon? That's barely a month away."

"Come on, Jackie. I've got it all figured out. Pete's going to Frankfurt for the book fair, isn't he?" Jackie nodded. "Let him go there and do what he has to, and then the three of us can meet him in Paris. We can take the Mistral to Lyons and then rent a car and drive through Burgundy to Nice. Do you realize how many starred restaurants there are per square inch on the map?"

"God, it's tempting. You're right about the timing, too. But do you realize what this'll do to our exercising and—"

"As the prophet once said, 'Indulge yourself.' A week away from jogging won't kill you, will it? Come on, say yes."

"All right. It's yes for me. I'll convince Pete tonight, and then I'll call you. Are you sure you're up to it?"

"I feel terrific. No sign of morning sickness. Tell me, are you and Pete still thinking about it? Having a kid?"

"We still talk about it, but the moment somehow has passed. Maybe it's time to start thinking about it again. I'm so excited for you!"

"Me, too. Tell you what. Let's make a date now to spend an evening together making plans. The sooner the better."

"Okay. How about dinner on Saturday? Complete with maps and the Michelin guide."

"It's a deal."

"Good. And we may have something else to celebrate."

"What?"

"This Saturday, for the first time, Pete's running in competition. A five-miler in Van Cortlandt Park. Ben's been prepping him for the last two weeks. I really think he's got a chance of finishing in the top fifty to a hundred. Over three hundred are entered."

"Then we'll also have a victory dinner," said Trish. "Our baby would never pick anyone but a winner as its godfather."

22

The Yankees were down by a run with one out left in the bottom of the ninth against the Red Sox when the lights in the apartment went out. The TV dissolved to a lozenge of light and then that disappeared, too.

Pete, who was watching the game with the kind of intensity that generates triple-bypass operations, waxed eloquent: "Oh, fuck, what happened?"

Before he could scramble off the sofa, Jackie came into the room, a candle in one hand and, in the other, a censer of musk incense, tendrils of smoke making miniature contrails in the air.

"Game called because of carnality," she said, just short of a whisper.

"Oh, baby, there was only one out left. And Reggie was up."

"Follow me, and you'll find something of a more

exciting and memorable nature in the 'chambre de dormir.' "

Pete, feigning reluctance, followed Jackie into the bedroom. He continued to bitch through half a joint and two sips of Courvoisier. And then when Jackie started massaging him with Oil of Olay he became very quiet.

"I hope the customer won't mind the masseuse removing her scanty bikini briefs?"

"Uh . . . yeah . . . great idea."

She ran her tongue down the length of his spine. He arched up, consumed by ecstasy and expectation. Her hands and mouth became one. And then he was demanding her. With just the slightest show of resistance at having to exchange one pleasure for another, she turned in toward him. For what seemed like hours, they devoured each other.

As he entered her, Jackie said, "Do I feel different, love?"

"Baby, you feel beautiful."

"I'm not wearing that Close Encounter of the—"

"I don't care about anything," he moaned, "except being in you."

"This could be dangerous. . . ."

"Shut up and kiss me. I love your taste."

They awoke a little after three, when a cold draft slipped over their still enmeshed bodies and caused them to part and scramble under the covers.

23

"Here's to us, and to our trip," said Pete, clicking glasses first with Jackie, then with Trish and Allan.

"And to *you*, darling," added Jackie. She described the race that day in Van Cortlandt Park. Pete had come in in the top quarter, and Jackie was shining with pride for him.

Before settling down to the serious business of deciding where in France they would eat, they chatted about running, the upcoming baby, and Allan's pleasure in just having been named a member of the board of one of the bank's subsidiaries. Then Pete signaled John Ballato, the energetic, elderly proprietor of the restaurant, for the menus. Ballato's was a small, convivial place on the edge of Little Italy, with superb Italian food. This was the first time Jackie and Pete, who used to be regulars, had come here since the restaurant had re-opened after its summer closing, and Mr. B. was particularly attentive. They decided to split a large cold antipasto and follow it with half portions of green fettucine with a tomato and ricotta sauce. They finished with osso bucco—mammoth veal knuckles— served with small forks to scoop out the marrow.

Spotting a copy of the *Guide Michelin* on the floor next to Jackie's chair, Mr. B. teased them about meeting at an Italian restaurant to plan a trip to France. Pete ordered a third bottle of Frascati, and their conversation grew thick with references to the heavy hitters of French cuisine: Troisgros, Bocuse, Bise, Point. By the time the waiter arrived with the espresso, they'd mapped a wildly zigzagging route southward from Lyons to Nice.

"Has anyone ever died of an overdose of mousse?" asked Allan, an evil grin crossing his face.

As they paid the bill, Allan suggested they go to Ferrara's, an Italian pastry shop, for baba au rhum. The others laughed and groaned.

"Mega-calories, here we come," said Jackie.

"I'll never be able to face Ben again," said Pete.

Catching the half-serious note in his voice, Jackie asked, "What are you training *for*? The Super Bowl?"

"No, I just want to get in shape."

"Pete, you loony. Don't you realize? You *are* in shape. The best shape ever. Ben is delighted, and you should be, too. You're in peak condition. I can't even fantasize any more about making it with a young guy. *You're* in better condition."

"Not after this trip. But the hell with it. The old body needs a bit of R and R."

24

He was breathing hard, each gasp of air punctuated by a thin, wheezing noise, like a nail being filed, that rose unbidden from somewhere between his ribs. He was grateful no one was around to witness his miserable performance though he knew the very fact of running alone, with no one to distract him with conversation, made this morning's effort doubly difficult. He checked his stopwatch after his first lap of the reservoir and was dismayed to see that his time was off by a full minute.

"Fuck you, Remy Martin," he muttered to himself. "I only drank two snifters . . . so okay . . . three."

He willed himself to pick up his pace, though a fierce stitch worked overtime on his left side and his mouth tasted like a beaver den.

"And you, John Ballato," he continued his litany, "your pasta is *not* going to sink this kid. I feel great. And remember, I didn't finish all my osso bucco."

He was really pressing now. And though he was pushing, he knew what he was working against: He was hung over. His stomach churned with the intensity of the Snake River.

He clicked his stopwatch as he completed his second lap. He was pleasantly surprised when he looked at the watch. Just twenty-five seconds off. Not bad. He'd made up thirty-five seconds on the last 1.6 miles. But, boy, did he feel like shit. Bill Rodgers didn't have to worry about Ballato's. Had he ever run in the morning after osso bucco *and* fettucine sorrento verdi *and* baba au rhum *and* Uncle Remy? No. Fucking-A-No. He smiled to himself. He was so pleased with his wit and insight that he almost ran into Ben and Sylvia Goodman.

"Oh, hi."

Ben nodded soberly at Pete and then pointed at the pocket of his warm-up jacket. He clucked softly and shook his head. At first Pete didn't understand. And then he saw the lanyard looping out of the pocket. Son-of-a-bitch. It was his stopwatch. Ben had timed him.

"Celebrating last night?"

Jesus, was he direct. Pete immediately felt as if he had brought home a bad report card.

"A little. Remember our friends Allan and Trish?"

"The banker."

What a memory. Sylvia seemed embarrassed and

was engrossed in embroidering tulips in the dirt with the point of her sneaker.

"That's right. Well, they're—I mean, she—that is, Trish is having a baby. And, you know . . . I guess we celebrated a little too—"

"Pete, you're a big boy and I don't have to lecture you."

Here it comes.

"But eating heavy Italian food is good for no one. Not even Italians."

"But, Ben—"

"And I'm sure your celebrating included wine. And brandy."

It wasn't a question.

"You know what that does to your cholesterol levels, not to mention—"

"Ben, Ben, I think Pete has gotten the point," said Sylvia in a small girl's voice.

Bless you, Sylvia. Pete silently blew a kiss toward her. Maybe it was growing up with no one caring that made him want Ben's approval.

"Hey, Pete. Sylvia's right. I'm sorry. I was only upset because you're doing so well. And that combined with my . . . well, damn it, affection for you. Well, I'm sorry."

"Stop it. I understand. I shouldn't do this sort of thing to my body. Apart from . . . *this* morning, I've never felt better in my life, and it's all attributable to you. And Sylvia."

"And don't forget the other Twelvers," Sylvia added quickly.

"Who could forget?" Pete laughed, and Sylvia joined in. "I haven't told anyone yet, but Jackie and

I and our friends, the Andersons, are taking a trip by car through Burgundy. But don't worry. We'll let the Andersons do most of the eating. This kid will *mange* lean and spare. And I'll have my running shoes with me, so I'll work out every day."

"Trip? What trip? When?" asked Ben, his voice suddenly tense.

"Next month. Right after the Frankfurt Book Fair."

Ben stared at Pete as if he'd forgotten his name. Then he turned abruptly to Sylvia.

"What time is the repairman from Home Box Office coming to fix that wire?" he asked.

"Ten, I think."

"Well, we'd better do our laps now. We have some errands to do before that, too."

And without a goodbye, they took off, Ben only pausing long enough to click his stopwatch. They moved off easily, running together in stride, more like skaters than joggers.

It wasn't until Pete was out of the park that he stopped to wonder how the hell Ben knew they'd gone to an Italian restaurant.

25

SEPTEMBER

Jackie, dressed for bed in a pale gray silk and white lace nightgown, sat in her favorite fat chintz chair, her legs slung over one of its arms. Cushioned on her stomach was the red *Guide Michelin*. She was wrestling with the delightful problem of which restaurants they should go to in the Lyons area. They'd settled on a three-night, five-meal (not counting breakfast) stay. Bocuse and Troisgros were easy choices, but there were fourteen other starred restaurants. Pete was stretched out on the couch reading a manuscript that was on multiple submission and supposed to be "very hot." He did not look impressed.

It was after midnight when they got the call. Pete answered the phone on the first ring. His tone made Jackie look up at once. "Hold on," he said. "We'll be right there." He hung up and looked at Jackie, his facial muscles suddenly taut. "That was Trish. It's Allan. He's been mugged. It's not good. He's at Lenox Hill."

The lobby of the hospital was deserted except for a very pregnant young woman arguing with her husband and the night duty nurse about getting into a wheelchair to ride to the labor room. The nurse looked up with a harried smile and pointed them toward the elevator. On the fifth floor, they walked through a set of double doors, and there, in a small waiting room, looking very scared, was Trish. They embraced in an awkward three-way huddle. Then Pete stepped back, and Trish fell against Jackie's shoulder, crying softly. After a few moments of release she regained her composure, then answered the question they'd hesitated to ask. "The doctors say he'll be okay. They're ninety percent sure that there's no permanent damage." Her voice wavered as she thought about the other ten percent. Jackie held her hand tightly, and Trish started to explain what had happened.

A little after eleven o'clock, Allan had taken their dachshund, Debenture, out for a walk. About a half hour later the telephone rang. It was a policeman calling from the Emergency Room of Lenox Hill Hospital. He had found Allan lying unconscious on the sidewalk under the scaffolding of the new building going up on Seventy-second near Lexington. Trish had better hurry. They might have to operate. As she was leaving the apartment, the doorbell had rung and the elevator man had handed her Debenture. He had wandered into the lobby trailing his leash.

When she arrived at the hospital, Allan had just come to. He had suffered a severe concussion, but so far, it seemed, none of his vital functions had been impaired.

While she spoke, Trish kept her eye steadily on the small pane of glass in the door to Allan's room. A nurse tapped lightly on it and signaled that she could make another short visit. Pete went in first with Trish. Even though Trish had whispered to him as they started through the door that Allan looked awful, he wasn't prepared for what he saw. Allan's face was framed by bandages that encased his entire head. An IV snaked down into his arm. The skin beneath his eyes was deeply discolored, and the lids were badly puffed and swollen. Leon Spinks in an ugly mood would have had a softer touch. Hearing their approach, Allan cracked open one lid.

"Hey, man," said Pete, "good to see you."

"Thanks," said Allan, attempting a smile that curved in the wrong places.

"You gave Trish a real scare." The hell with hospital small talk, he thought. He lowered his voice, and asked urgently, "What happened?"

"Guy jumped me." Pete nodded encouragement, and Allan continued. "I heard this voice say, 'Hey, Allan, you got change for a five?' I stopped to check the pockets of my jacket. Hearing my name took me completely off guard. It was so dark where I was standing, I couldn't really make him out.

Then he was on top of me. Came at me with some kind of metal pipe. He kept coming and coming."

"Christ, you *are* lucky. But you saw him then. What did he look like?"

"Black. Not too old. Weird orangey hair."

"What do you mean, 'weird'?"

"Well, you know, a big, wild Afro."

"Sort of copper colored?"

"That's the color. Why?"

"No reason, no reason." He squeezed Allan's hand. "Look, I'm going now. You shouldn't get too tired. I'll send Jackie in for a quick hello. We'll see you in the morning."

Jackie had been in with Allan for a minute when Pete heard the gravelly drinker's voice of Allan's mother. He hadn't seen her since Allan and Trish's wedding three years earlier, but he remembered her vividly. The late-model showgirl. She leaned on her husband's arm, her large boozy eyes panicky. Pete moved quickly to calm her. The doctor, he told her, had assured Trish that Allan would suffer no long-term effects. As soon as it was established that the senior Andersons would be spending the night with Trish, he and Jackie said good night.

As they stepped into the elevator, Pete said, "You're not going to believe what I'm about to tell you. You remember that son of a bitch who stole my wallet? In the park? Last May? Well, this guy who went after Allan sounds like the same cat. Black. Big copper Afro."

"Are you sure?"

"I can't be sure it's the same man, but something

tells me it is. And there's one more thing that bothers me."

"What's that?"

"Allan told me the guy called him by his name. Just before he went for him."

"That doesn't make sense. How could he possibly know his name?"

"I don't know. But one thing is certain. It wasn't your average mugging."

26

If anything bugged Jackie more than people who let their dogs foul the sidewalks, it was people who got on the "six items or less" line at the supermarket with enough groceries to sit out the siege of Stalingrad. Like the woman in front of her. A solid fifty without anyone pushing her, togged out in gold lamé boots and a mini-skirt, she obliviously pored over a copy of *TV Guide*.

Easy does it, Jackie, you're in New York. Remember, you love the place. If you want good manners go to Dayton.

Jackie checked her cart to make sure that she hadn't forgotten anything. Three steaks, each one big enough for a linebacker in training; two heads of Bibb lettuce; a bottle of pickled green beans; five pounds of potatoes; and a bottle of tarragon vinegar. So, okay, it was eight items, but it wasn't even a snack compared with what the geriatric Dolly Parton in front of her was buying.

She could see Pete waiting outside in Allan's Peugeot. Allan would be all right, but it would take time. The doctors were still worried that he might not have complete movement in his right leg, but they thought there was a good chance he'd be perfect. It would take time, they repeated again and again.

And poor Trish. Her face looked like it had been washed away. And with a baby coming. Naturally the trip was off—Pete had arranged with his company to cancel the Frankfurt part as well—but that was the least of it. Jackie had been with Trish all day, after she and Pete had got a big three hours sleep the previous night. Trish needed them, and they wanted to be with her. This was the first time Jackie had left her all day, so she could shop for dinner for the three of them. They were scheduled to pick her up back at Lenox Hill in twenty minutes.

"That meat is just pumped full of destructive steroids and coloring agents."

Jackie turned to see Eileen Cole, their nutritionist neighbor, staring balefully at her shopping cart.

"Oh, hi, Eileen. I didn't know you shopped here."

"Their greens are acceptable," said Eileen, still peering into the cart, "but those beans, or whatever they are, have at least five chemical additives in them. Try placing one in a goldfish bowl some day. It will dye it as green as the Sargasso before the day is out."

"But they taste great," answered Jackie, the annoyance in her voice barely disguised.

"You and Pete are much better off not eating all that terribly cholesterol-laden food that they serve in France."

"Who told you we weren't going to France?" said Jackie, almost jumping on Eileen.

Easy, girl.

"I don't remember. I think it was Ben. He said Pete told him this morning."

"Ben said that Pete told him?"

"And that vinegar you have there," Eileen said, pointing an accusatory finger, "is as much a corrosive agent as nitric acid."

Jackie was white hot when she got into the car. She almost tossed the shopping bag at Pete.

"Don't we have a semblance of a private life anymore? Or have we traded it for a swimming pool?" she asked.

"What are you talking about?" he said.

"I just saw Eileen Cole in Gristede's, and she said something to me about our not going to France. And guess how she found out? She said that Ben told her and *you* told Ben."

"I did no such thing."

"I'm not making this up. Why would she have said that if it weren't true?"

"I don't know, but so what? Okay, I did see Buddy this morning when I went out to get the *Times*. I must have said something to him about his not having to water our plants after all. And he probably said something to Ben."

"Well, damn it, what business is it of theirs whether we're going or not?"

"You should be happy that we live near people who care about us."

Damn Pete's reasonableness.

"And, while we're at it, I'm sick of Phoebe's teas and her cute little organic casseroles. And Ben's pep talks. And our cozy evenings chez Number Twelve. The whole bit. They're a bunch of bloody snoops."

"Honey, you know you don't mean that. They're just being kind."

"Aren't they being *too* kind?"

"What do you mean? They're just good neighbors."

"Maybe."

"Why are you so paranoid? You still sound like a West Sider. Everything's a plot. The delivery boy's a rapist. The man who reads the meter is another Reverend Jones. Everything's a federal case. Why don't you call in your favorite ex-Congress*person* to investigate?"

"Okay, okay," sighed Jackie, her own nastiness echoing unpleasantly in her ears. "I'm sorry. I'm being unfair." But was she? She wasn't at all sure of that. "Tell you what, though. Let's make ourselves a lot scarcer. At least socially. They're nice, but enough's enough."

"Whatever you say, Bella."

27

The sound of violently churning water filled the gym. Three men were swimming laps in the pool. Side by side, stroke for stroke, a rhythmic troika of power and grace. Then, very gradually at first, one figure began to pull ahead of the other two, first by inches, then widening the gap by a foot, then two feet. Coming out of the next turn, the lead figure had gained almost a half-length on the other two. He began to move ahead inexorably, now leading by a quarter of a lap, then almost a half lap.

Jackie stood by the pool, stopwatch in hand, counting the laps. They were up to eighteen. She traced the swirling, eddying path of the leader with her eyes, transfixed by the perfectly synchronized movement of his arms and legs. The leader turned now at the far end of the pool. Jackie blew a sharp blast on the whistle looped around her neck. The winner lifted his head from the water and smiled. It was Ben Goodman.

"Five minutes, twelve seconds," said Jackie. "Congratulations." She and Ben watched first Jerry McDonald and then Pete complete their laps. As they clung to the pool's edge, gasping for air, Jackie read off their respective times.

"Jee-sus, Ben," said Pete as soon as he could talk. "Who suggested this race anyway?"

By way of answering, Ben nodded his head at Pete.

"Me and my bright ideas," groaned Pete. "And here I've been thinking, all along, that *at least* I could beat you in swimming, if nothing else. When was our last race? I remember distinctly that I won. Dave and I *both* licked you."

"You did indeed, Pete. That was sometime in July, I believe." All three men were toweling themselves dry. Ben paused to give emphasis to his next comment. "No more late nights, I hope."

"That I'm no longer guilty of."

As she listened, Jackie thought with amazement of Allan and Trish and all that had happened in the few weeks since their evening at Ballato's. Allan had been released from the hospital after six days, with the understanding that he report back regularly for testing and physical therapy. Trish was still feeling pretty rocky, but no longer in danger of an emotionally triggered miscarriage.

"Everybody has off days, you know," intoned Ben in his best coachlike manner. "Neither of you men should be discouraged. I am extremely impressed with the progress you've been making.

Now, if you will excuse me, I promised Sylvia I'd be back early this evening."

"You know," said Jackie sardonically after Ben's retreating footsteps had faded away, "I've never considered Ben a model of tact. I still don't. Like just now. When he's playing the big coach in the sky, he tends to overlook the fifty percent of the world that's female: I didn't hear any compliments on *my* progress, did you? But I will say this. He was really the gentleman just now. He didn't remind you *why* you and Dave beat him so badly in your last race."

Pete looked at her questioningly. "What're you talking about?"

"I hate to say it, but he was a pushover then. Don't you remember, Ben and the others all had that summer flu?"

"Christ, you're right. We talked about it that time in the sauna with the Barnetts."

"So much for your moment of triumph."

"Don't rub it in," said Pete, then, glancing at Jerry, he asked, "You ever hear from the Barnetts?"

"Nope. You?"

"No, neither do we. But I'm sure it's just the mañana mail in the Caribbean. We'll probably get four letters and six postcards at the same time."

28

It was a joy to be able to just schmooze on the phone again with Trish. In the last twenty minutes they'd covered a number of important items ranging from Halston's new Lauren Bacall Forties look to a Hunan restaurant that had recently opened in Soho. Twenty whole minutes without a medical bulletin on Allan. God, normal life could be exhilarating.

"Hey, Jackie, remember our friends, Don and Sarah Bingham?"

"Vaguely. She the one with the art nouveau jewelry?"

"*Exactement.* The Binghams are looking for a new apartment. Where they live now, every time Sarah plugs in the hairdryer in the bathroom, the lights blow in the kitchen."

"Well?"

"They were the ones I was thinking about for the apartment in your building. You said it hadn't been rented yet."

"As far as I know, it's still empty."

"Would you ask the owners about it?"

"Why not? It would be nice to get some people we know in there. And I definitely could use a buffer between myself and the others."

Phoebe picked up the phone on the fifth ring. She sounded out of breath. She had, she explained in truncated sentences, just got back from running in the park.

"Is the Barnetts' apartment still available?"

"Yes . . ."

"Great! I was hoping it would be. We have some people we wanted to tell you about. The Binghams. They couldn't be nicer. You'd really like them." And, thought Jackie greedily, *she'd* like to have a neighbor with dynamite jewelry that perhaps she could borrow occasionally.

Phoebe made interested-sounding noises. "Tell me more about them," she said.

"They're quiet, attractive people. Don's an avid squash player. I think he's rated high at the Yale Club. He and Sarah also play a lot of paddle tennis together on weekends. Somewhere in Connecticut."

"Uh-huh."

"Now what else? Don's a vice-president in our friend Allan Anderson's bank. Citibank. Sarah does PR for a small cosmetics company."

"How old are they?"

"About our age."

"Where are they from?" Phoebe was beginning to sound almost eager for information.

"Sarah's from California—Eureka. Don's from an old New York family. His dad's a partner in . . ."

"Jackie, my dear, thank you for thinking of us," interrupted Phoebe, her voice turned crisp. "Actually we do have another couple in mind, but if there's a change we'll be back to you. I've got to go now. 'Bye."

Jackie heard the click of the connection being broken and slowly lowered the receiver. *Got to go now?* Who was Phoebe kidding? She'd seemed prepared to spend the morning discussing the Binghams. What had come over the old girl?

29

OCTOBER

"Jackie?"

"Yes?"

"It's Doctor Nash."

"How are you, Doctor?"

"I've got good news for you and bad news for a particular rabbit family."

"You mean—"

"Yes, Jackie. You're pregnant."

"When?"

"These things usually take nine months, and using the date you gave me, we're going to see an early June baby. Probably a Gemini."

"Oh, Doctor Nash," said Jackie, unable to hold back her tears.

"Go ahead. It's one of the few things worth crying for."

* * *

It was a perfect fall day. A good day to fly a kite and a good day to lie on the grass. Jackie and Pete were seated on a low rise of ground just west of the kids' pony-cart track in Central Park. Jackie leaned back, her arms cradling her head, and tilted her face up to the sun for a long, delicious moment. She opened her eyes and grinned at Pete, "This is glorious."

"I agree. But I'm starved. What've you got for us?"

"This," said Jackie. Ignoring the shopping bag filled with pâté and French bread, she reached into her L. L. Bean canvas carryall and pulled out a large box wrapped in light blue tissue paper. She'd always been a lousy keeper of secrets and by now, with her news almost three hours old, was itching with impatience. "Come on, open it up," she said, thrusting the blue package into Pete's hands.

"What have I done to deserve this?"

"A lot. Though you had fun doing it. Now hurry."

Pete tore the paper off, lifted the cover of the box, and looked inside. There was another box, this one wrapped in pink. "Oh, no. Not the old box-within-a-box trick," he groaned. He opened that box and then another and another until he held in his hand a box the size of a cake of soap. He pushed aside the white tissue paper inside it and held up a tiny pair of Adidas sneakers. "What are these for?" he asked uncomprehendingly.

"They won't do *us* much good. I guess we'll have to find someone small enough to wear them."

There was a long beat, and then Pete grabbed

Jackie in a tight hug. "Oh, wow!" he shouted. "Are you sure?"

"I'm not, but Doctor Nash is. He called me this morning just as I was leaving. It's definite. The beginning of June. A Gemini."

"Fan-tas-tic! How're you feeling?"

"Wonderful!"

"Great. I can't wait to tell—"

"No, don't," said Jackie quickly. "Let's not tell anyone yet. Not even Trish and Allan. It's too early, and I'm superstitious. Now where's that bottle of wine you promised to bring?"

Pete uncorked the bottle and filled their glasses. Children's laughter drifted across to them from the pony track. Catching the sound of it, Jackie shivered with anticipation.

"This is going to be a lucky kid," said Pete. "A beautiful mommy with a great body, able to run a mile in under eight minutes. And a sense of humor to boot."

"What about the daddy?"

"Daddy's too modest. He'll brag later," answered Pete, as he reached over and kissed her. "This baby is going to get a lot of love."

"Make sure you save some for Mommy."

He drew her close and kissed her again.

30

The following Saturday afternoon Pete and Jackie decided to poke around Soho. Soho is that small slice of Manhattan real estate west of the Bowery and north of Chinatown whose vast lofts and derelict iron-facaded factories the city's artists had discovered and appropriated at the beginning of the seventies. Those who had moved in then were urban pioneers. Now they had become merely chic. On Saturdays and Sundays young and trendy uptown New Yorkers flocked onto West Broadway, milling along the sidewalks and in and out of galleries and shows, looking rather than buying, giggling at the absurdities perpetrated in the name of art but sometimes spotting serious new artists whose work two, five, or ten years from now they might not be able to buy. The mood was cheerful and relaxed, and strangers, who shared the bond of having sought out this particular place on this particular day, smiled at each other.

Jackie and Pete headed first for the patriarch of Soho galleries, the O. K. Harris. Although it was still early afternoon, the room was dense with people.

A man's voice called "Pete," and there, ten feet away, was Frank Donovan. Pete grabbed Jackie's hand and tried vainly to edge past a young couple intently contemplating a rectilinear slab of copper with a jagged scar running diagonally top to bottom. Donovan and Pete had been lab partners in a biology course required of freshmen at Columbia, and together they had groused, kibbitzed, crammed, and joked their way through it. After that they had gone their separate ways, but they would occasionally meet at the West End Cafe for a beer or catch an old flick at the New Yorker or Thalia. Donovan had stayed on for three years of law school, while Pete had gotten his first job as an editor (on a trade magazine for pharmacists) and first apartment (a walkup on Thirty-ninth and Third), and the two had lost track of each other. Suddenly they were shaking hands and making introductions all around.

Donovan's thin Irish face, perennially the choirboy, seemed worn. Even as they spoke, Pete was conscious of his own excellent condition and felt guilty when Donovan commented on how great he looked. Jackie—God, he was proud of her, looking super in her tight jeans and a short khaki flyer's jacket—shook hands with Donovan's wife, Sue, a short, thin girl with pale blue eyes, and his father-in-law, Dr. Burns, a stocky, balding man. Donovan said they were on their way to grab a bite to eat.

"We'll join you. At least for a glass of wine. I know just the place," said Pete.

"*And* something to eat," said Jackie. "I'm ravenous."

Pete smiled and lightly brushed his hand over Jackie's stomach in a quick and private movement. He felt a strong surge of emotion and, for a sweet but brief instant, the reality of his impending fatherhood.

At WPA, a stylish restaurant around the corner, they settled down at a small, round, smoked-glass table beneath a huge black and white mural showing welders, in the thirties' style of work-as-nirvana, dreamily laboring at their trade. After they'd ordered sandwiches and wine, Pete turned to Dr. Burns who was seated next to him and asked, mostly out of politeness, "What kind of doctor are you?"

"Oh, that's my son-in-law's affectation. I'm a Ph.D. I teach. American history. I'm in my last year before retirement. At Brandeis."

"Did you know Ben Goodman? He used to be athletic director there," asked Pete.

"Of course. Everyone at Brandeis knew him. He was a legend."

"He's a good friend of ours."

"He's still alive?"

"What do you mean? I ran with him this morning!"

"I'm not disputing you," said Dr. Burns, with the calm manner of someone accustomed to doing just that and then being proven correct, "but I am amazed. The man has to be in his eighties by now. Minimum. He retired in 1956, which would make him, by my reckoning, eighty-nine."

"There's no way he could be eighty-nine. Are you sure you're not mixing him up with another Ben Goodman?"

"I'm sure."

"The Ben Goodman I know isn't even sixty yet. I'd bet my life on it."

"Well, you'd lose your bet, my boy," continued Dr. Burns, unperturbed.

"What bet?" asked Jackie, picking up on the conversation. "Pete, please okay the wine and let this lady pour us a little something to drink."

"Never mind that, Jackie. Do you know what Doctor Burns just told me?"

As she listened to Pete, Jackie's eyes dilated with astonishment.

Dr. Burns glanced from Pete to Jackie, then chuckled, breaking the mood. "Give Ben my regards. He got me back on my feet after I had a heart attack back when I was forty-one. You mentioned running a moment ago. Are you working out under him?"

Pete nodded.

"You're lucky people. He was one of the finest trainers in the United States."

31

Jackie placed the new Electric Light Orchestra LP on the turntable, put on a stereo headset, and sat back and listened. She tried to clear her mind of everything but the music. All day she had been obsessed with what she had read that morning. She couldn't assimilate it. It was too strange. She hadn't mentioned it to Pete over the phone because she wanted to see his face when she told him. How could he possibly explain *this?*

ELO were on their fourth cut when Pete walked into the bedroom. Jackie was so deep into the music that she jumped when Pete touched her shoulder. She took off the earphones and gave him a quick kiss. Then, stalling for time, she asked in a carefully matter-of-fact voice how his day had been. He had already started to sort through the papers in his open briefcase.

"I had lunch with Thornton Lieberman. Remember, he's the agent for those two Steloff novels I edited? He's not the only agent who'd double-deal a publisher, but he's the only one who'd do it for a lifetime supply of Gucci loafers."

He glanced over at Jackie, then back to his briefcase, scowling at the sight of a particularly large manuscript resting in its interior that he had to read that evening.

"Thornton is even lower than my previous low opinion of him. We were having lunch to settle the terms for Steloff's third novel. You remember, on the first one, *Quentin's Game*, I had to make a passionate plea at our editorial meeting, stopping just short of going down on my knees, in order to sign it up. And what happened? We sold a big thirty-seven hundred copies. No paperback sale, no book-club action, nothing. With the second, for which I had to do another number on how he was just a book away from doing it, we reached the lofty sales Matterhorn of fifty-two hundred copies. No book club on that one either, but we did get a paperback sale. Four or five thousand, but at least it was something. So, taking both books together, maybe we made enough to pay for today's lunch. And what happens now? Steloff hands in half of his next book. And it's good. Very good. And sexy. And, potentially, very commercial. Now what does my good friend Thornton Lieberman want as an advance for this half-written book? After I've paid three thousand for the first and thirty-five hundred for the second? On faith."

Pete paused for effect, and Jackie gave him an appropriately engaged look.

"Well, I won't keep you guessing. This Cardin eel blithely asks me for seventy-five fucking thousand dollars. Can you believe it? I wanted to jam my shrimp cocktail fork through his ear. Instead, I dredged up my old mantra for a few moments and told him there was no way I could come up with that kind of advance. So what does he say to me? He says, 'Go to a paperback house and lay it off.' Jesus, I could kill that guy. A few fast scenarios flashed through my head about drowning him in the pool right there at the Four Seasons, but I couldn't figure out how to get away with it. Meanwhile he's just smiling, his head swiveling like a lawn sprinkler, he's so busy waving to people and being seen. You've got to laugh. How was your day?"

When the question came at last, Jackie was ready. She began slowly.

"I stopped by the library on the way to work to look up a couple of things. That little shocker we heard about Ben Goodman on Saturday sparked my curiosity."

Pete grunted. He'd picked out the new issue of *Variety* from his briefcase and was rapidly thumbing through the pages.

"Marvelous thing about the Donnell branch. It's got a great reference room. *Who's Who* going back to the turn of the century."

"Come on, what are you getting at?" said Pete.

Surprise. He was listening.

"I didn't think our friend Ben Goodman would be listed. A gym teacher? But it did occur to me that Arnold Jensen might be. He's always implied that he's a hotshot in his subject. Don't frown. You know he has. All that jazz about that special tribe he discovered in South America, in that country the name of which I can never remember. Anyway, turns out he hasn't been putting us on. There he was. Nice big listing. Only he didn't make the real *Who's Who*. Just *Who's Who in America*."

"Jackie . . ."

"Okay, okay. I also found an entry for Victor Macrae of Squibb and Sons fame. Now, listen to this," said Jackie. She picked a call slip from the library off the top of her bureau and began reading: "Arnold Jensen, graduate of Williams College, Class of 1912. Phoebe Jensen, Mount Holyoke, 1914. Victor Macrae, Williams, again 1912 . . ."

"What are you talking about?" Pete put down *Variety*.

"Don't you see? Look when they graduated! They're all in their late eighties. If not older. Just like your friend's father-in-law said Ben Goodman was."

"That's wild."

"Wild? Don't you think it's quite a bit more than that. Like a little . . . weird. Arnold, Victor, Phoebe, none of them looks even sixty! But they must—all of them—be twenty-five or thirty years older than that."

"It just proves they're right about this whole exercise and diet thing. And enough sleep. And so on."

"But, Pete, if that's so, then everyone would be doing it."

"Look around you. Millions are. The Twelvers are just ahead of their time. Haven't you seen those Dannon Yogurt commercials? All those one-hundred-ten-year-olds galloping around on horseback, only they don't look more than eighty? Same difference. Arnold is eighty-five—or more!—and looks fifty-five. So what. I say, great for him."

"You're too much. If I told you that Buddy came to this country on the same boat as Kunta Kinte, you wouldn't blink an eye. You'd just say, too bad he didn't have the good luck to have Alex Haley as a relative, so he could be the star of *Roots*."

"And I could be his publisher. Come on, Jackie. Look at it this way. Assuming that what you read in *Who's Who* and what Donovan's father-in-law told us *is* true, and that Ben and Arnold and probably the rest are really that old—and I tend to believe it—then we have a great opportunity. What I plan to do is to follow their advice to the letter. Everybody always says that they want to live to be a hundred. Hell, we have a real chance of doing it."

32

Early one morning later that week, after they'd completed three laps around the reservoir, Pete, Ben, and the Jensens stopped at a small health food store on Madison Avenue. While they stood at the narrow bar waiting for their glasses of papaya and Tiger's Milk, Ben turned to Pete. "I haven't seen Jackie for the last two days. She okay, Pete?"

"She feels a bit punk."

"Not serious, I hope?"

"No, no. Her stomach's been bothering her just a bit, that's all."

"In the mornings?"

Pete shook his head no, but felt his cheeks flush. It hadn't occurred to him that he might have to start fielding questions of this kind now, and he'd been caught off guard.

"Hey," Ben continued happily. "I think you've

been holding out on us, haven't you? I thought I noticed something. You've got a blossoming woman there. I keep my eye on her. She's expecting, isn't she?"

"Well, I promised I wouldn't mention it to anyone. She's a little nervous about it still. Don't let on you know, okay?"

Ben smiled and squeezed Pete's arm conspiratorially. "Sure won't," he said.

33

Jackie woke slowly, shifting from her side onto her stomach. The tenderness of her breasts reminded her instantly of the baby and a feeling of contentment and well-being swept over her. She glanced at the bedside clock: 9:10. Pete must still be out running. On Saturdays, in a display of sheer hedonism, the Twelvers pushed their jogging time back a few hours. Running had begun to seem less important to Jackie, and now she stretched out her arms and legs, luxuriating in the comfort of the wide, empty bed and in the pleasures of being lazy.

She had a date with Trish to go treasure-hunting in the thrift shops on Third Avenue, but that was not till eleven. She dressed unhurriedly in a pair of forest-green gabardine pants that went sensationally with a tweed Ralph Lauren blazer that she'd bought the month before (she'd decided to wear the hell out of her tailored clothes while she still could), plugged in the electric coffeemaker, and then ran lightly down the two flights of stairs to the lobby to pick up their mail. The mail was neatly divided and stacked on the dark mahogany lowboy. It was a homey, old-fashioned way of handling it and a simple code of honor prevailed: No one ever looked through anyone else's mail. Not even for sales notices from department stores. To the left of the no-smoking sign, where the Lawrences' mail always was placed, Jackie found the new issue of *Publishers Weekly*, bills from Con Ed and Paul Stuart's, a letter from their congressman, and, tucked under this, a folded note with her name on it. She opened it, saw Miriam's signature, and read: "Am out jogging. Back soon. Victor and I stopped at an orchard near us in Connecticut yesterday. We brought back apples for the whole crew. McIntoshes and Pippins. They're in the garden. Help yourselves. Please!" Jackie smiled to herself as Miriam's face, round and coquettish under its awning of Mamie Eisenhower spit curls, flashed before her. Miriam spoke often of her and Victor's country house in Roxbury, but mainly, or so it seemed to Jackie, because it gave her the chance to mention, just in passing of course, all the well-known neighbors they had: the Warrens, the Styrons, the Millers. For someone who seldom read anything more challenging than *Town and Country*, she still knew which names to drop to somebody in the book business.

Jackie opened the door to the garden. She stepped onto the small landing at the top of the staircase. From there she saw two bushel baskets of apples and several large pumpkins resting on the round dining table. Sunlight splintered off the glass top, and the air stirred softly, carrying with it a familiar, slightly sharp but not unpleasant smell that she couldn't quite identify. Then, as she started down, she felt the step suddenly begin to give out under her. She stumbled heavily against the railing, catching hold of it just in time to prevent herself from pitching headfirst to the ground. She stood on the bottom step for a moment, swaying weakly.

Almost at once, Buddy was at her side. "Are you all right, Miss?"

Had he been there all along? She felt confused. Still stunned, she breathed in deeply, not yet able to speak.

"If I'd seen you was comin' down them steps, I would of shouted a warnin'. I just finished layin' some varnish on that new step and was waitin' for it to dry before nailin' it down proper. Damn!" He peered anxiously at Jackie. "You okay?"

"I think so," she said, rubbing her abdomen where she'd bruised it against the railing. Then, with a shock, she remembered the baby. Oh, my God, was everything all right? She closed her eyes. Calm down, she thought. It took a calamity to make a healthy woman miscarry. She'd read that in one of the books about pregnancy. She knew that by evening her body would be stiff, but nothing else really seemed wrong. She was silly to worry. Everything was fine. It had to be.

34

The sky would have turned on El Greco. A blue that was almost cobalt, laced with shards of black clouds moving with the speed of a kite. The sun was beginning to dip behind the Palisades, and Jackie felt a strong intimation of winter. It was funny, she thought, how suddenly, in just one day, you could sense the intensity and rhythm of the next season. Try to explain that to a Los Angeleno.

Leaving Bendel's, Jackie pedaled her bicycle east on Fifty-seventh. She didn't like the traffic (especially the cabs), so she always ducked into the park the first chance she had. That was at Fifty-ninth and Fifth, where she was headed now. Though she had tried many different routes home since they'd moved to the East Side, she had come to favor the one that paralleled Fifth, taking her through the zoo, around the boat pond, and out at Seventy-ninth.

She rode toward the park at a leisurely pace. She still felt a little sore from the fall she'd almost taken on Saturday in the garden. It had really been careless—no, stupid—of Buddy not to have put up a sign of warning about the loose step. But there was no point in being angry. Nothing had happened— to her *or* the baby, thank God!

As Jackie started to cut across Fifty-ninth, a horn blared sharply behind her. Distracted, she realized all at once that she was about to crash into a stout woman roller-skating on the sidewalk in front of her. She braked quickly and swung the bike around the woman. The woman skated on, oblivious to how close she had come to setting an assisted-sprint record.

It was amazing how many people were constantly moving in the park. Joggers and bicyclists were by far in the majority, but in any kind of weather short of a jungle rainstorm, unicyclists, skateboarders, and roller skaters were venturing out in burgeoning numbers. Jackie loved to watch the roller skaters at night. With warning lights strapped to their legs, they looked like lightning bugs as they skated out of view.

It was on the approach to the zoo that Jackie decided she was being followed. She had stopped to adjust the clip on her right ankle when she noticed the man. He was also on a bicycle and was trying to give the impression that he was checking the pressure on his front tire. He was about fifty yards away, and in the increasing darkness Jackie couldn't really see what he looked like. But she had no trouble registering the bright plaid deerstalker hat the man wore. She had first spotted the man, actually the hat, as she turned onto Fifty-ninth.

Come on. Drop the paranoia bit, she told herself. Get on your bike and get the hell out of here before it's completely dark and you've grown fangs on this man with the silly hat.

Jackie swung out behind a young couple on expensive Peugeot ten-speed bikes. The couple was serious: leather racing helmets, gloves, European-style shorts—the works. She could only stay with them for a moment before they pulled silently away.

She looked behind her. Sure enough, there he was, the man in the hat. He was still too far away to distinguish his features, but she was sure, now, that he was following her. A wave of panic hit her. She had to find help. If she could just find somebody to stand next to, she knew the man would have to leave her alone. But there was no one around. She couldn't believe it. Where was everybody? Had the cold weather scared them off? That was crazy. Why hadn't she listened to Pete? Just that morning he had said she ought to quit going home through the park, now that it was getting dark earlier.

Directly ahead was the entrance to the zoo. Thank God. Even in the worst weather there was always someone gazing at the oily water in the seal pool, waiting mindlessly for a glimpse of the animals' backs. But this time there was no one. She took in the whole of the zoo grounds in one desperate look around. Not a soul! But it wasn't too late for the zoo attendants. Where were they? A light from the lion house gave her her answer. God, what ridiculous, rotten luck. Feeding time!

Now she knew she had no choice but to tough it out alone.

She put her head down and started to pedal as hard as she could. She glanced over her shoulder, and saw that the man was closer. Ahead was the pedestrian tunnel leading to the children's zoo. If she could just get through it into the park proper, there had to be other people around. The tunnel yawned darkly. She could hear the man now, his breath coming in raspy snorts.

As she entered the mouth of the tunnel, she knew he was right behind. She willed herself not to, but she had to look back. She turned, and suddenly she felt a stinging flash against her neck, and then she was flying off the bike.

"Take it easy, lady. You were just knocked out."

Jackie looked up. A policeman was looking down at her. And there was another next to him. They were both young. Two joggers and a woman with a small poodle completed the ring above her.

Jackie rose unsteadily to her feet. Her first thought was of the baby. She knew with a terrible certainty that this time something awful had happened.

One of the policemen held her arm securely.

"Think we should take her to Lenox Hill, Billy?"

Dr. Nash had been able to see her almost immediately. He was in the hospital, delivering twins. At the words she dreaded—and expected—to hear, Jackie felt tears welling into her eyes. Her throat went dry, and she did not trust herself to speak. Dr. Nash assured her that bed rest and a light liquid diet would set her right in no time at all. He also said that there was no permanent damage and that within a few months she and Pete could try again. The next time everything would be fine.

He continued speaking without missing a beat, a practiced smile on his face. "Naturally," he said, "you feel depressed. But you're young and healthy. You'll be able to have another baby without any difficulty. Just get back into the swing of eating well and exercising regularly as soon as you feel up to it. And, Jackie, remember, what happened was an accident. Don't blame yourself for it. Promise?"

After they had taken Jackie to the hospital, the two cops had been called over to York Avenue and Seventy-eighth. Some young punks had trapped two rivals in the drained swimming pool in John Jay Park and were throwing empty bottles at them. Two hours later they stopped for coffee at a luncheonette on Lexington and Ninety-fifth.

"Fucking kids."

"Your boy busting chops again?"

"Nah. That young broad we picked up. Didn't you see the fishing line?"

"What are you talking about?"

"The fishing line on the ground by the broad who fell off the bike. Some kids must have held it up across the front of the tunnel. I'd sure like to get a hold of those little bastards."

35

In the first few days following the accident, it seemed to Jackie that wherever she went she spotted mothers-to-be. The swell of their midriffs made her look away. They were members of what surely was one of the least exclusive clubs in the world, yet *she* had lost her membership in it in little over a month.

Soon afterward, however, the sharp anguish of it gave way to wistfulness. She knew it would, be a long time before she would stop thinking of the lost baby, but Dr. Nash was right. She and Pete could try again. She was strong and healthy and anxious to resume her life.

She began to run regularly and work out in the gym again. She avoided the Twelvers (it gave her an odd feeling to know how old they really were) and plunged into Bendel's strategy-planning for next spring's fashions. Though Jackie could scarcely credit it, military was on its way in. Again. With a difference, of course. Out were khaki and olive drab. In were peach and lime green and blush pink. Thus had the genius of high fashion struck again. It was Jackie's job to believe in this nonsense, and she pursued her sources with enthusiasm. "Mädchen in Uniform," here we come.

One morning, after an exhausting session at an importer's showroom looking over a new line of Italian ready-to-wear modeled after Mussolini's brownshirts, Jackie returned to her office to find that a Lieutenant Rogers had called her. *Lieutenant* Rogers?

"Yes, dearie, 'Lieutenant,' " said Tyrone, flashing what he referred to as his wiseass, fieldhand smile. "Don't you think you're carrying market research a bit far? Calling in the U.S. Army? Or is it the Navy?"

"Don't be a bitch, Ty. This whoever-he-is has nothing to do with Bendel's. I've never heard of him."

"Her."

"Huh?"

"It's a she. A lady-type person."

"So?" She glanced again at Tyrone, then laughed. "Oh. *That* explains your smirk. You, my pet, have a very active tabloid imagination. Remind me to mention you to Rupert Murdoch when he decides to launch a gay weekly." She dialed as she spoke, frankly puzzled. The voice on the other end identified herself as Catherine Rogers, Lieutenant, j.g., in the U.S. Navy. And as Dave Barnett's sister.

Which explained everything, and nothing. "I must speak to you," she said without preamble.

"I'll be home about six-thirty. Why don't you come by?"

"No. I can't do that. I'll explain later. Where else can we meet?"

Unnerved by the urgency in the woman's voice, Jackie suggested the Russian Tea Room. It wasn't until after she'd hung up that she realized that she hadn't asked why Lieutenant Rogers wanted to see her.

Jackie slipped into the curved red leather booth opposite the bar, ordered a Campari and soda, and kept a watchful eye on the customers wheeling through the revolving door. At precisely the appointed time, a slender, dark-haired woman entered alone. She was dressed in the classic female naval officer's uniform—skirt, jacket, and tie—but she was stunning. Jackie could see, in the line of her nose and the shape of her eyes, Dave's features softened and perfected. Why hadn't he mentioned a sister?

Jackie caught the other woman's eye, waved her over, and introduced herself. She contained her curiosity by asking how long the lieutenant had served in the Navy.

"Since college. The Navy put me through the nursing program at Skidmore. I had to promise them at least two years. I liked it and decided to stick around. Though not as a nurse. By the way, I can't stand civilians calling me 'lieutenant.' It's Catherine, but my friends call me Cat."

A waiter placed Jackie's Campari on the table and Cat asked for the same. In the moment of quiet that followed, Jackie became aware of Cat's rhythmically clicking her thumbnail against her forefinger.

"I'm here because of Dave," said Cat, suddenly coming to the point.

"How is he?"

"That's just it. I don't know. He and Kim have disappeared." Cat's voice wavered, then she continued, speaking rapidly, as if to outdistance her fears. She hadn't heard from Dave for quite a while, but she didn't think much about it because they were both lousy correspondents. She'd been stationed at Guantanamo for a couple of months setting up a recreational activities program, and so she hadn't telephoned him either. Then when she got stateside again last week, she decided to call him to say hello. The operator said his phone had been disconnected. She telephoned IT&T, and they gave her an awful run-around. Finally they told her that their records showed he had resigned. They couldn't—or wouldn't—give her any other information.

"Resigned!" said Jackie.

"Yes. It surprised me, too. I decided I'd better get up here fast and find out what was going on. I got in last night. This morning I went to the address I had for Dave—your apartment building—and I saw your neighbors, what's their name? Johnson?"

"Jensen," said Jackie urgently. "Go on."

"They told me the opposite of what I heard from IT&T. That Dave didn't resign but in fact was promoted and transferred to Santo Domingo. When I tried to find out more, they were almost . . . unfriendly. And, frankly, they acted a little peculiar. They didn't seem to understand who I was."

"What do you mean?"

"They kept repeating that it was impossible. That Dave didn't have a sister."

Jackie shook her head in confusion. "I don't get any of this. Certainly I can't believe Dave quit IT&T and didn't tell any of us. We've assumed all along that they were in Santo Domingo. Tanned and happy and having a ball. In fact, we got a note from Kim soon after they arrived."

"Could I see it?"

"Sure. I'm pretty certain I saved it. I'll dig it out. How about meeting tomorrow at noon?"

"No, I can't do that. Someone from IT&T called me at my hotel this afternoon. He said he had some information about Dave. So I agreed to meet him for lunch."

"Where're you staying?"

"The Worthington. It's off Madison."

"That's right near Number Twelve. Tell you what. I'll drop the note off tomorrow evening on my way home from work."

They arranged to meet at the hotel's outdoor cafe at six the next day. While Jackie tried to catch their waiter's attention, Cat pulled her handbag and gloves onto her lap and wound a wide white silk scarf around her neck. It was smashing next to the inky blue of her jacket and the dark sheen of her hair.

"You know," she said, allowing herself to smile

for the first time, "I feel better about all this. At least something's happening. Dave's my only brother. And I'd hate to lose him again."

"What do you mean, *again?*"

"Didn't Dave tell you?"

"Tell what?"

"Well, it's a bit complicated. You see, what happened was, we were split up when we were very young. Our parents were flying home from a ski vacation, and they crashed into a mountain during a snowstorm. They were killed instantly. Dave was almost six, and I was just three years old. My mother's sister, who was the only family we had, died a year later, so we were turned over to the state. I was adopted right away. It was much harder on Dave. Poor guy, he got stuck in foster care for almost four years, and by the time he was finally adopted legally by one of his foster-care families, he was already a loner. He's never gotten over the feeling of not being wanted and I guess he never will."

"Hold up a second," interrupted Jackie. "Let me take care of this." She quickly calculated the tip and signed her name and account number to the bill the waiter placed in front of her. "Please, go on. If you don't mind talking about it."

"I don't at all. You see, the key thing as far as Dave and I were concerned was that when we were growing up neither of us knew that the other one existed."

"What!"

"Yes, it sounds crazy, but my adoptive family didn't know I had a brother, and I was too young to remember. Of course, Dave was old enough to remember me, but the agency let him believe that I'd died. We would have gone on forever not knowing about each other if I hadn't joined one of those new groups made up of adopted children searching for their natural parents. It took awhile, but I did find out who my biological parents were and that they were dead, but I also found Dave. That was only five years ago. I had just turned twenty-two."

"God, that must have been a traumatic experience."

"Well, it was, but it was wonderful, too. When you discover, as an adult, that you have a brother you didn't know you had, believe me, it makes him all the more precious. You don't take anything for granted. Look, here I am. I'm twenty-seven. I'm not married—Rogers is the name I grew up with, which is why some people don't realize I have a brother, or that Dave has a sister—and who knows if I'll ever get married. I've been involved . . . oh, that's another *long* story. Dave is my family. He's it. And I love him very much."

Cat's face tightened and Jackie reached out for her hand, which she did not pull away.

"I don't know what I'll do if I . . . if . . . I can't . . ."

"Don't worry, you'll find him. Pete and I will do everything we can to help you. I know it's going to work out. People don't just disappear. There has to be some explanation. Come on, let's share a taxi uptown. I want to start looking for Kim's letter."

36

Jackie checked her watch again. It was twenty past six, which surprised her. She'd expected Cat to be on time. She took another swallow of white wine. Damn, she thought, is Almaden the only wine that's sold by the glass? At 6:30 she pushed back her chair and went indoors to the front desk.

"I'm waiting for Lieutenant Rogers," she said to the young, uniformed clerk. "Would you please give me her room number, and tell me where the house phone is?"

The clerk turned to the register. "Lieutenant Rogers checked out this morning," he said.

"I think there must be some mistake," said Jackie.

"No, her husband paid the bill."

"Her husband! That can't be."

"Well, it is. I checked her out myself at about eleven this morning."

"What did her husband look like?"

"Why do you ask?" asked the clerk, suddenly guarded.

Jackie turned away from the clerk wordlessly. She knew he was within his rights in not responding to a question of this sort. Halfway across the lobby, she heard the clerk call out to her, "Are you Mrs. Lawrence?" Jackie turned and nodded. "Lieutenant Rogers left this for you," he said, waving an envelope.

The note was brief and cheerful: She had found out where Dave was. The man she had spoken to from IT&T had located him and she was on her way to see him now. She thanked Jackie for her concern.

Well, at least that explained the so-called "husband," thought Jackie, puzzled that she didn't feel a greater sense of relief. Maybe it was the formality of the signature: Cat had suddenly become Catherine.

The desk clerk watched Jackie walk out the door. He appreciated a good derriere. His hand went to his pocket. He patted it once. The smooth outline of the hundred dollar bill the old geezer with the lousy rug had given him was there. People sure are strange, he thought. Then he started to plan again how he was going to spend the money.

37

"I've told you a hundred times, dummy. Always make the five point. It's not my analytic breakthrough. Read Tim Hollander. Read Barclay Cooke."

"All right. I'll remember next time," said Jackie petulantly.

"Debenture could give me a better game."

"That's it!" yelled Jackie in mock anger as she dumped the backgammon board onto Pete's lap. He grabbed her around the waist and they fell on the large hooked rug. They wrestled for a moment until Pete pinned Jackie under him.

"What's a four-letter word beginning with 'r' and ending with 'e'?"

"Rate."

"No."

"Rote."

"No."

"Rare."

"You're not playing the game."

"Okay. How about *rice?*"

Pete laughed and pulled her close to him, kissing her deeply.

Later, after they'd made love, Pete gently stroked the inside of Jackie's neck. They were still lying on the hooked rug, their clothes strewn around them.

"I love you so much," he said quietly and then, the tone of his voice changing, added, "And I'm proud of you."

"For what?"

"For not doing your paranoid number when Dave's sister checked out of that hotel before meeting you."

"I don't think that's a very nice thing to say."

"Well, lately you've been so damned suspicious. You don't even know what you're suspicious of. I'm surprised you didn't call the Navy to ask about . . . what was her name?"

"Cat Rogers. And I already did."

"You did? Jesus!"

"She's AWOL."

"So? All that means is she's late checking back in. She's probably utilizing the 'magic fingers' in some motel bed with the IT&T man right now."

"That's your answer to everything."

"It's not such a bad answer."

"Well, I'm going to locate her. If only to tell her that it's pretty pissy behavior to stand someone up. She could have reached me earlier in the day."

"The Navy's not going to give you her address, baby."

"I know. I asked. But she told me where she went to school. If I could just remember where, maybe they'd help me find her."

"You're in the wrong profession. But before you sketch out the rest of this caper for me, let's take a breather. I feel like breaking training. You game?"

"I don't believe what I'm hearing."

"Believe it. If you move that cute little butt fast enough I'll buy you a Baskin-Robbins for dessert. With sprinkles."

"Feets, do your stuff," said Jackie, jumping up and gathering her clothes.

Jackie and Pete were four houses away when they noticed the Jensens silhouetted under the front light talking to a couple on the steps. They both started to wipe away any trace of ice cream from their mouths, then caught each other's eye and laughed.

"Thirty years old and afraid of getting caught eating ice cream," Pete whispered to Jackie.

"Shh. They see us," said Jackie as they came up the path to the front entrance.

Arnold and Phoebe were standing with a couple in their late twenties. The man was tall with wavy brown hair that flopped down into his eyes. Either he was extremely fit or he had a great tailor. He wore old-fashioned horn-rimmed glasses. The woman, a strawberry blond, was almost as tall and dressed elegantly in a slim-fitting light tweed suit.

As Jackie and Pete approached, the couple smiled tentatively.

"Pete and Jackie Lawrence," said Arnold, taking charge, "I'd like you to meet Jorge and Rosanna Santos. They're going to be your new neighbors. I know you don't speak Portuguese, but do either of you speak French or Spanish?"

"Only to order in restaurants," said Jackie regretfully.

"Well, I'm sure Jorge and Rosanna will be speaking English within a few months. They're from São Paulo. Jorge is an economist."

"You won't believe what they said about New York," said Phoebe. "They wanted to know if the air was always so clean. Imagine that!"

"The air in São Paulo is notorious," said Arnold. "Eight million people and almost as many cars."

Everyone shook hands once more, smiling broadly. On their way up the stairs to their apartment, Jackie turned to Pete. "They seem nice—what were their names?—but I guess we won't be making any movie dates with them."

"So? That suits you, doesn't it? You've been saying you wanted to see less of the other people in this building."

38

Sunday night was the first home game of the World Series, New York versus Los Angeles, and Jackie and Pete were guests of Jerry and Francie McDonald who were, via the good offices of CBS, guests of the Yankees' owner. Their box seats were directly behind first base. New York was ahead, 3 to 2. It was the bottom of the eighth, which was just as well because the night air had grown cold (the Series was later than usual this year), and Jackie was exhausted from ducking and dodging in her seat each time the ball was thrown to the first baseman. What if he missed?

She and Francie were ready to leave, but the men would not hear of it. "I won't even comment on that," Pete had said. Jerry gave them both a look of utter disbelief. The last out finally came, a New York win, and the four eased their way out the stadium exit ramp, then sprinted through the jubilant crowd to the McDonalds' BMW.

"Thanks, Jer, for a great evening," said Pete as Jerry unlocked the car door.

"Don't thank me, thank CBS. Not only do they pay me for what I like to do best, but the perks are unbelievable."

"Wasn't Victor going to try to set you up with something on ABC?" asked Pete, directing Jackie ahead of him to the back seat.

"Yeah, but it didn't work out. Which doesn't bother me. My hours *are* pretty shitty, and they will be as long as I'm producing the eleven o'clock slot, but what the hell. I've got visibility. My name's up there on the screen every night. And this is the town to be in. Now," he continued, glancing at his watch, "it's a little after ten-thirty. What about Chinatown?"

"Great," said Jackie. "I just got a tip on a new place. It's on Doyers. The decor is supposed to be dreadful and the service lousy, but the food is billed as Hunan hot and very good, and they're open until one."

Once they were free of the crush of cars and people surrounding the stadium, they slid rapidly down out of the Bronx, across the Harlem River, and onto the East River Drive. Jerry got lucky and found a parking spot on Mott, and an hour and a half later, four sated, MSG-dosed people were walking up the short flight of steps leading to Number Twelve to finish off with coffee and Francie's special chocolate chip cookies.

As they started through the tall, paneled front

door, Jackie heard a low, creaking sound coming from the direction of the garage doors. She nudged Pete, who paused to listen.

"Must be Buddy," he said. "He brings the cans out about this time of night." He leaned over the iron railing toward the garage. "That you, Buddy?" he asked.

A muffled "yes" came from the other side of the door.

"What's wrong? Having a problem?"

"Door's stuck," said Buddy.

Pete and Jackie looked over the exterior of the garage, confirming what they already knew: There was not a fingerhold to be had.

"I'll give him a hand from inside," said Jerry, heading for the stairs that led to the basement and the connecting garage. Moments later the garage door rolled silently open, its sudden upward motion knocking Buddy off balance and onto his knees. He rose unsteadily to his feet. Even from the distance at which she stood, Jackie could see the drops of sweat standing out clearly against Buddy's forehead. Without comment, Pete and Jerry went into the garage and carried six garbage cans out onto the sidewalk. Pete touched Buddy lightly on the shoulders. "See you tomorrow," he said. The others waved good night and began to climb the two flights to the McDonalds'. As they passed the Goodmans' apartment, a harsh, rasping cough rang out. Pete raised his eyebrows. When they had closed the McDonalds' door behind them, all four began to talk at the same time. They looked at each other and laughed.

Pete held up his hand for attention. "I think we're all thinking the same thing. It sounds like the Magic Mountain meets Lake Saranac. What the hell's bothering them?"

"They really are in a slump," said Jackie. "Worse than last summer. Remember that, Pete?"

"I do. Seems as if one of them gets sick, they all get sick."

"Maybe they hang out together too much," said Francie.

"I know one thing," said Jerry. "If Ben's cough keeps up, he isn't even going to make it to the track tomorrow. I've been training with him the last couple of weeks for that ten-kilometer race on the second. And, the last few mornings especially, he's had an awful time of it. He says he's just fighting off a cold. Some cold! I never thought I'd have to fake a sprained ankle for Ben to be able to keep up with me!"

"He'll be able to pass you tomorrow, dear," said Francie, as she handed Jerry a large platter of thick, chocolate-studded cookies. "*No one* moves very quickly after eating my cookies."

39

The next morning, while she was reading a piece in the *Times* on last season's Saratoga Arts Festival, it hit her. Skidmore. That's where Cat Rogers had gone to college. The campus was only a few miles from the festival grounds.

As soon as she reached her office, Jackie telephoned the college. Yes, Lieutenant Rogers was an active alumna and, yes, they had a recent address and number for her in Pensacola Beach. Jackie dialed the number. No answer. She tried again an hour later and then, just before packing it in for the day, took one last shot at it. This time, after several rings, a man's voice, low and guarded, responded. Jackie asked for Cat. At first the man said nothing and then, to Jackie's horror, he began to cry. He seemed to be trying desperately to bring himself under control and at last he succeeded sufficiently to ask Jackie who she was and why she wanted to speak to Cat.

"Well, I'm Chris Tompkins, Cat's . . . friend," said the man, apparently satisfied with Jackie's explanation. "This is going to come as a shock, but Cat's . . . she's . . . she's dead."

"What!"

"Yes, she's . . . she killed herself."

"Oh, my God!" Jackie shouted. Tyrone, who'd been whispering and giggling over his own phone for the past ten minutes, turned and gave her a peculiar look. She dropped her voice and continued, "I'm sorry, I don't know what to say. I don't want to bother you at a time like this, but how did it happen?"

"It's all right. I mean, you're not bothering me. I have to get used to talking about it," said Chris Tompkins, though the despair in his voice suggested he never would. "I went to Milwaukee to see my kids, and Cat flew to New York to see if she could locate Dave. When I got back here to Florida it was all over. The police were waiting for me. They'd been notified by the police in New York. They had found Cat's body somewhere in Brooklyn. She'd . . . jumped off a bridge. There was a note. To me. She said she was despondent over her brother. She thought he didn't like her, and that's why he had disappeared without telling her where he was going. And she mentioned me at the end. She said I shouldn't blame myself for what she was doing."

It took Jackie a few seconds to realize that Chris

had stopped talking. "I don't understand," Jackie murmured.

"*You* don't understand? I don't either!" said Chris, angrily. "Sure she was concerned about Dave. It was only natural. But she had her own life, and she was happy with it. We had talked about what her reaction would be if she discovered that something had happened to Dave. Dying wasn't part of the equation. It's not like Cat. But nothing adds up, not even the note. Cat's a very warm . . . she was a very warm and open woman, so loving, but her letter was distant. Almost businesslike. It was not the kind of letter you leave someone you love. And I *know* she loved me."

"Of course you're upset," Pete said to Jackie that evening. "I'm upset, and I never even met the woman. It's always a shock, no matter who does it. Someone you've known all your life, or someone you don't know at all. That's what you've got to remember, this was somebody you met only once. How can you have any idea what was going on in her head? Didn't you tell me she was living with a guy? A guy with kids? Someone who probably couldn't get out of his first marriage?"

"Yes," said Jackie tentatively.

"Well, that kind of scene is hell. Think about it. What was the official explanation again? This pretty young chick, Cat, knocks herself off because she can't keep tabs on her brother? Well, I agree. That's not convincing at all. But this is what the boyfriend chose to tell you. What about what he *didn't* say? Look, here's this gal—she's gorgeous, you said so yourself—she joins the Navy. Who knows why. Maybe she needs to feel she belongs to something. She's sure she's never going to get married, never have her own family. Then, bingo, she falls in love. But there's a catch. The guy isn't free. She's back to square one. Maybe she just couldn't take the situation any longer. Something snapped. You know, if you knew what really was going on in Cat's life, you'd probably be able to make a pretty fair guess about why she did what she did."

Later, after finishing a Gobi-dry Tanqueray martini (how long had it been since she'd had one? she asked herself), she realized that Pete's logic was impeccable. But, damn it, she still felt that something was wrong.

40

Jackie waited until Pete turned on the shower. The
sound of the running water combined with the
cheerful buoyancy of the newscaster on the CBS
Morning News made it unlikely that Pete could
overhear her, but, to play it safe, she picked up the
phone extension in the living room instead of in the
bedroom. She didn't want him to catch her doing
what she was doing, but she felt she had to find out
more about Cat's death. Not why she killed herself
(after her conversation with Pete, she'd given up on
that), but how.

Chris Tompkins had given her little to go on beyond the fact that it had happened in Brooklyn.
The telephone operator sounded personally annoyed that Jackie didn't know which precinct to
ask for, but finally put her through to one, probably
the first on her list. No surprise that they didn't

have a clue to what she was talking about. When
they realized, however, that Jackie was calling
about a deceased (their expression), they connected her with the central Brooklyn morgue. There, a
clerk asked her for Cat's name and date of death
and put Jackie on hold. Almost ten minutes later,
just as she was about to give up, he came back on
the line. "You want Officer Perciatelli," he said.

"Officer *who?*"

"Perciatelli. That's P-e-r-c-i-a-t-e-l-l-i. He was the
officer on duty in the Twentieth when they found
the deceased. He works the noon-to-eight shift. You
can reach him then."

"The Twentieth Precinct?"

"For the second time, lady, yes, the Twentieth.
Do you want me to spell that too?"

"No. But thanks anyway. You're a real charmer.
Just remember that not everyone you work with is
dead," she said, then hung up.

At five past twelve, Jackie picked up the phone
in her office and dialed the number for the Twentieth Precinct.

When Perciatelli came on the line, Jackie explained that she was a friend of Cat's. She had just
learned of her death and wondered if he could give
her any more information about it.

"What kind of information?" asked the officer.
His voice was noncommittal.

"Any details about what actually happened. I
find it hard to believe that she did this to herself. If
I knew more about it, it might be a little easier to
accept." Jackie spoke in her most sincere voice.

When she paused and the officer said nothing, she guessed that he was considering how much to tell her, and she hurriedly continued.

"She was an old and dear friend. We'd known each other since we were kids, and I just found out about this, and it's . . . very upsetting. I don't know if it's against regulations or what, but anything you can say to me about it, I'd appreciate."

"Well . . ." said Perciatelli, and in the way he said it, Jackie knew she had won him over. "I'll massage the rules a bit for you. Let me get my report."

Perciatelli returned a few minutes later. She could hear him breathing on the other end before he spoke; he must be looking over what he had written.

"Okay, I've got it here. I remember this one now. It was the usual kind of thing. Here, I'll read you part of my report: 'Subject's purse, black leather with a shoulder strap, was found at seven fifty-two A.M. on the Marine Parkway Bridge, East Wall, by a Mister Eugene Sopkin, who was operating a black nineteen seventy-two VW. Mister Sopkin, who was attempting to repair a flat tire, noticed the purse and upon perusing its contents, brought it directly to the Twentieth Precinct. Presence of apparent suicide letter was noted and judged serious. Marine Police notified at eight forty-three A.M. and commenced sweeping Rockaway Inlet area for subject's remains at nine-twenty A.M. Subject located at two fifty-six P.M. in shallow water at Breezy Point.' You know," said Perciatelli, interrupting himself, "we were lucky to find her at all. We caught her just before the tide shifted. We lose a lot of floaters to the Lower Bay every year. Once they get that far, they drift right out to sea, and that's it. Nobody sees them again. Let me see, where was I. Autopsy. Okay, 'Autopsy performed by Dr. Jason Monash.' Are you sure you want to hear all this?" asked Perciatelli, suddenly seeming to remember that he wasn't just chatting it up with one of his police mates.

"Yes, please, go ahead," said Jackie weakly. She was horrified by the officer's calm recitation, but determined to hear him out.

"All right. 'Autopsy revealed the presence of Valium and Nembutal in subject's bloodstream. Ratio was not toxic.' This means," said Perciatelli, interpreting the report, "that there was more of it present than is considered normal, but not enough to have killed her. Perhaps she started to take an overdose, and then changed her mind. You know, for every successful O.D. you read about, ten have tried and not made it. Most pill poppers want to be found alive. So perhaps your friend decided to make things more final. Now, what else? Ah, yes, the bruises. 'The body was bruised about the upper torso and arms, but not to a degree inconsistent with a jump.' That just about does it, miss. All in all I would say that what we have here is a fairly straightforward suicide."

The doors of the elevator opened on the ground floor and Jackie stepped out into a crowd of smartly dressed women waiting to be let loose on the floors above. To her right, "Shoe Biz" was doing a brisk business. There must have been at least a dozen customers in the small shoe salon. Each could be counted on to purchase a minimum of two pairs of shoes at a hundred dollars each. Twelve times two hundred dollars made twenty-four hundred dollars. Not bad for five after one, with the better part of the shopping day yet to come. Ahead of Jackie, an elegant blond tried on one of YSL's giant night wraps. In the men's boutique, one alcove over, two Italian businessmen, probably executives fleeing kneecapping and getting their money out of Italy at the same time, leaned against a display case, joking, while a saleslady wrote up a sale. You could always count on Bendel's for a bit of perspective, thought Jackie wryly. Detective Perciatelli's grim rundown on Cat still echoed in her mind. She'd better hustle if she didn't want to be late for her lunch date. Screw training. What she needed was a double Stolichnaya, straight up.

41

NOVEMBER

A cheer went up from the crowd standing at the halfway point when the first knot of runners rounded the bend at Seventy-second Street, near the Daniel Webster statue. Pete and Jackie searched intently for Jerry McDonald. Then they spotted him, running easily, head high. Pete quickly looked down at his watch, then back to Jerry. "He's doing beautifully," he said to Jackie, then nodded toward Ben Goodman and Arnold Jensen, who stood on his other side. "He's almost eighteen minutes for the first five-thousand meters. That's just under six minutes per mile. Fantastic. Did you expect him to do this well, Ben? Can he keep it up?"

"Not only do I expect him to keep it up, I expect him to finish in the top quarter," said Ben, with a look of deep satisfaction. "You'll have to give me a full report on him."

At that moment, Jerry passed the small group from Number Twelve. "Go to it, man," shouted Pete, drowning out Ben. He reached over to Francie, who was standing with them, and hugged her. "Now that's what I call a payoff. Not that you're in such bad shape yourself," he added, before turning back to Ben. "Sorry, but what were you saying?"

"I said, you'll have to bring me the good word on Jerry. I'm going to head home now. You know, the little woman's been a bit under the weather lately, and I don't want to leave her alone for too long. Arnold's decided to accompany me."

Pete glanced from Ben to Arnold. "You know, I've been worried about *you*. You just don't seem up to par, either of you. Are you all right?"

"Couldn't be better, my boy," answered Arnold for both of them. "Haven't you learned yet that the more fit you are the thinner you are?" He turned to Ben. "We mustn't tarry. Remember, you have a prescription to pick up for Sylvia."

"Right. We're off," said Ben, suddenly brisk. "Goodbye, Pete, ladies. Buzz our bell when you come back, and give us the good news on Jerry."

Pete, Francie, and Jackie watched as the two men cut across the grass in the direction of East Eighty-third Street. Their backs were bent, and they moved with a rigid, awkward gait.

"The big experts," sneered Jackie under her breath.

"Funny, their taking off before the race is over," said Pete.

"You mean, *tottering* off. Looks like they'll be lucky to make it to Fifth Avenue."

As if to confirm Jackie's words, Ben suddenly lost his footing and stumbled against Arnold. For a moment it seemed as if both men might tumble ignominiously to the ground. When they righted themselves, they turned around, but instead of seeming chagrined at revealing their physical frailty, they were smiling broadly, as if nothing could quench their good humor. They waved merrily at their young observers and continued on their way.

42

"Come on, Jackie, I want to get back in time to watch the game," Pete said to the closed bathroom door.

"I'll be finished in a minute," came the muffled reply from the other side. "My makeup isn't—"

"Jesus! Makeup! We're just going to buy a plant, for God's sake. The damn place is only four blocks away."

He was just warming up to a second plateau of exasperation when the front doorbell rang.

"Good," said Arnold Jensen as Pete opened the door. "It's so nice out, I wasn't sure you'd be in." He didn't look any better than he had the day before.

"We were just getting ready to go out, in fact," Pete replied.

A small man in his late forties stood next to Arnold. He was dressed in a gray leisure suit with navy piping that would have guaranteed him an audition on *The Gong Show*. He stared intently at Pete. He looked so displeased that Pete immediately felt uncomfortable.

"Excuse me," said Arnold. "Mr. Morton Landers, meet Mr. Pete Lawrence."

The little man had an amazingly strong grip that took Pete by surprise. He felt a small click as two joints castanetted against each other.

"Mr. Landers has been talking to us about Kim and Dave. Mr. Landers is from Diners Club."

"Credit Consultation and Research Systems, Limited, Mr. Jensen. Diners Club is our client."

"Of course. Well, anyway, Mr. Landers would like to speak to you—why, good afternoon, Jackie. You look marvelous. I was just telling Pete that Mr. Landers is here about Kim and Dave. He's from—"

Jackie actually pushed Pete to the side as she moved closer to the man.

"Do you know where they are?"

"No," he said quickly, sounding rattled. "That's why I'm here. To find them."

"That was what I was trying to tell Pete before," said Arnold, with more than a dollop of irritation. "Mr. Landers is an investigator from a private firm in the employ of the Diners Club. So if you'd just give him a few minutes—"

Landers strolled past Jackie and Pete into the living room, looking around him with the appraising eye of a real estate agent.

"I'll see you later," said Arnold. "I have to get

back to Phoebe. She's in the garden. We're bone-mealing today."

Before either of them could say goodbye, Arnold was gone. Pete closed the door and turned to see Landers seated regally on the middle cushion of the couch.

"'I can see that you two are sensible folks. Good living, but within your means."

He sat farther back and allowed a tiny smile to butterfly at the corners of his mouth.

Jackie and Pete stared at Landers.

"You're wondering how I can say that? It's not easy. Believe me. Takes years. I've been in this game for a long time. And let me tell you, I don't think there's a better nose around than mine for deadbeats. I can't stand them." He paused. "Now these folks, the Bensons—excuse me, I mean the Barnetts . . ."

Landers' smile became knowing.

"Benson is not exactly wrong, you see. That was the name they used when they lived in Costa Mesa. Kay and Douglas Benson. That's what they were in Costa Mesa. But they were Kelly and Dean Bishop in Terrell. That's outside Dallas. That's what they used before Benson."

"What are you talking about?" Jackie asked.

"Deadbeats. Seventeen-thousand-dollars-and-change deadbeats. Deadbeats with style: Advent TV, vacations on Paradise Island, designer dresses, four-hundred-dollar suits. The Barnetts have been raping my client, the Diners Club, for almost a year. That's not to mention what they've done to every other major credit card company, including Barclay's."

"I don't believe it," said Pete.

"Neither do we," replied Landers. "Our grab rate is usually under two months. I've been chasing these cuties for eight months."

Pete looked toward Jackie.

"You can't be serious," she said. "Kim and Dave are not the kind of people who would do what you're saying."

"My dear young woman," Landers said, sounding very tired, "I don't have the time to sit down and educate you here and now, but take my word for it, you are very young and very naive. You are thinking, these are the most normal people in the world, right? Solid midwesterners. Salt of the earth, yes?" He paused like a teacher who had made the point many times before. "You just learned lesson number one. The All-American straight can be as crooked as a capo di capi."

Landers reached into an inside pocket of his jacket and brought forth a worn black leather notepad. He withdrew a slender mechanical pencil from a holder on the side and looked at them. He was back to being displeased.

"Where are they? And please don't give me any more of this Santo Domingo crap that your neighbors have been shoving at me. I've closed that number already. My last tracing is Boca Raton, and that was a little under a month ago. You're not helping them by keeping quiet. And they need help. My clients only want their money back. They won't prosecute. They'll give them every break they can.

These are two intelligent, potentially productive people. There's no reason they can't function in our society. But they need therapy. We can't help them if we can't locate them."

"I'm stunned," said Jackie.

She sounded stunned.

"I understand what's going through your head," said Landers, "but look at it this way. They're just a couple of decent people playing out the American dream without the right checkbook balance. It's like drinking: When it's become a problem, that's when you think you can handle it."

He stared at them a long time before Pete could speak.

"The last we heard was Santo Domingo, too."

Landers got up slowly from the depth of the cushion.

"Okay, you win. You *all* win. I don't believe any of you, but I'm not going to let it slow me down. I hate deadbeats, though that's a Twinkie to what I feel about these two players. You know why I feel that way? It's because I can feel these two laughing at me for shopping at Korvettes, for taking three years to pay off a Pinto. But I say, let them laugh. That only whips my ass harder. I'll get them."

He walked out the door without closing it.

"Wow," said Pete, almost to himself.

"Wow, is right," said Jackie, slumping down into the cushion the small man had just vacated. "I hate to say it, but that terrible man has left me very confused. It's crazy, but do you think that maybe Cat found out about—"

"That's just what I was thinking."

43

Pete was not pleased at having to appear on the morning panel, but it was part of the price he had to pay to justify his company's sending him on this swing through southern California. A week of wining and dining and bullshitting with West Coast literary mavens—fewer, thankfully, than their Eastern brethren—with a weekend of pure vacation tacked on at the end. Jackie already was stretched out on the beach in front of the hotel, doing her best to obliterate all memory of the cold and rainy weather they'd left behind in New York.

They'd arrived in Santa Barbara for the writers' conference the night before, just in time for a reception for Pete and the other visiting lit-biz luminaries (small-wattage variety) from New York. Over twenty students immediately had gone to work on him and extracted promises that he would give them objective opinions on their manuscripts. What he had read thus far did not inspire confidence in the future of the novel.

He now saw several of his fellow panelists entering the auditorium. Their subject: "Whither the Hardcover? Renaissance or Armageddon?" On the stage where they stood there was a flurry of handshaking and cordiality for the benefit of the members of the audience ranked expectantly before them, then they seated themselves at the direction of the eager, bow-tied moderator, a published novelist known in the business for high productivity and low sales. A man destined to teach. To Pete's right were a leading homosexual in the industry, whose nighttime forays were regularly gossiped about over Perrier and lime at the Four Seasons Grill; next, a young, apprentice killer-shark at one of the more aggressive houses; and then a tailored, underpaid woman editor, disarmingly pretty in a profession whose female representatives Pete characterized as—savoring the crudity of the phrase—oinkers. Beyond Pete, to his left, was the sole emissary from the side of the business that had caused the hardcover houses to push the panic button in the first place—a paperback publisher. He was a short, intense man, transmogrified by the California sun into a leisure-suited Polo Lounger, two heavy gold chains lassoed across his open-shirted, hairy chest.

After a preliminary round of throat-clearing and filling of water glasses by the occupants of the stage, the moderator nervously welcomed the students to the first official event of the Sixth Annual Santa Barbara Writers' Jamboree. (What was wrong, Pete thought sourly, with the good, old-fashioned word *conference?*)

"In the year two thousand and one," the moderator asked, "will you," he nodded solemnly toward the audience, "be publishing your Great American Novel between coated boards or Mead Mark One, which is to say, between hard or soft covers? To be brutally blunt, do hardcover publishers have a future? My dear—" the moderator looked toward the female editor—"why don't you lead off?"

The editor smiled, but before she could speak, the junior shark put into practice corporate guerrilla tactic number one—seize the initiative—and interrupted.

"I hope you don't mind," (I mind, thought Pete, offended for her), "but I think I'm in a unique position to answer that question in view of the recent acquisition of my firm by a large conglomerate. It is self-evident, I believe, that Leisure Resources International would not have invested in us if they did not endorse and support our abilities to successfully develop and distribute the written word. . . ."

And so on, and so on, thought Pete as he listened wearily to the young mako invoke the joys of conglomerate publishing. Pete glanced surreptitiously at his watch. Two more hours on stage, followed by two hours of lunch, followed by two hours of seminars on the campus lawn (the famous "Ponderosa Pine Chats") followed, thank God, by his and Jackie's escape southward to Beverly Hills. Pete was not by nature a cynic, but he could not help asking himself as he looked at the audience in front of him, then back to his copanelists: Who was massaging whose ego? Some good, at least, was coming from this Santa Barbara stopover: Jackie was getting a headstart on her California tan.

44

The pink towers of the Beverly Hills Hotel had never seemed more inviting. The smiling, blond parking attendant eased their Datsun, courtesy of Hertz, between a Mercedes that Goering would have felt comfortable in and a cream-colored Rolls that glittered with status. Its license said simply, ENVY. The tastefully realistic fake fire in the far corner of the lobby radiated good cheer. Gregory Peck strolled by in conversation with a small, freckled man whose radiantly shining bald head reached as high as Peck's tie-clip. On the way to their bungalow, Jackie slid her hand lightly over the dark glossy leaves of the luxuriant and perfectly groomed tropical foliage that surrounded the hotel, smiling in anticipation. As always, the Beverly Hills delivered.

In the week that followed, while Pete made his

rounds of agents and writers, beginning each day, as was the local penchant, with a breakfast meeting in the *lanai* of the Polo Lounge, Jackie delighted in the pleasures of vacation living. Fresh-squeezed orange juice served on the patio of their bungalow. Mornings poolside. Bountiful salad lunches in tiny garden restaurants hidden behind Sunset Boulevard. By late afternoon, his business over, Pete would run with her up Sunset Boulevard and into the hills, finally looping back to finish at the hotel pool for a swim. Then, later, they would case the shops on Rodeo Drive or glide in their car through the eerily silent streets of Beverly Hills, speculating on the current value in the feverish Los Angeles real estate market of the properties they passed. In the evenings, intoxicated by the heady atmosphere of competitive spending that lit up the lives, so it seemed, of even the humblest toilers in the show business world, Pete and Jackie gave his expense account a run for its money.

On the day before they were scheduled to return to New York, a Saturday, Pete and Jackie settled in at the pool for the day. It was a perfect, smog-free day, with a summery softness in the air. Jackie had with her Edith Wharton's *House of Mirth* and Pete carried the inevitable manuscript. The sounds of gin rummy and backgammon games in progress and lazy, relaxed conversations blended with the monotone of the telephone operator paging guests over the loudspeaker system. Shortly before noon, they heard Pete's name being paged.

"Damn," said Pete, "what is it going to be? An anxious writer or an uptight agent?"

He trotted over to the phone near the tennis courts, gave his name to the operator, and waited for his call to be put through.

"Pete?" The voice on the other end was familiar, but low, almost a whisper, and Pete strained to identify it. "Pete, it's me, Jerry. Jerry McDonald."

"Hi, Jerry," said Pete surprised. "Boy, is this a lousy connection." A burst of static underscored his remark, and he paused. "What's up?"

"Francie's mother and father have been in a bad automobile accident. The doctors think they'll make it, but it's pretty touch-and-go, and we're leaving immediately for Cleveland. We'll probably only be gone for a week, but we wanted to let you know where we were because we didn't want you to worry about us and we also wondered if you could do us a special favor. Sylvia will be watering our plants and feeding the fish, but our car is in for repair at the Volvo place. Loomis Motors, on First near Twenty-fifth. Could you possibly pick it up for us and keep it parked on the street? It'll be ready on Monday." Jerry paused.

"Yes, yes, of course," said Pete quickly.

"That's terrific," continued Jerry, his voice thin and attenuated. "I really appreciate that. The miserable sons-of-bitches charge an arm and a leg per day for cars that aren't picked up after they've been fixed."

Pete tried to interject—he was so sorry to hear about Francie's parents, and was there anything else he could do—but Jerry plowed right ahead. Static continued to crackle in the background.

"Look, I'm really wiped out by what's happened, and I can't talk now. We've got to rush to get our plane. I'll slip the receipt for the car under your door. Thanks again. See you soon."

Before Pete had a chance to respond, Jerry hung up. Pete stared at the receiver, puzzled. He could not put his finger on what accounted for his feeling of Jerry's remoteness, but it was certainly not a matter of the three thousand miles that separated them. He ordered two gin-and-tonics from a waiter who was lounging against a cabana, then headed back toward Jackie. Two people finally had decided to go for a swim, and the sunlight danced off their backs as they gracefully stroked the length of the pool.

"Who was it?" asked Jackie.

"Jerry McDonald. I just had the weirdest conversation with him."

"What was *he* calling about?"

Pete explained what had happened and that Jerry and Francie were going to have to go out to Ohio for a few days.

"The strange thing, though, was that I just couldn't get a word in edgewise. He wouldn't let me interrupt. He just kept on talking. Well, what the hell, he must be upset."

Jackie wasn't really listening to Pete at this point. She was shocked by what he'd said, but not by the news of the accident, as terrible as that was. It wasn't that. No, it was something else. It was a strong feeling that she would never see the McDonalds again. Of course, she had no *real* reason to believe anything other than what Jerry had told Pete. They would return in a few days. As simple as that. But what if they didn't? Involuntarily, she shivered under the huge, orange California sun.

45

They had been back from California for almost a week when a letter from Francie McDonald arrived. Jackie at once recognized Francie's firm, rounded handwriting.

Dear Jackie and Pete,

Mom and Dad are out of the hospital and doing fine. We were really worried about them at first, but things looked worse than they actually were. Dad ended up with a compound, spiral fracture of the left leg and has a hip-to-toe cast which won't come completely off for another six months. They don't expect any complications, but it does take time. I'm more concerned about Mom. She looks like her old self, but the crash was an awful shock to her and she's become very vague. Jerry's offered to run Dad's office (he's a big gun in real estate here) until he can get around himself, and naturally I don't want to come back to New York without Jerry. So here we'll be for another month at least. CBS has been generous about a leave of absence for Jerry, and I can always get my job back at Cinandre. About the car: Jerry wonders if you would mind taking it down to an outdoor lot on Twelfth Street and Second Avenue? It's for long-term parking. You keep the keys. Hermie, the man who runs it, knows Jerry, so there'll be no problem about his asking you to ante up in advance. Say hi to everyone and, again, thanks for taking care of the old wheels.

> *Love,*
> *Francie*

P.S. Jerry just ran twelve miles at seven minutes per!

The letter was postmarked Cleveland. Jackie noticed there was no return address, but she usually didn't put one down either. It was reassuring to have proof of their well-being. And if she and Pete wanted to get in touch with them, she could easily get their address from the Jensens.

The Jensens and the other oldtimers (which was just what they were, Jackie thought malevolently) had bounced back from their spell of poor health and again were jogging with élan around the reservoir in the early morning hours as if they'd never missed a day. Jackie had seen them pull it off before. Just as they were at their lowest ebb, really showing their age, they snapped to, all of them at once, so it seemed.

Pete slipped back into the habit of running with the golden oldies, but Jackie, though she wanted to work out with him, shied away from joining the group. The disparity between their apparent and their real ages led Pete and Jackie into a series of arguments that always followed the same line and reached the same conclusion:

"So?" Pete would answer when Jackie brought up the matter. "Since when has anyone over forty—hell, thirty—wanted to tell the truth about their age?"

"Well, sure, I can see people claiming to be a couple of years younger than they are. People do it all the time. But they don't write off twenty or thirty years."

"If they can get away with it, why not? It just proves they're doing something right. Their diet and their exercising work. Look, Jackie, I know you don't care much for them and nobody says you have to, that's your prerogative, but don't crucify them for a human failing. If Albert Schweitzer had dyed his hair, would that have made him less a person? If you don't want to aggravate yourself, stay clear of them."

"What do you think I've been doing? You're incredibly dense sometimes."

"Don't pick a fight with me just because you're not the neighborly type," said Pete, sweetly reasonable.

"Some set of neighbors. You still don't understand what I'm talking about, do you?"

"No, I don't," said Pete in a maddeningly patient tone.

"Nothing bothers you." Jackie struggled to contain her anger. "Don't you see? They deliberately let us draw the wrong conclusion. They lied to us. And not only that, they see nothing wrong in it. And, sadly, neither do you."

Pete shook his head, and Jackie shouted, "Okay, okay. Let's drop the subject."

Jackie was angry and hurt that Pete did not see and accept what was so obvious to her. Liars cannot be trusted. Trust is the essence of friendship. Ipso facto, liars cannot be counted as friends. But so be it. If Pete wanted to spend time with the Goodmans, Macraes, and Jensens, that was his problem, not hers.

When Pete and the Twelvers turned north toward the reservoir for their morning workout— Jackie noticed that the new Brazilian couple frequently joined them; Jorge was supposed to have been one of Brazil's top amateur soccer players— Jackie, leaving five minutes later, headed south. She entered the park at Seventy-ninth Street, then circled down past the children's playground, around the model boat pond, then back up along the edge of the main north-south automobile route. She also always tried to swim laps in the pool or work out on the Nautilus during those times of the day when the gym was otherwise empty.

One day, as she was hurrying down the hall stairs, already late for the office, she met Ben Goodman coming up. She smiled pleasantly and slowed to a walk. The less she saw of the older people, the more polite she had become, her cordiality as insincere, she felt, as their own.

"You're looking good, young lady," said Ben, firmly patting her lower back.

"That's because I'm always running to catch a bus," said Jackie. "Like right now."

"I won't keep you, but I hear your times are really something. You've got a proud hubby."

"And he's got a proud wifey," Jackie replied, the edge to her voice betraying her antagonism.

"We miss your company, but I know some people like to work out alone. You know, a true test for you would be to race in the Perrier Open as an entry with Pete. Think about it. Now off you go," said Ben, dismissing her with a pat on the fanny.

As she waited on Fifth Avenue for the pod of buses that she could see migrating toward her from further uptown, she thought about Ben. Evidently, the more obvious results of her exercising had made an impression on him. His hands had been all over her. But almost absentmindedly. He'd had something else on his mind, and she recognized it for what it was. He was challenging her, daring her to push herself further. And it was clear to Jackie that he didn't think she could do it.

The Open, which was to be held on the third Saturday in January, was Perrier's newest race. It was set up as a competition for couples. The separate running times for the two members of each team would be averaged for the final score. The new-wave seltzer company was having a field day with the race, passing around customized, bubbly warm-up jackets to several thousand New Yorkers, and although this was its first year, the race already had become the chic sporting event of the season. When Pete had asked Jackie somewhat wistfully if she wanted to sign up with him for it, her instant reaction was, no way. It would be a fifteen-kilometer race, a mere tuneup for serious marathoners, yet tough enough to eliminate all but the hardiest of the weekend joggers, and she did not want to risk the public humiliation of not being able to finish it or, worse yet, collapsing. On her best days, she was running up to five miles, and although she knew the rule of thumb was that you could run at least twice as far in competition as you normally did, she nearly swooned at the idea of trying.

Now, because Ben and the others didn't think she could do it, she began to have second thoughts. A childish attitude, perhaps, but did it matter what her motivation was? She had doubled her distance once before. Of course, that had only been from one lap of the reservoir to two, and this meant a jump from five to ten miles. Could she do it? She rehearsed in her mind six circuits of the reservoir. That would be 9.6 miles, just over fifteen kilometers. It would take her the first lap to get warmed up, as always; the second, third, and fourth times around probably would be manageable; the fifth and sixth? Who knew if she'd still be on her feet, much less moving forward. She would try it that afternoon after work, and if she was successful, she would surprise Pete by entering them in the Open.

* * *

The run itself was every bit as difficult and painful as she had imagined. No. It was worse. But she knew, as she came into the final stretch of the sixth circuit, that nothing could stop her now. Her calves and shins ached with a delicious agony envisioned only by a Dr. Mengele or a de Sade. With each step, she gasped for air, but her determination carried her. She was amazed. She had been running for almost an hour and a quarter. And she had almost finished her 9.6 miles. She imagined her name in print in the *New York Times* in the full-page ad that Perrier would take out to honor the finalists in its race. No, that was going too far.

The giant snail shape of the Guggenheim Museum came into her field of vision. Thank God! It was only a matter of yards before her finish line. She forced herself to quicken her pace, fighting the signal her brain was sympathetically sending to her body that it was hurting too much. Only fifty more yards to go. Just then a figure stepped from around the wall and onto the edge of the track. It was Ben Goodman. What was he doing here? As she drew nearer to him, she noticed a stopwatch in his hand. How dare he! A wave of anger swept over her, and she realized that she must keep running, and run until he was out of her sight, or risk the temptation to punch him. How far she ran and how fast was her business, not his. Just as she passed him and began to pull away from him, she heard him cheerfully call out her name. She tensed.

"Jackie," Ben said. "Sorry, but that's not good enough. You're too far behind Pete. You know," he continued, laughing, "your husband's a competitor.

He doesn't just want to finish. He wants to win. I'm going to have to suggest to him that Allison run with him instead."

Jackie felt as if someone had kicked her in the solar plexus. She staggered, but managed to keep going. As soon as she knew Ben could no longer see her, she collapsed onto the ground, and, though her chest was heaving and each word she spoke hurt, she said, pounding the ground for emphasis, "No, you won't, you miserable, freaky old bastard. I'll show all of you."

46

DECEMBER

In the next couple of weeks, Jackie ran seven to eight miles each day and often ten. She was becoming faster, too. (She remembered how excited she'd been last summer to run a mile in under eight minutes. Now she was consistently closer to a seven-minute pace. Pete had been thrilled with her decision to compete in the Open—she hadn't said a word to him about Allison and, apparently, neither had Ben—and he ran with her instead of the others as much as possible. Apart from a day off to celebrate Thanksgiving with a large, old-fashioned turkey dinner (on this day even more than Christmas they were nostalgic for the families they didn't have), they were training in earnest now.

When Pete was unable to join her, Jackie frequently put together offbeat running courses for

herself, sequences of streets that pleased her because they carried her through unfamiliar neighbor-
hoods or on errands that she'd been putting off.
Recently she had run down to Chinatown for fried
dumplings (she figured she'd earned them) and on
the Sunday before last to Orchard Street to check
out the latest stock at her two favorite discount
dress stores.

On this particular Saturday morning, Jackie
mapped out a route that would take her up Fifth
Avenue to Ninetieth Street, into the park for two
laps around the reservoir, across Ninety-sixth Street
to the top of Carl Schurz Park, then past Gracie
Mansion and onto the promenade bordering the East
River. She would loop the promenade three times to
increase her mileage, then from there run onto the
lower promenade down to Sutton Place some
twenty blocks further south.

It was a perfect running morning—sunny and in
the mid-thirties by ten o'clock when Jackie set off.
She quickly settled into a comfortable, easy stride
and held it for the length of her course. Once on
the city streets again, she zigzagged west, finishing
her run at the Maginot line of impenetrable, reso-
lute shoppers in Bloomingdale's vicinity. Anyone
with real business to accomplish or a timetable to
meet was forced to walk in the gutter. As she
slowly flowed with the crowd past the store's gleaming blue-gray walls, she had to fight with herself not
to enter. Bloomingdale's at high noon an a Saturday. Customers ricocheting from counter to counter
like moths around a two-hundred watt bulb. It was
tempting, but it would have been madness.

Now that she'd completed her morning workout, though, her credit cards itched for action. At moments like this, Jackie the consumer took over from Jackie the athlete. This other Jackie loved to shop—browse, poke, consider, bargain—and to spend money, lots or little, it didn't matter so long as the prize was worth having. Still regretting Bloomingdale's, Jackie idled northward, glancing absentmindedly into shop windows along the way: Swedish glass, art nouveau silver, wicker furniture, marble garden statuary, lamps from Milano and baskets from Mexico.

On Sixty-third Street she stopped and entered a small thrift shop no larger than a storefront laundry. Her eye had been caught by a small evening bag dropped casually into one corner of the display window, as if its owner had just the moment before rushed onto the dance floor. It was made of black silk, strewn with delicate petit point roses ranging from pale to deep pink. On hearing what Jackie wished to see, the elderly saleslady pulled the bag from the window and placed it on top of the glass jewelry case for Jackie's inspection. It was even more exquisite up close, with only the slightest bit of fraying at the clasp to betray its age. It was exactly what Jackie had been looking for.

"How much is it?" she asked the woman.

The woman, whose hair was gathered into a cotton-candy-like bun, took the bag from Jackie, pulled a small white tag from its interior, and adjusted the glasses on the end of her nose.

"Seventy-five dollars."

"I guess I'm not in the market for that bag today

after all," said Jackie mildly. The woman knew what she had; the bag was worth every penny of that and more. Jackie peered past the bag down into the jewelry case at the trays of gold and silver, beads and glass.

"I'll take a look at some of your jewelry, though."

At Jackie's direction, the woman lifted out an art deco silver spider and a pair of earrings that resembled candle-wax drippings.

"Let me see *that*, please, that bracelet over there," Jackie asked suddenly.

The woman groped around the tray, unsure what interested Jackie.

"No, no. That one, the one with the rust-colored stones," said Jackie impatiently.

Her heart had begun to beat wildly, and her voice was taut. She had almost missed it, but the stones were so special that the bracelet had seemed to leap up at her from the depths of the case. The stones were the size of a big man's thumbnail, and they were a deep, earthy-red color like slices of pet-rified wood. There were four of them set into a heavy, burnished band of silver. It was a gorgeous piece, and Jackie knew she had seen it before. She was almost positive of it.

The woman lifted it out of the case, and Jackie, immediately conscious of its authoritative weight, draped it across her wrist. "It's a beauty," she said. Then she asked as spontaneously as she could, "Where on earth did you get it?"

"Well, after people have done their fall cleaning, they come see us. A lot of people still think of us

, bless their hearts. We have one lady who moved to Marco Island thirteen years ago, but every year she sends some lovelies."

"Oh, yes, I know these are all contributions," said Jackie quickly. "It's wonderful that people are so generous. But what I mean is, where did you get this particular piece?"

"Heavens, I have no idea."

"But you do, I mean, you do keep records, don't you?"

"Yes.

"Well . . ." When the woman failed to make the connection, Jackie plunged on. "Would you be kind enough to check your records to see who brought this bracelet in? It's very important to me."

The woman's geniality faded.

"No, young lady, I certainly cannot do that," she said stiffly. "We respect our patrons' privacy, and their charities—to whom and what they give—is surely a private matter."

In other circumstances, Jackie would have been amused by the woman's self-importance. She looked again at the bracelet itself. With trepidation, she turned it in her hand, opened it, and stopped and stared. There, in the center of the back of the band in tiny letters, she read:

> To F from J
> Because you are . . .
> 1/24/75

She *had* seen the bracelet before. She had seen it encircling the wrist of Francie McDonald.

* * *

As Jackie closed the front door of Number Twelve behind her, she felt that special stillness a house has when all its occupants are absent. Although it was almost noon, the others must still be in the park. A lucky break. She paused for a few moments to listen for any hint of sound—there was none—then ran up the staircase to their apartment. She had bought the bracelet because it seemed important to have proof; proof of *what* she did not know and could not yet bring herself to seriously consider. She placed it on the table in the foyer and, hesitating for only a few seconds, reached into the silver and enamel bowl where they kept important odds and ends. She knew the McDonalds' car keys were there, and she'd noticed before that the key ring held several extra keys. Before she could change her mind, she opened the door to the hallway and, though there was no one to hear her, crept silently down the flight of stairs to the McDonalds' apartment. She took a deep breath and slipped one of the keys into the lock. When it did not yield, she tried a second key. This time the lock clicked, and with a small push, the door swung open.

Inside, the Venetian blinds were drawn and only small wedges of daylight sliced into the room. Jackie hung back in the entrance, waiting for her eyes to adjust to the dusky light—and for the courage to make her next move. She yearned for more light, but hesitated to switch on the lamps for fear of seeing too much too quickly. She planned to search the apartment—one room at a time, nice and easy—for something, she didn't know what it would be, that would tell her where the McDonalds were: either, pray to God, where they said they were, in Cleveland nursing Francie's parents, or . . . she could not complete the other part of the puzzle. The discovery of Francie's bracelet had filled her with anxiety, for there was no way to explain satisfactorily how an object so precious and so personal had come to be where it was, knocking about a thrift shop which, despite its respectability and the worthy cause it no doubt served, was just an upper-income-bracket excuse for a tax deduction. Francie would not—could not—have brought her bracelet there. Someone else must have, and Jackie shuddered at the implications.

Jackie turned first in the direction of the bedroom. Now that her eyes had adjusted, the murky light was sufficient to see that the bed was neatly made up and everything was in order. She opened one closet: Jerry's suits and sports coats were arranged by color, with luggage on the shelf above them and shoes below. She stuck her head only briefly into Francie's closet. The intimacy of doing so embarrassed her, but, Lord, what a clotheshorse! She hadn't realized how many outfits Francie owned. The clothing rod was packed, and there were still more suitcases and over two dozen pairs of shoes.

In the bathroom, Jackie stood in front of the shower curtain for a long beat, then yanked it sharply to one side . . . but, of course, there was nothing. She felt silly, and giggled aloud in relief. On the shelf above the sink she saw makeup in pale green cases—compact, lipstick, mascara, foundations. On the sink edge there was a wrinkled, half-used tube of toothpaste, cap missing. In a small plastic glass were two toothbrushes.

Back in the foyer, she paused to decide what direction to go in next. Something about what she had just seen bothered her, and now as she ran her eye over the furniture in the living room, she realized what it was. She backtracked to the bathroom and looked again at the objects scattered over the shelf. Toothbrushes and toothpaste? Okay. These were the classic items left behind when people went off on trips. But the makeup? These were not extras, but the essentials, the basics that some women wouldn't even go to the corner drugstore without. A woman, for instance, like Francie—born with an eyeliner in one hand, a lipstick brush in the other. She would have scooped the stuff into her handbag, even if the house were on fire.

Jackie became aware that her shirt was wet just as a drop of sweat fell off the tip of her nose. She turned, walked rapidly toward the door, then stopped, her hand on the knob. She was torn between wanting to get the hell out and a perverse and pressing curiosity. The makeup shouldn't have been there. Something was wrong. Uneasy though she was, she wanted to know what.

She stepped into the living room, sliding her eyes over the couch, armchairs, coffee table. No tale to tell here. The furniture had a pleasantly rumpled look, as if Jerry and Francie had just gone off for the day and would be back that evening. Lifting her gaze to the wall of windows at the far end of the room, Jackie stopped abruptly. This was where

Francie kept her plants. Why were the blinds drawn?

Jackie had admired the plants on the evening that she and Pete had come by for coffee after the baseball game. There had been wandering Jew, Swedish ivy, and begonias hanging down from the walls and ceiling, and cactuses, a handsome crown of thorns, and geraniums heading up from a long tray of pebbles that ran the length of the windows. The effect was stunning, a lush mass of greenness, vibrant and alive, slashed by bursts of red. Now, as she peered through the gloom at the plants, Jackie could see that something was off; their silhouette was altered, distorted in a way that she could not precisely determine from where she stood. She drew closer and then, with horror, she realized what was wrong: The plants were dead. The soil in the pots was caked and split and the leaves were shriveled and curled under. All were utterly devoid of life. For the first time, she became aware of a heavy invisible blanket of rot hanging in the air.

"Oh, my God," Jackie whispered to herself. Sylvia Goodman hadn't been watering those plants. *No one* had. What would Francie say when she saw them? *If* she saw them. . . . The thought rose unbidden, and as it crashed into her consciousness, she whirled to the right, remembering that on that earlier evening she had also seen, mounted on the wall somewhere in the vicinity of the plants, a fishtank. The fish! Sylvia was to have been feeding them, too.

There they were. Floating at the top of the tank, covering the surface in a tide of death, their vivid golds and pinks and purples reduced to an ashy gray. The front of the tank was made of magnifying glass, and Jackie stood rooted before it, her gaze locked by a fish's eye enlarged to the size of an overcoat button.

It began as a low moan, expressive of anger as well as pain, and then it burst forth, loudly and unmistakably, as a cry of pure terror. Jackie, realizing all at once that it was she who was making this hellish noise, recoiled as if she had been struck. She tried to contain the sound but it was as futile as swimming against heavy surf. She gasped and then screamed again and, screaming still, turned and ran. Not for the front door. Not yet. She rapped her hipbone sharply against the edge of the counter as she stumbled clumsily into the kitchen. She pulled open the refrigerator door. The oranges and lemons in the vegetable bin were blistered by large splotches of green mold, the contents of several small dishes had ceased to be identifiable, and over everything hung the acrid smell of decomposing milk. Jackie slammed the door. She needed no further confirmation that the McDonalds' apartment had been abandoned. It was true then. First the Barnetts, now the McDonalds. Jackie was afraid to take the thought any further.

On the floor by the front door, a piece of crumpled paper caught Jackie's eye. Instinctively, she picked it up and jammed it into her back pocket. She let the front door bang behind her with the recklessness of a panicked animal and, half-hiccoughing, half-sobbing, raced up the stairs and into the safety of their apartment. She looked at her watch. She had been downstairs less than five minutes. In one rushing motion, she grabbed her pocketbook and flung its strap over her shoulder, tore a sheet of paper from the notepad by the kitchen telephone and quickly wrote: "P: I'm at Trish and Allan's. Come there as soon as you get home. Urgent. J."

47

Jackie arrived without warning on Trish and Allan's doorstep ten minutes later. Allan had gone to pick up a crib they'd chosen from the local baby-furniture store, but Trish was home working at a small desk tucked into a corner of their front hall.

"Boy, am I happy to see you," said Trish, chattering over her shoulder as she led Jackie into the living room. "You've just spared me the ghastly task of trying to balance our checkbook. It's like asking Christo to wrap the Philippines. Too big a job. I haven't had the guts to do it for the past six months, though Allan doesn't know that. If I were really rich, I'd have a personal accountant do the dirty deed for me." Trish abruptly stopped talking and stared at Jackie. "What's wrong, Jackie? You look terrible."

"Everything."

"Oh, my God. Nothing's happened to Pete, has it?"

"No, thank goodness," said Jackie. And then she started to cry.

"Jackie, what is it?" said Trish anxiously. She lowered herself carefully onto the couch—she was so huge that she looked as if she might have the baby tomorrow—and patted the cushion beside her. "Here, sit down. Now, tell me what's going on."

Jackie, talking rapidly, described the exhilaration of her run and then her impulse stop at the thrift shop. She had just gotten to the part about finding the bracelet when Allan's portly figure struggled through the door. He entered back first, pulling a large, flat cardboard carton behind him.

"You can pay a fortune for something, and they'll still ask you to assemble it yourself. And now the stores have made it chi-chi, with their knockdown this and their knockdown that. I'll tell you, knockdown or not, this son of a bitch crib weighs a ton. Hard to believe it's designed for an eight-pound baby."

"Honey, Jackie's here."

"Oh, great. Hi, love," said Allan to Jackie, glancing briefly over his shoulder at her, then back to the carton, which he propped up against one of the foyer walls. "To what do we owe the pleasure of your company?"

"Cool it a second," said Trish. "Something's happened. She's just telling me about it."

"Allan, can I bum a cigaret?" asked Jackie.

"I thought you had joined the ranks of the untainted ones."

"Knock it off, Allan. Give her one," snapped Trish.

"Sure thing," said Allan. He unzipped his jacket and reached into his shirt pocket for his pack of Winstons.

Jackie inhaled deeply, once, twice, three times, and then the doorbell rang. "That's Pete. I told him to come here as soon as he got home."

As Pete walked through the door, Jackie hugged and kissed him. Then she cleared her throat. "This is what's bothering me, though 'bothered' is not the word for it. I'm terrified. I'm glad you two are hearing this also. Pete keeps telling me I'm crazy, and I'm not!"

She began with Kim and Dave Barnett's relocation to Santo Domingo. "Which was rather sudden," said Jackie, "but even so, I was ready to go along with it. Until Dave's sister showed up. You remember my mentioning her, don't you, Trish?"

Jackie quickly recounted the details of her brief acquaintance with Cat Rogers. How Cat had called to ask for help in finding Dave. Then Cat herself had disappeared. And then Jackie had learned of her so-called suicide.

"So-called?" asked Pete. "The police were satisfied that that's what it was. But what the hell do they know? They should have stepped aside and turned the case over to Agent 36-B. Besides, after what we learned from that credit investigator, the whole thing does make sense. You said so yourself."

"Yes, I know I did. But I've thought about it some more, and I'll tell you something, I don't believe the Barnetts went out and spent all that money. I don't believe they're chasing all over the country under madeup names. And I don't believe that Cat killed herself because she discovered her brother was in trouble. That's ludicrous. I think somebody helped Cat do what she did. I think somebody didn't want her making waves."

"There you go again, Jackie. Cooking up a good old-fashioned conspiracy."

"God damn it," said Jackie angrily. "You make it sound as if this whole thing was a figment of my imagination."

"Hey, listen, you two, pipe down," said Allan. "If we wanted referees' jobs, we would have signed on with the NBA. I, for one, want to hear Jackie out. She's a nervous wreck, and I want to know why."

"I'm sorry, darling," said Pete, putting his arm around Jackie's shoulders and pulling her close to him. "Allan's right. It's just that I hate to see you so upset. I'll shut up. I want to help you, but I still don't know what's wrong."

"Don't you see, Pete?" said Jackie excitedly. "First the Barnetts. Now the McDonalds. Two couples literally disappear overnight from the same apartment building. Within a few months of each other. Doesn't that seem just a little bit strange to you?"

"Well, yeah, it would *if* that were the case. But how do we know the McDonalds won't be back when they said they would be? Jerry called me on the phone, and Francie wrote you. What more do you want? And as for the Barnetts, I don't know where they are, but they're probably having a good time wherever they are. I don't understand: What's bothering you now, right this minute, that wasn't bothering you before? You've known about all of this for a while."

"I'll tell you what," said Jackie, her voice surprisingly level. "This morning I discovered something that proves that the McDonalds' . . . mercy mission to Ohio," her voice shook, she wasn't really up to sarcasm, "is just as phony as everything else."

Quickly Jackie told them about finding Francie's bracelet in the thrift shop and then about the dead fish and plants in the McDonalds' apartment.

"I agree that a bunch of belly-up goldfish isn't the prettiest of sights," said Pete, "but you know Sylvia. She's probably been so busy with those inane card parties of hers that she forgot to stop in at their place. I see your point about the bracelet, though. That is odd. Unless Francie lost it and someone else turned it in. That could happen, you know."

For a long time no one spoke.

Allan, looking distressed, stood up and announced that he imagined they could all use a glass of wine. "On second thought, maybe we need something stronger, like brandy," he said, heading toward the sideboard.

Jackie, exhausted, slumped against the back of the couch. She followed Allan's progress through glazed eyes. There was a slight hitch to his gait. Suddenly it reminded her of something.

"Pete," she demanded, "doesn't it seem like too much of a coincidence, even for you, that the man who stole your jacket in the park resembled the same person who mugged Allan?"

"You never told me that!" said Allan.

"I decided I was wrong. It wasn't the same man."

"Well, thank God for that at least," said Allan. "You know, Jackie, maybe these things that are bothering you *are* coincidences." He held up his hand to silence Jackie before she could protest. "It *is* possible. But I don't like the smell of this whole situation. Unfortunately, I don't think you have a strong enough case to bring in the police." He paused and turned from Jackie back to Pete, then continued. "I don't want to interfere with your lives, but given the way Jackie feels, I think you should move out of your apartment."

"What!" said Pete, incredulous. "Move out of the best apartment with the best rent in the whole of New York City? You must be kidding."

"Pete, I don't think you understand what Jackie's going through. You're so into that apartment you're oblivious to what's going on around you."

"What do you mean?"

"Look, maybe you think Jackie is going through some kind of sick fantasy, but one thing you can't dispute is how upset she is."

"That's not fair."

"It is so!" said Allan and Trish. Pete, clearly taken aback by their unanimity and vehemence, remained silent. Trish seized the initiative.

"You're in great physical shape now, both of

you, but apart from that, it hasn't been the happiest of times for you."

"Here," said Allan, who was holding a bottle of Remy Martin. "Let me pour us some of this high-octane stuff. I think we need it."

"I don't like to sound like a superstitious nut," continued Trish after Allan had sat down again, "but maybe this apartment is some kind of jinx for you. Did you ever think of that, Pete?"

"Okay, enough, I give up," said Pete wearily. "Jackie, you've been awfully quiet through all of this, but it doesn't take an Einstein to figure out that you agree with all that's been said, and I guess it's probably the right thing to do. Obviously, you're more important to me than the apartment. So let's get out. It'll take a month or two, but we'll find something else."

"Hold it," said Jackie. While the others had been talking, she'd rooted around absentmindedly in her pockets and had felt the scrap of paper she had picked up earlier in the McDonalds' apartment. Now, staring down at what was written, she felt alone and vulnerable. It didn't matter that her husband and her best friends were with her. A fear as real as the room they sat in gripped her.

"Look at this," she said, smoothing out the wrinkles in the piece of paper and laying it on the coffee table for the others to see.

There, repeated a couple of dozen times, was Francie McDonald's signature. No one spoke. They seemed puzzled.

"What is this?" Pete finally asked.

Jackie silently turned over the piece of paper.

They could see now that it was a small sheet of personal stationery, folded outward. In the middle of its upper half were the initials "SG."

"Oh, my God!" said Pete, his voice shocked.

"What is it? I don't get it," said Trish.

"'SG' stands for Sylvia Goodman," said Jackie, exhaling a thick cloud of smoke. "She's the person who was supposed to be watering the McDonalds' plants and feeding the fish. She's a handwriting expert." Jackie gave a short, bitter laugh. "It looks like she was practicing Francie's signature. Getting herself in shape to write me a little note from Ohio."

"Call the police!" said Trish.

"I'm afraid you may be right, Jackie," said Pete, "but how do you prove it? Do you know how difficult it is to verify a person's signature? They're still arguing over which of Howard Hughes' wills is authentic, and it's more than two years since he died."

"What are you saying?"

"Simply that I don't believe the police are going to be interested in the McDonalds, one way or the other."

"Why not? You just said yourself that I may be right. Well, I'm worried to death about Francie and Jerry, and I want to know where they are. And knowing that would answer some pretty basic questions for us, too."

"What do you expect the police to do?"

"For one thing, they could contact the police in Cleveland."

"You must be joking!" said Pete, looking at Jackie as if she'd lost the power of reason. "Do you

think the New York City Police Department goes
in fishing expeditions? Don't you think maybe they
have enough to keep themselves busy right here?
Enough dead bodies, without having to go poking
round the boondocks for ones that might not exist?
And where are they going to look? Who knows
Francie's parents' names? And why should they
look? Missing persons? If anyone had filed a missing
persons report, the police would be getting in touch
with *us*. Not the other way around. Jackie, don't
you see? The police would just laugh at us."

What Pete said made sense. Jackie felt sick with
impotence.

"Besides," added Pete, "if the police were to take
this thing seriously, I'll bet you they wouldn't want
us to move out of the apartment. They'd want us to
stay right where we are. To see if anything else
happens."

"Nothing's going to make me stay in that apartment one night longer!" said Jackie.

"I'll tell you what," said Trish. "No one's going
to be moving into our nursery for two months—the
doctor says three, but the way I feel, I know it's
two—so why don't you guys stay here until you get
this business straightened out? Maybe everything
will turn out to be all right, but I know how Jackie
feels. Pete, why don't you go back there and get
some clothes? Jackie can wait here with me."

"I'll go with you," said Allan. "And I'll get us
some more cigarets." He picked up the empty pack
and hooked it into the wastepaper basket in the
corner.

Jackie and Pete conferred about what clothes

Pete should pack. As he and Allan headed for the door, Jackie said, "And don't talk with anyone. *Not anyone*. I don't want them to know where we are."

"That's crazy."

"Maybe, but that's the way I want it."

48

One large suitcase and two smaller ones. The portable typewriter. His navy blazer and a glen plaid suit. Jackie's camel's-hair coat and her boots. His briefcase and Jackie's. Pete surveyed these belongings, which he'd piled near their entrance, then turned to Allan. "I guess these'll hold us for a few days." He glanced regretfully toward the living room, filled now with late afternoon sun. "Until I can persuade Jackie to move back."

"That's not going to happen, my friend."

"No, I suppose not," Pete answered, smiling ruefully. "From now on I'm going to let her play it her way. Right or wrong."

"Do you think there's any truth in what Jackie thinks is going on here?"

Pete stared at Allan.

"How could there be?" he answered. "It's preposterous. Things like that don't happen. Maybe all this . . . this paranoia is a delayed reaction to losing the baby. I hate to give up this place, but seeing her miserable is a lot worse. She's always had a hyper imagination, but this story she's pieced together happens only in . . . books."

They both laughed.

Loaded down like a pair of Sherpas, Pete and Allan made it down to the foyer in blessed silence before the front door banged open. And there were the Macraes . . . and the Jensens . . . and the Goodmans. They were dressed in their powder-blue jogging outfits, and they were still flushed from running. Phoebe Jensen's dark hair spilled from under her blue knit cap and curled damply and becomingly around her face. She had never, thought Pete ironically, looked so charming. Almost girlish.

"Well, well, well," boomed Arnold Jensen. "Where're you off to? I thought you just got back from somewhere. California, wasn't it? Surely you're not going on another trip, are you?"

"Hi, everybody. No, we're just moving in with some friends for a couple of days. They've had an illness in the family, and we have to help them out." Pete noticed Arnold looking at the amount of luggage they were carrying. "Well, we may be there longer," he added quickly. "A week or so."

"Dear me, I hope it isn't serious," said Phoebe.

"Not very. They just need us to watch the kids," answered Pete, sounding unconvincing to his own ears.

Arnold switched his attention to Allan, reaching out to shake hands.

"Forgive me for not saying hello earlier. I didn't recognize you at first, Mr. . . ."

"Anderson. Allan Anderson."

"Of course, Mr. Anderson. It's a pleasure to see you again. So," he asked, turning back to Pete, "you and Jackie will be staying with Mr. and Mrs. Anderson?"

"Oh, no," said Pete too quickly. "We'll be with some other friends. Allan's just giving me a hand. Now, if you'll excuse us, we're a bit late. . . ."

Pete tightened his grip on the heavier of the two suitcases and, balancing the typewriter and the loose pieces of clothing with his other arm, edged toward the door.

"Will you be joining us in the morning?" asked Ben Goodman. Sylvia was standing at his side. As Pete took them both in in a quick glance, it occurred to him that in Sylvia's sharp, steady gaze there was nothing whatsoever that suggested an absentminded person. Could Jackie be correct?

"I'll be working out, but it may not be convenient to do it with you. But don't worry, I'll stick to it. Promise! Now, we've got to go," Pete said, as he backed out the door.

Pete and Allan hurried down to the sidewalk. A taxi was turning in from Madison and, after a round of cheery goodbyes, they made their escape.

"That was a mistake," said Pete.

"What?"

"Didn't you notice? Arnold figured out immediately that we're staying with you. I might as well have announced it straight out." He laughed drily. "God, I'm getting as suspicious as Jackie. You'd

think they were some kind of gray-haired Tong
from the way we're carrying on. Promise me one
thing though, Allan. Don't tell Jackie that they
know where we're going to be. It would really
spook her."

49

Jackie fixed her eyes on the towering plume of water that exploded skyward in the distance from a small pile of rocks in the middle of the East River. A light wind caught the cascade of water and sprayed it outward in a sweeping, fluttering arc. The Delacorte Fountain was New York's answer to the Jet d'Eau in Geneva, and for Jackie, it provided the perfect distraction from the mechanics of her morning run. Shifting her gaze from the fountain and from the river traffic moving around it, she saw that the halfway turn was just ahead of her. At the fence by the heliport, she reversed direction and began her swing northward toward the Andersons' apartment. Another week of these East River round-trips, and then on to a new course.

After a frantic two-week, flat-out search, Jackie finally had found a new apartment. They had

signed the lease the previous day, and they expect
ed to move in the following week. If the movers co
operated.

The apartment was in Gramercy Park. Though
they weren't on the park itself, they would have a
key to its elegant private gardens. The gardens
with their well-tended gravel paths and flower beds
discouraged anything more vigorous than walking
(Or pushing a baby carriage. Trish's proximity had
rekindled daydreams of motherhood.) For running
there were footpaths and promenades circling lower
Manhattan's riverfront and, on high-energy days
the glorious span of the Brooklyn Bridge would be
within striking distance. But what really mattered
was that the move entailed a complete change of
neighborhood. There would be sixty-four people-
packed blocks between East Eighty-third Street and
their new address, and little likelihood that Jackie
and Pete would accidentally encounter the denizens
of Number Twelve.

Of course, the new apartment was a distant second to the one in which they'd been living. The
ceilings were lower, the rooms smaller, and the
pullman-style kitchen as tight as the one they'd left
behind in their old West Side apartment. The rent
was one hundred and seventy dollars more a
month. None of these things concerned Jackie in
the least. She knew they could be happy there, and
when she expressed this thought to Pete, she realized with a jolt that she had ceased almost entirely
to think in those terms. Worry and anxiety had
been the staples of the past half year. Now, even in
the short time they had been with Trish and Allan,

Jackie had felt a return of confidence. She was sleeping better and her energy seemed limitless. As she thought about this she lifted her legs higher and stretched her muscles into a longer stride, half in a parody of the fine amateur athlete that she was, half in earnest. Damn it, but that felt good. She still intended to run in the Perrier Open. She certainly didn't plan to alter her lifestyle because of their break with the "old folks." It was Pete who'd noticed that she'd begun to refer to the Twelvers in that way. She supposed it was because she no longer saw them as a threat.

The more she thought about it, the more she was willing to concede—to herself, if not to Pete—that she had become obsessed with them. She forced herself to confront the full implications of her actions the day she'd run in fear from their apartment. Without saying it, she had been accusing them of murder. From the unfeverish perspective of the present, the idea seemed . . . farfetched. There were rational explanations for everything that had happened, including the appearance of Francie's bracelet in the thrift shop. What it came down to, she admitted now, was that she didn't like the Macraes, the Jensens, and the Goodmans. More accurately, she despised them.

She'd seen nothing of them in the last two weeks, thanks probably to her decision to shift her running route from Central Park to the river. Now, straight ahead, the end of her run came into sight. It was funny, but she had never felt comfortable running here along the river. She felt somehow as if the regulars were keeping tabs on her, taking her measure.

Often she deliberately looked other runners in the eye to see if she could determine by some flicker in their expression how she was doing, but she never saw anything there except disinterest. At these moments she rebuked herself: She was being paranoid again.

Gratefully she turned off the promenade and walked up the slight incline toward York Avenue. She did not look back. Had she, she might have caught sight of Ben Goodman and Victor Macrae standing against the railing that ran along the river. They examined the stopwatch Victor held in his gloved hand, then hurriedly left the promenade.

They exchanged no words. They had no need to, for each man wore a smile of deep satisfaction.

50

The movers had finally promised them a date, and the Lawrences were to move on the following Tuesday.

Pete thought it would be a good idea to pack up their valuables and a few personal items themselves, and in her new mood of calmness, Jackie agreed. It wouldn't hurt to see the old folks just once more. Besides, she'd done a small calculation of her own that was like taking out flight insurance: It guaranteed a safe landing. Recently she'd noticed another connection between the Barnetts and the McDonalds. The Barnetts had left for Santo Domingo in late July. Jackie remembered the pleasant time they'd all had relaxing in the sauna only a few days before then, and Dave's commenting on how out of shape they had been when they'd moved into Twelve East Eighty-third the previous November.

Which would have made it nine months earlier. When the McDonalds had left for Ohio, they had been in residence precisely the same period of time. She and Pete had moved in at the beginning of May. That would mean, if one subscribed to this morbid bit of reasoning—*if*—that they had a month's period of grace before *their* nine months were up. Not that Jackie believed in this kind of nonsense, but it was comforting somewhere deep down.

Pete rented a Ford station wagon from Avis, and by half-past eight Saturday morning they were on their way back to Number Twelve. The building was quiet when they arrived. The old folks must be out on one of their long weekend runs. Bless them for their predictability. Jackie didn't kid herself that they'd be lucky enough to avoid seeing them altogether, and so she and Pete had concocted an explanation for their departure from the building: Jackie was moving up in the world of Bendel's. The store was giving her a crack at designing store campaigns, including windows. The catch was she had to do it on her own time. She'd need space to work in at home and lots of it. The room they'd made into a study for Pete wouldn't do. Jackie would need her own studio, even though this meant giving up the apartment. They hated to have to do it, but this could be her big break. Naturally they'd honor any rent obligations.

Though their tale couldn't pass a logic muster on *Zoom*, they thought it would play.

As soon as they walked into the apartment, Jackie felt a surge of nostalgia. Everything looked

> pretty. She let the charm of the scene wash over
er, then, with a wrench, turned her back on it. She
ulled a cavernous suitcase down from the shelf in
ne bedroom closet and began to empty into it the
ontents of her bureau drawers. Pete went to work
a the living room, clearing tables and shelves of
ne mementos and art objects they'd collected since
hey'd been together. Jackie had just finished pack-
ng a drawer full of sweaters, velour pullovers, and
hallis shawls when she heard glass shatter. She
valked into the living room, and there was Pete
eaning their Paul Jenkins litho against the wall. A
ine of broken glass, like a failing corporation's for-
unes, zigzagged down across the face of it.

"It slipped from my hands. Now the move's offi-
:ial," said Pete sheepishly. "Here, help me with the
est of these pictures."

Pete and Jackie were balancing a large botanical
orint of a sunflower between them when they heard
a knock. Jackie opened the door on the third knock
:o find Ben Goodman and Arnold Jensen.

"Well, hello!" said Ben expansively. "Great to
:ee you! We've been wondering when you'd come
1ome. We hoped it would be in time for Christmas.
Arnold and I are just back now to pick up jackets
'or the others—it's colder than we thought—and
we heard sounds from your apartment. We couldn't
resist poking our heads in. How're your friends?"

"Just fine, thanks," said Pete hastily, realizing at
once that Ben was referring to the mythical family
with the unnamed illness with whom he and Jackie
were supposed to be staying.

"Marvelous," said Ben. "Then that means you'll be moving back any day."

"Well, not exactly. . . ."

Jackie took the cue and plunged in. "I'm the one who's to blame here," she began, then she quickly fed them the story she and Pete had agreed on. The men's faces sagged as they listened.

"Why didn't you tell us you needed a studio?" cried Arnold. "We can easily arrange that for you in the gym. The light's perfect. We'll carve a little portion of it off for you. A little corner just for you. How about that, Ben?"

"Absolutely," said Ben. "No problem. What we'll do is take the section to the left of the sauna, move the treadmill out of there and over by the Nautilus, where it belongs anyway. Then we'll—"

"Wait a minute," said Jackie. "I'm afraid you don't understand. We've signed a lease for a new apartment. We're moving in on Tuesday."

"Are you serious?" asked Arnold bleakly.

"I'm afraid so."

"Oh, dear," groaned Arnold. "Phoebe's going to be crushed. She and I—all of us—think of you as part of our family."

"Don't worry. It's not as if we're moving out of the city or anything like that." Jackie spoke gently. The two old men seemed so genuinely distressed that she felt a tremor of guilt. She knew the feeling was irrational. She and Pete were the injured parties, not the other way around. "We'll come for lots of visits," she added, with less conviction.

"Well, what's done is done," said Ben with a show of good humor. "Can we give you a hand?"

"No, thanks," said Pete. "We've got everything
ader control."

"All right, then, I'm sure we'll see you before
ou leave. In fact, we'll make a point of seeing
ou." Nodding goodbye, the two men closed the
awrences' door behind them and retreated down
e stairs.

"Do you think they bought our story?" Jackie
hispered.

"Does it matter?" asked Pete.

Jackie thought for a moment, then shrugged.
ete was right. The only thing that mattered was
aat they were getting out of here. If the old folks'
elings were hurt, that was too bad. She was sorry,
ut that was their problem.

Pete found some good rock on the radio, and he
nd Jackie got back to their packing. Two hours
ater they stopped to contemplate the impressive
aound of possessions piled by the front door: a
alf dozen cartons filled with their Wedgwood
Wild Strawberry" service for twelve, their silver-
are—still unmonogrammed—and, wrapped in the
ages of a Sunday *Times,* all the trinkets gathered
ff tabletops and bookshelves. There were three
uitcases of clothing, Jackie's two favorite Chinese
orcelain lamps, and all their wine and liquor. Pete
nd Jackie were debating whether to take a break
or sandwiches before or after loading the car,
vhen the front doorbell rang.

"That'll be Ty this time," said Jackie.

"What do you mean?"

"I forgot to tell you. Tyrone wanted to help, so I
uggested he come by around ten. It's now . . ."

Jackie looked at her watch, saw that it was almos
twelve, and didn't bother to finish the sentence
"Oh, well," she continued, "at least his heart's i
the right place."

"Sure thing," said Pete, snickering and rolling hi
eyes upward.

"Be quiet," said Jackie, laughing. "He migh
hear you."

She opened the front door. There stood Phoeb
Jensen staring soulfully at her, large teardrops i
the corners of her eyes poised to cascade down he
cheeks at the smallest provocation.

"Arnold's told me your news, and I'm devas
tated," Phoebe snuffled. "Do you mean it?" Sh
waited a moment for an answer and, receivin
none, continued. "I see that you do. Well then, yo
must do us one last kindness."

"Yes?" said Pete obligingly. Jackie tried an
failed to catch his eye.

"After you've finished your packing, please won'
you stop by for a short farewell drink at ou
place?"

"Of course. We'd love it," said Pete.

As soon as Phoebe had left, Jackie hissed,
"What's wrong with you? Jesus!"

Pete shook his head. "I know how you feel, but I
think you're going overboard. I think they really
will miss us. Be a sport. It won't take more than a
half hour."

"Okay. *You* go. I'll wait in the car."

"Come on, Jackie. You're being silly."

"All right. All right. I'll play the good wifey. I
still say she's one of the world's great phonies,

though. My God, couldn't you see what a performance that was? But, never mind, let's get this stuff downstairs, then we'll stop by. But no more than a half hour. *On the clock.* Then we'll celebrate with a real lunch. Omelets at the Westbury."

"Sold."

"I'll tell you one thing, though," said Jackie, venturing a little joke, "you can bet your life I'm not going to drink any more of that organic witch's brew."

51

They were all there. Phoebe and Arnold, Miriam and Victor, and, of course, Ben and Sylvia. All dolled up in their running blues. And Richard Kelly. Now that was a concession. On a Saturday—one of the two big business days a week for real estate heavies. Who would have guessed he cared that much about them? And Eileen Cole, and Buddy and Lil, and—Jackie was relieved to see them—the young Brazilians, Rosanna and Jorge. She exchanged greetings with Rosanna, who had made dramatic strides with her English. She was so warm and open that Jackie regretted she wouldn't get to know her better.

Arnold walked up and kissed her on both cheeks.

"We all agreed we couldn't let you two go without some kind of little gathering, impromptu though it might be."

The others hung in a circle around them.

"It won't be the same without you dears," said Miriam Macrae, reaching out to pat Jackie on the arm. "Now tell us about the new apartment and the promotion. I understand you're destined to become a fixture of the *Women's Wear Daily* columns."

Jackie launched into their story of what she would be doing at Bendel's. Victor stood beside Miriam, listening intently, his head cocked. Jackie noticed that a small tic pulsed sporadically in the corner of his left eye. Now and again by some tiny gesture or mannerism the old folks betrayed their age, and though Jackie never really let herself forget it, it always was jolting to be reminded of their true chronology. Suddenly she caught sight of Phoebe wielding her pitcher of pink punch. Nudging Pete, she nodded in Phoebe's direction, just as Phoebe looked over toward them.

"I have a confession to make," said Jackie, grinning at Phoebe.

"As if I couldn't guess . . ." Phoebe raised the pitcher toward Jackie in a salute.

"That's it exactly. But it's me, not your punch. I just can't drink anything sweet. Pete makes up for me."

"He's such a dear," Phoebe said fondly. She handed a glass of punch to Pete, who drained it in three gulps and held the glass out for more. "Well now, Jackie," she continued, "if you're going to pass up my punch, the least you can do is try one of my Granola-plus cookies, or my feelings really will

be hurt. Here . . ." She commandeered a glass plat-
terful of dark brown knobbly homemade cookies
from Sylvia. "This is my own adaptation of one of
Adelle Davis' classic recipes."

Jackie reached out for a cookie and nibbled it
politely. It was surprisingly good, like the cook or
not. She took a second and put it down on one of
the shelves of the bookcase beside her. "For later,"
she said to Phoebe conspiratorially, playing at
Phoebe's game of being best buddies. Perhaps she
had been too hard on the old gal.

Turning again to the Macraes, Jackie saw that
Eileen Cole had intruded herself into their group.

"Been to Brownie's lately?" Eileen asked.

Jackie shook her head negatively, her mouth
filled with the cookie.

"Well, I'm happy to say, there's no need to any
longer. Did you realize our neighborhood is burst-
ing with new establishments? Why just last week I
tried one on Eighty-ninth and Madison. 'The Eating
of the Green' they call it, and it's every bit as good
as Brownie's. Of course, they don't dare call themselves 'health food' restaurants. But it amounts to
the same thing—lots of veg and grains, the best
darn fuel a person can give his or her system."

"Absolutely! You're so right!" said Jackie, managing to keep her voice free of even a hint of irony.
And then she heard herself throw out a question
that almost startled her: "What do you hear from
the McDonalds?"

"Oh, didn't you know?" said Victor. "They'll be
coming into town in about ten days. Only a little
later than they'd originally planned. They decided,

since they were already there, to spend the holidays with Francie's parents, who're doing just fine, apparently."

"I'm so glad," murmured Jackie. Oddly, she believed Victor. She took a couple more cookies from the plate which Phoebe had left on a table within reach. She had not realized until now how hungry she was. Oh, how good the cookies tasted. She felt happy. Warm and safe. She just wished everyone wouldn't talk so loudly.

"We're pleased, too," Victor was saying. "For Francie and Jerry's sakes. And *ours*. It's a relief not having to look for more new tenants. It's *so* hard finding the right people."

"Ladies and gentlemen," said Arnold suddenly, in a strong, clear voice. "May I have your attention? We have a special presentation to make to two special people. Jackie and Pete Lawrence. This is a sad occasion for us, but, though they will soon be gone, they most assuredly will not be forgotten."

"Hear, hear," said Ben Goodman.

Jackie felt herself blushing. She glanced nervously toward Pete, who leaned nonchalantly against a doorjamb. He seemed to smile at a secret joke. A band of sweat circled his brow.

"Most especially," continued Arnold, "they will not be forgotten next month. I refer, of course, to the Perrier Open. We think of you still as *our* team, and we will be rooting for you all the way. Now, on behalf of all of us, I want to give you a small token of our affection." Phoebe handed him a package wrapped in red tissue paper. "Don't be shy. Who's going to do the honors? Jackie? No? All right, Pete, here you go."

Pete moved forward and shook Arnold's hand. "This is mighty nice of you," he said, smiling in formal acknowledgment. He called Jackie over. Together they pulled the paper away, and there, in their hands, were matching red satin running shorts and zippered jackets. On the left pocket of each jacket their names were embroidered in royal blue script in the best 1940s gas-station-attendant style.

"These are wonderful," exclaimed Jackie, whose embarrassment had given way to real delight. "Where on earth did you get them?"

"You are viewing the handiwork of our own nimble-fingered Mrs. Goodman," said Arnold, gesturing toward Sylvia. They were both terribly solemn and Jackie realized that neither one had a clue as to what charmingly campy outfits they had produced.

"We had planned to give them to you on the eve of the race," continued Arnold, "but . . ."

"You are very sweet, all of you!" Jackie suddenly found herself hugging Arnold. Then all at once she was surrounded by the others, kissing and embracing her, eyes moist, voices melting. She felt lightheaded, drunk with emotion, and all her anxieties and apprehensions were fading away with the certainty that they were leaving and that these were good and warm and affectionate people—whom, yes, she would miss—when she realized, in a frozen instant of chilling clarity that cut through her euphoria, that she was the only person eating the cookies and that Pete was the only one drinking the punch and, in the same split second of horror, that the other young couple, the Santos, were no longer there. Suddenly the voices of the others seemed terribly far away, and she knew that something was very wrong.

Part Three

52

It was a marvelous party. The music was supplied by six musicians who played languidly and wore white tails. It floated in and out of hearing, but sounded mostly like a brook. That's it, thought Jackie, a babbling brook. Boy, was that wild. She saw that everyone was in white. Must be my wedding! Wait a sec, Pete and I were married in Larry Fraiberg's apartment, and the only people wearing white were the bartenders. But everyone at the party looked so elegant. There was Ben Goodman, beatific in icy white satin robes—he was dressed like a Bedouin intern!—twirling about the room like a dervish. Around his neck hung a huge, shining stopwatch.

Wow! Look at Eileen Cole! There she was in a pearl-white body stocking gracefully pirouetting around a shopping cart full of organic vegetables, gleaming with freshness. She waved gaily to Jackie. Jackie waved back. And then she felt terribly embarrassed. There, next to her, lying on a couch made of spotless brocaded silk, Pete slept! God, what bad manners! His rudeness would make Eileen angry. She pssst! at him again and again to no avail. He just slept on. Suddenly a big, shaggy St. Bernard, with a coat as white as a glacier, began to lick her forehead. At first, Jackie was scared. But then she realized that Victor Macrae was holding the dog's leash.

"Don't be afraid," said Victor.

As a matter of fact, it felt good. Her brow was hot and dry and the dog's tongue was cool and smooth. But wasn't a dog's tongue supposed to be rough? No matter. Take it easy, kid, and enjoy it.

"That's it, Jackie. Relax. That's a good girl."

Hey, you creep, I'm nobody's good girl! Pete could never understand why she got so irritated by the way they treated her. They treated them both like dumb kids.

"Ben, how's her blood pressure?"

"One twenty-one over seventy-three. She's stabilized."

"Good. She's in excellent condition, Ben, for such a truncated training period."

"Thank you, Victor," said Ben. He moved forward and leaned over Jackie and smiled reassuringly at her.

"Hi, kid," he said, his face inches away from hers. "You're fine. Just take it easy. Everything is going to be all right."

Jackie saw now that he had discarded his satin

robes for a smock of some kind. He was so close to her that she could see the oil in the pores of his face. His breath was strong and sour.

"Get away," she shouted. Ben didn't blink an eye. His smile deepened as it hung above her. She felt a rush of loathing and reached up to push him away. It was then that she realized she couldn't move her arms or her legs. She tried desperately to shake her arms free. Jesus! She was strapped in place. A wave of confusion and fear swept over her, and it was only her chance sighting of the bottle of liquid suspended above her that saved her from going under. Of course! She was in a hospital. Hospitals restrained patients so they wouldn't harm themselves tossing and turning. Her relief at this discovery made her smile, but even as she did, she came up against another question that sent a sharp chill through her: If this was a hospital, what was she doing here?

"Why am I here?" she whispered. But there was no response. Victor and Eileen now stood beside Ben. Damn them. Were they deaf? "Why?" she repeated. *"Why?"*

She knew she must be yelling, but when she stopped to listen to herself, she couldn't hear a thing. There was silence, except for the murmur of the brook. She followed the murmur to a corner. There it was. A plastic contraption that tumbled back and forth like one of those silly wave machines. Except the liquid inside wasn't blue. It was dark red.

"Easy does it," said Victor. "Stop trying to talk.

Arnold's due on the next shift, and I'll recommend to him that we remove your gag."

Gag! Now she understood. The words she had spoken aloud were only in her mind. Mercifully, she dropped into a deep black pit and sank into the bottom without a sound.

Jackie had no idea how long she'd been out, but it must only have been for minutes. Nothing had changed. Above her was the same frieze of blurred faces. Her eyes began to focus, and she recognized the thin, bony face of Eileen Cole. Was Eileen still angry at Pete? Pete! She had forgotten all about Pete. Terrified at what she might see, she jerked her head to the side. And there, to her left, he lay on a stretcher. So peaceful, so calm. Too calm. Just as fear began again to well up in her, Pete moaned and stirred.

"He's fine," said Victor reassuringly. "He'll be coming around soon. We gave him a bit too much atropine. Every now and then, we overcompensate for the weight factor."

"If you and Arnold would listen to me, you wouldn't keep making these dangerous miscalculations," said Eileen snappishly.

Victor chuckled patronizingly. "How does telling college kids to eat a proper breakfast make you the expert on physiology?" he asked. Then he turned back to Jackie and continued in a voice as smooth as a skipping stone. "But it's not Pete that concerns us, dear. It's you. You just gave us a real fright. Please try to relax. We've given you a mild Thorazine compound that is extremely restful if you don't

resist it. It's important to you, and to us, to keep
your blood pressure steady."

Victor's voice went in and out like a shortwave
radio. Jackie's mouth felt dry and gummy. Victor
kept talking, but Jackie had trouble following him.
She couldn't take her eyes off the IV bottle suspended above her, its snakelike tubing coiling down
into the crook of her arm.

"The exsanguination process is not affected by a
patient's being unconscious. But Arnold and I have
always felt that it was important for our young
helpers, like you and Pete, to understand, to really
share, this glorious adventure."

Victor paused, as if waiting for Jackie to ap-
plaud his sentiment, and in the quietness of the moment, Jackie thought, what process? What
adventure? She looked desperately toward Pete for
an explanation, and saw that he had drifted off
again. Turning back, she caught only the last of
what Victor was saying: ". . . will be here any
minute. So, please, just rest."

Rest! As if she had any choice in the matter.
Well, maybe she did. She should try to figure out
where she was. Really open her eyes. There must
be a giveaway.

Damn this nightmare! Wake up!

She looked around her. Every surface in the
room was white, from the shiny tile floor and lac-
quered walls to the lowered ceiling. Above where
she and Pete lay were two rows of high-intensity
lights, but there must be others as well, for the
room seemed to shimmer. It was like being in the
center of a sunburst after a heavy rain, and yet she

saw no windows. Pulleys, cords, bottles, tubes, and dials engulfed their beds. Victor, who stood beside a sleek, highly polished console studying what looked like a printout, caught her eye and nodded genially to her. Ben and Eileen were now seated at a low white table near the wall opposite them and, though Jackie could not raise her head high enough off the pillow to absolutely confirm it, it appeared that they were playing Scrabble. How peculiar. Scrabble, indeed.

Just then a sound intruded itself on the hushed room. It was puzzling, yet somehow pleasant too: a low, whirring noise that carried with it a hint of promise, like the tickle of a roulette ball running against its wheel. By the time Jackie realized she had been listening to a combination lock being turned, the ticking gave way to the sound of well-oiled tumblers falling into place and then to the sharp, authoritative crack of a bolt being thrown back smartly.

Now Jackie knew exactly where she and Pete were. And terror streaked through her like a gazelle fleeing a predator.

The door opened, and there stood Arnold Jensen. He loomed in the entranceway just as he had that day long ago when she had surprised him here. Only then she and Pete had been on the other side of the door.

This was no hospital. This was the basement of Number Twelve East Eighty-third Street. They were in Arnold's laboratory, and she and Pete were his . . . patients? No, nothing so simple as that. They were . . . guinea pigs. No. Worse than even that. Sacrifices. Yes, that was it. A wave of nausea coursed through her. She stared at Arnold as he glided calmly toward her.

"Hello, my dear," he said, when he reached her side. "You're looking well." He gently brushed a strand of hair from her forehead. At his touch, Jackie wrenched away from him, her face flushed. "Your eyes have never looked lovelier," he continued, unperturbed, "but you mustn't upset yourself. You'll only make it more difficult. I know you're frightened, but you needn't be. You won't suffer in our hands. You and Pete are like our own to us. Now, if you can, think back on all the happy times we've had together, while we attend to Pete. It's time to wake him."

Arnold signaled to the others, and they crowded around Pete, blocking off Jackie's view. She stared helplessly at their white-smocked backs, praying they knew what they were doing. Then she heard Pete groan, and her eyes stung with tears of relief. Arnold flashed her a smile of accomplishment, as if he'd just delivered a baby.

"You and Eileen take your break now," he said to Ben. "Who's scheduled to come on next?"

"Sylvia. And Miriam, too, I believe."

"Fine. Tell them there's no rush, though. We'll buzz them when we need them. How soon can we begin phase two, Victor?"

Victor nodded toward the dark red liquid cresting back and forth. "The process is a little slower than usual, but the product's excellent."

"Good, that's all that counts, and this time we

can afford to wait for it. Ben and Eileen, go get some sleep. We'll keep you posted on our progress."

Eileen, carrying the maroon Scrabble box under her arm, hurried out the door after Ben, and Arnold bent silently over Pete. His eyes kept blinking open, then fluttering shut again. Jackie strained her head in his direction and tried furiously to catch his attention. It was no use.

"As you can see, Jackie," Arnold said, approaching her, "Pete needs a bit more time to himself. Now, in the meantime, if you promise to behave yourself, we'll remove that adhesive. Do I have your word? No fuss?"

Jackie nodded, and Arnold began tenderly to ease the adhesive from her mouth. Before it was half off, Jackie started to scream.

"Stop that," commanded Arnold. "Look what you're doing to Pete."

Arnold's voice had the force of a slap in the face, and Jackie fell silent immediately. She looked quickly at Pete and what she saw shocked her: He was fully awake now, but his eyes shone with unalloyed terror.

"Oh, Pete, honey, I'm sorry," said Jackie in a choked whisper.

"Now do you see why we felt we had to gag you? Not because we were afraid of sounds reaching the outside world. No," he paused to laugh drily, "this room is a marvel of engineering. I only wish more people could have the opportunity to experience it. It is the flip side of an acoustically great concert hall. A sound-dampener, rather than a sound-amplifier. A Carnegie Hall in reverse. No, what we were afraid of is what just happened: You've upset yourselves by trying to communicate. There's no need to speak to each other. We will make everything clear in due time."

While Arnold had been speaking, Jackie murmured over and over again, "It's okay, Pete, I'm here. It's okay." Gradually his neck muscles relaxed, and then once again he fell asleep.

"What time is it?" asked Jackie abruptly.

"Quarter to two."

"That can't be. It must be much later. We didn't get to your apartment until noon."

"Quarter to two at *night*, Jackie. You've been here for over twelve hours."

"Twelve hours?" repeated Jackie, struggling to absorb what Arnold had just told her.

"It was a close call, too. We didn't know your effeminate black friend was planning to join you. But our timing was fortuitous. He showed up on the front doorstep a mere five minutes after we brought you down here. It took a lot of talking to persuade him to leave. He has, by the way, a filthy mouth."

"Why are we here?" asked Jackie.

Arnold ignored her. "What do you say, Victor," he said, raising his voice slightly. "How much more time does Pete need?"

"Ten minutes. Maybe fifteen."

"We'll answer all your questions then, my dear."

Arnold reached for a fresh towel from the side table between the two beds and wiped the film of perspiration away from Jackie's forehead.

"Don't touch me," she snapped, startling herself by the loudness of her voice.

"Now, now, Jackie," said Arnold admonishingly. "Remember your promise to be quiet. Think of Pete."

Jackie fought off a wave of dizziness. "What are you going to do to us?" she managed to ask.

Arnold watched her silently, without a flicker of expression.

"Look, I don't know what you have in mind. I don't want to know. But that's just it. Pete and I haven't any idea what's happening. We couldn't explain this to somebody if we tried. And I swear to you we won't try."

"You called the police once before," said Arnold coldly.

"What are you talking about?" asked Jackie, her mind blank.

"Come now, Jackie. Think. You can't have forgotten Dave's sister already."

"That was different. But how did you know about that?"

Again Arnold did not answer, and this time there really was no need. Her suspicion that Arnold and Victor knew everything there was to know about their lives turned to certainty, and the room began to spin violently. She had to clench her teeth to stifle her hysteria. Intense fear tore into her, like a branding iron in her guts.

"Please," said Jackie, her voice dropping to a whisper. "Please don't hurt us. We haven't done anything to you."

Arnold remained silent.

"Please let us go," Jackie pleaded openly. "If you untie me, I know I can get Pete out of here by myself. There'll be no witnesses. We'll disappear, and you'll never hear from us again. Your secret is safe."

More silence.

Desperately Jackie pushed off on another tack. "You've been like parents to us. We've always said that. Ask anyone. Ask Trish and Allan Anderson. We love you. And you've always said you love us, too. Like your own children. You wouldn't hold your children against their will, would you?"

She searched his face for some response and, seeing none, knew that nothing she had said made any difference to him. In the silence that grew between them she became aware again of fear pressing at the edge of her consciousness. And then she knew what it was. It was the fear that the same thing was going to happen to them as had happened to the others. They were going to die.

When Jackie opened her eyes again, she became aware immediately that Pete was awake.

"Hi, darling," he said. His voice was blurred, but he was smiling. "Don't worry. Arnold's told me . . . everything's . . . everything's going to be . . . everything's all right."

"Pete, they're going to kill us!"

"Be silent, Jackie," said Arnold. "Get control of yourself."

"It will . . . all . . . all be okay."

"Pete's right," said Arnold. "Of course, you're frightened. But you'll feel better in a few minutes. Victor is going to give you both a mild Demerol compound, and it will only be the briefest moment before you feel totally at ease and happy.

"Before your senses become pleasantly fogged again, I want to thank both of you for what you're about to give. We've all, by the way, liked the two of you enormously. Yes, even loved you. You represent so much of what is truly beautiful and wondrous in mature youth. And the way you both threw yourselves into training. Especially you, Pete. We had some doubts about you. Oh, not because of your desire. We saw you had that right at the beginning. No, it was your body type. Endomorph. A tendency to be . . . chunky. But Ben thought you could do it, and he was right.

"But I am getting ahead of myself. I've made this little speech many times before and I've found it works a lot better if I start at the beginning. That was in 1937. More than forty years ago. I was forty-seven at the time and attending the twenty-fifth reunion of my class. I was Williams 'Twelve. Without polishing my own apple, I looked pretty good, and by that time I also had accomplished quite a bit, though, as it turned out, I had not yet begun what I later came to consider my life's work.

"I had been fortunate enough to inherit a sizable income on my thirtieth birthday, which from then on made it unnecessary for me to work. I was able to pursue freely the two interests that I regarded as paramount and that filled me with immense satisfaction. One was my vocation: anthropology. The other my avocation: physical fitness. In those days, keeping fit, especially jogging, was thought of as being, well, eccentric at best. Jogging! No one had even heard of the word. And when most people thought cholesterol was a distant star, I stayed rigorously away from it in my diet. Well, you can imagine my surprise the first morning of our weekend reunion, to find a fellow jogger beginning to work out. We talked for a few minutes and then ran six miles toward Bennington. We hadn't been friends as undergraduates and, actually, only vaguely remembered each other. But we immediately realized that our interests, dreams, and fears were identical. That man was Victor Macrae."

Victor smiled and bowed in a courtly fashion toward Jackie.

"Luckily," continued Arnold, "we lived near each other. Victor in Greenwich. He commuted to New York where he worked as a research biochemist for Squibb. And I lived here. In this building. It was left to me as part of my inheritance. It was only a matter of a year before Victor and Miriam sold their house and moved in here with Phoebe and myself. We realized that we shared something that we never thought we could voice to ourselves, let alone to another human being. And that was that we didn't want to grow old. We didn't want our muscles to grow slack and listless. See our mouths tighten into small frightened sphincters, ready only to kiss death. And we didn't want to die. Of course, then, as now, everyone accepted aging and death as inevitable. But Victor and I said no. We wouldn't go without a fight.

"Back then, in the thirties, the idea of extending one's lifespan beyond what was decreed by nature was strictly a flight of fantasy. Of course, there always have been some people who believed you could trick death. Victor, you're the scientist here. Tell Jackie and Pete a bit about some of the experiments."

"Fascinating stuff from the very start," said Victor, setting down the needles he was sterilizing. "And sometimes a little offbeat. Hindus sought the fountain of youth by eating the testicles of tigers. Raw! Taoists believed that the secret of long life was in saving the male seed by—I always find this hard to believe—routing it through the spinal cord to the brain. In modern times, efforts to prolong life have been just as zealous. Freud tried a vasectomy, once thought a life-extending procedure. He lived until he was eighty-three, so it might have helped him. Other, more gullible men had primate testicles surgically added to their own, and many of them died from infection."

"The handiwork of a certain Middle European quasi-doctor," interjected Arnold angrily. "He should have been hanged!"

"Happily, abominations of that kind are a thing of the past," Victor continued calmly, ignoring Arnold's outburst. "Today aging is a subject for science, as it should be, and in the last twenty years the advances have been breathtaking.

"Consider that each of us has a biological clock inside us. It's set to run for a particular amount of time, and when the time runs out, that's it. *Finis.* We die. Now, however, gerontologists are beginning to think we can control the clock. Make it go slower so we can live longer. They don't know yet what turns the mechanism on or off. But they're determined to find out. They've accomplished wonders in their labs with mice, cockroaches, fruit flies. Doubled and quadrupled their lifespans, extended their ages dozens of times over. Hopefully we are next in line. By the way, they're not talking about increasing our lifespans ten or twenty years. They have in mind life expectancies of two, three, or even four hundred years. Heady stuff. But it hasn't happened yet. Until then, there are common-sense measures that all of us can take—they won't hurt us and they may help—like vitamin concentrates, enzyme punches, lots of physical activity, and low-calorie, high-fiber diets. As you know, we adhere to these practices at Number Twelve. But they are not, in and of themselves, enough to give us many extra years on earth."

"Let's get back to how it all began," interrupted Arnold impatiently. "For us." Victor nodded, and Arnold continued.

"If it hadn't been for a strange accident that occurred shortly after I met Victor at our Williams' twenty-fifth . . . well, probably none of us would be around today. Or, if we were, we'd be doddering in nursing homes in front of an *I Love Lucy* rerun. As it is, the work that's being done now, in the seventies, was first begun by us forty years ago.

"In 1938, a few months after Victor and Miriam had moved in here, I made one of my frequent trips to Central America. I had been doing research at Columbia on a pre-Mayan civilization that existed in what today is called Belize. Then it was British Honduras. My object was to trace some pottery fragments found near Merida to a pattern that I felt had its origins in Belize. I smile now when I think how desperate I was to find those few shards of pottery and what I finally came across.

"We were flying from Panama City to the dig, which was about a hundred miles northwest from Belize. We were in perfectly clear weather, no more than an hour from our destination, when we crashed. The pilot, a Mexican, had miscalculated our fuel. That error killed him and severely injured a young Ph.D. named Crawford. Crawford survived because he was in fabulous shape. He had rowed eights at Harvard and Oxford and had stroked them to a win at Henley. He stood six-four and his muscles were like whipcord.

"That night, however, it came home to me that probably both of us were going to die. Though I had escaped serious injury and only suffered from bruises and shock, the possibility of getting out alive seemed remote. Crawford only had moments of clarity, and I had never felt so alone in all my life. And then the Cluzares came. I had heard of them before, but had never expected to see them. They were probably one of the last primitive hunting bands in the new world that practiced, or so we thought, cannibalism.

"What was known of them came from the few missionaries who escaped with their lives. The semi-civilized tribes that abutted their region refused to go into their territory. With clockwork regularity a member of a nearby tribe would disappear while going for water or journeying to another village.

"The Cluzares were nude except each had a

small gourd, tied by a vine around his waist, that contained his sex. Their faces were painted vermilion with black raccoon circles around their eyes. They were all in excellent health, and none seemed to be over thirty.

"They were fascinated and delighted by Crawford. They stroked his limbs and made cooing noises at him as they patted his face. They made litters out of bamboo and carried us for hours. We reached a small village as dawn broke. Their camp was built around one large building where the men lived and the key ceremonies were conducted. It was surrounded by similar round houses for the women and children.

"In the weeks that followed, the Cluzares cared for Crawford as if he were the Christ Child. They fed him the choicest vegetables and fish. He rapidly recovered. Though they didn't pamper me with the same intensity, they provided me with ample food, and I, too, quickly regained my strength. It was then that they started to bleed Crawford."

Jackie stared at Jensen. She couldn't have spoken if she had wanted to.

"The bloodletting was crude and probably painful, but Crawford didn't complain. It was later that I realized that they had been feeding him some kind of narcotic in his food. Day after day they bled him. They would make an incision in either his thigh or his upper arm each day and take out a little less than a pint a day. To Crawford's blood they added a milky liquid that they made out of two roots.

"And so I slowly watched Crawford die. For the

first two days there was no discernible change. After all, there are eighteen pints of blood in the body and you can lose quite a bit before the effect is apparent. But by the third day Crawford's color was that of a frog's belly, and I shivered as I tried to wipe the sweat, which smelled like a root cellar in summer, off his brow. On the fourth day Crawford started to sing. His voice was low and it took me a while to identify the songs. They were mainly fight songs from prep school—I think he went to Kent—and when I tried to question him, he just smiled sweetly at me and called me Robbie, which was his brother's name. I noticed that the moons of his nails had enlarged and were as white as chalk. By the next day Crawford couldn't talk—his tongue was too dry. But he never stopped smiling. By the sixth day the body's failsafe system started to draw off fluid from wherever it could find it to try to stem the catastrophic process that it blindly fought. The tissues around his eyes started to sink in the way a child's rubber toy slowly deflates from an unintentional pinprick. His stomach began to hollow out as if he were holding his breath. I think he died during the night of the following day. Yet he wasn't at all scared and actually seemed more beautiful each day as he got closer to death.

"For some reason, I instinctively knew that the Cluzares weren't going to kill me. In fact, they really weren't interested in me. This concoction made from Crawford's blood and the roots, they drank daily, treating each drop with the reverence that we would give to a holy relic. Being a trained anthropologist and fluent in more than one Meso-Indian dialect, I was able to put together enough of a Cluzares vocabulary to begin to comprehend what was going on. I also found one of their calendars and quickly calculated that they were all a good deal older than they appeared to be, forty or even fifty years older.

"The Cluzares had found a way to prolong life by almost halting the aging process. Their secret was confirmed for me when, almost a week after Crawford's death, a Cluzares hunting band brought in two young men from a neighboring tribe. The men were terrified. They knew what lay before them. The good food and care that they received did not in the least allay their fears. Once again I witnessed the process that Crawford had undergone. But I had no fear for my own life at all. You see, I was too old.

"It took me almost two weeks to walk back out to civilization. The Cluzares provided me with food and escorted me to the borders of their territory. I carried as many examples of their ceramic work as I could. I also took several samples of the two roots. My 'escape' was hailed at the time and reported around the world. The names of Speke and Burton were even invoked in one of the more spirited accounts in the *New York Post*. By the way, it was quite a different paper then.

"About a year later I returned with Victor. People thought we were at best foolhardy; more likely, insane. But I knew better. All told, we made three trips to see the Cluzares and learn more about their great secret. Alas, as I once told you, they were wiped out by an influenza strain that was brought to them by some missionaries. But, fortunately, their most important gift had been passed on.

"Victor worked for over five years to synthesize and perfect the active ingredients contained in those two roots. By this time we had become friendly with Ben Goodman. Though we scrupulously watched our diet and exercised diligently under Ben's supervision, we were aging with a frightening rapidity. It was then we decided to take the big step. Not for just ourselves, but for all mankind.

"We knew we couldn't realize our goal without further help. And so, in short order, we gathered into our little band first Eileen, and then Richard. And through Ben, we were joined by Buddy and Lil. Buddy had once been in charge of athletic equipment for Ben. Later, after we had begun to perfect our methods, my niece Allison was brought into the fold. We've had our differences with Allison recently. She's finally joined another group, though the damage has already been done. Her retrogression is a sad and sorry sight, but we think fondly of her still. That surprises you, Jackie? That there are other groups like ourselves? It's true. We are no longer alone.

"Vanity, fortunately, I feel, is not served by the process. We have found that it actually takes almost two years of treatment before aging stops. And then there's only stabilization of aging, not return to youth. So we can't go back to a thirty-inch waist and a facial tone as taut as a drum. Luckily, we were able to seize an age that still contains an amazing amount of vigor. Though we gaze less appreciatively as we pass a mirror, life, in its most important sense, is fuller.

"One day, not too far in the future, we'll be able to show the world the miracle we've accomplished. And that miracle will be your doing also. In the beginning we had great difficulty in locating subjects like yourselves and getting them motivated enough to let us condition them until they reached that peak, what we call 'the glow'—when they were ready, or rather their blood was ready, to help seek the true miracle of life. The thing that enabled us to have a steady supply of helpers was the housing shortage that sprang up full-blown after the war. It gave us just what we needed: mature, healthy people. And we gave them what they needed: a great apartment on the fashionable East Side."

"Arnold, I think it's time," said Victor.

"Of course."

And before she could unscramble the maelstrom of grotesque thoughts that were slashing her mind, Jackie felt the cool breeze of alcohol wiped on her arm, followed by a sharp prick. And then nothing.

53

As soon as Jackie woke, Arnold leaned into her line of vision. "Hello, there," he said cheerfully.

"What time is it?" she asked. Although she was groggy and slurred her words, she was instantly aware of the situation. It seemed essential to get her bearings.

"You've slept through almost an entire day. It's nearly nine o'clock at night. We debated waking you earlier, but you seemed so exhausted we let you sleep. I hope it'll reassure you to know that you are almost halfway through the process."

"Is Pete all right? When's he going to wake up?"

"Soon. Don't concern yourself, by the way, with the fact that he's had a stronger reaction than you to the drugs. It sometimes happens. He's not feeling discomfort. He's in remarkable shape."

As Arnold spoke, Jackie let her eyes slide away

from him to quickly take in Pete lying next to her. She realized that there was something changed about him. He was lying on his side. His restraints had been removed. Slowly Jackie raised her own hands up.

"That's right. I was wondering when you were going to notice. At this stage we always remove the straps. It gives the proceedings more dignity. But go easy. You'll find if you try to move too much you'll pass out. You're very weak."

Arnold was so voluble, thought Jackie. The professor in him had taken over again. He needed to explain. He needed understanding and approval. It occurred to her that if she could keep him talking, maybe he would give away some small piece of information that she could use. She knew she must act. If she didn't do something soon, it was all over. She *was* weak. But she knew that she wasn't as weak as Arnold thought she was.

"Why us?" she said, asking the most important question first.

"You've asked the question I hoped you would, dear Jackie," said Arnold. "As I mentioned before, we want you to know everything. Both of you. Unfortunately, though, I know from past experience that Pete will be too hazy when he regains consciousness to follow our conversation, so there's no point in delaying.

"We chose you partly by chance, but mostly by design. You were thoroughly screened weeks before Pete 'got lucky' and found your apartment here at Number Twelve. You were the right age, you had the right physical characteristics, you came from the right background.

"We've always demanded that our helpers be splendid physical specimens and, so far, we haven't had to compromise our standards. You were in pretty bad shape when we recruited you. You ate too much. You drank too much. You were incredibly lazy. And, Jackie, the number of cigarets you smoked was a gross insult to your body. We knew, however, that you had both been first-rate athletes in school, even though Pete has always had a tendency to put on weight. And, more important, we knew that you had the drive, the *will* to achieve 'the glow.'

"You were the right age. At first, years ago, we looked for younger helpers. Seventeen- and eighteen-year-olds. But the results were unsatisfying, like undercooked chicken. We soon concluded that our candidates had to be between the ages of twenty-eight and thirty, an age at which the body had the ideal proportion of muscle to fat tissue.

"Lastly, we've required that our helpers have no immediate family. No parents. No siblings. Yes, I know the question you're going to ask, and the answer is, it was a mistake. We didn't realize Dave Barnett had a sister. Can you blame us really? You know the circumstances. It was the first mistake of that kind that we've made in eight years, and it made us all desperately unhappy. Taking someone's life is a very serious thing, and we have never been willing to do so unnecessarily. Such a pretty girl, too. But we had no choice.

"And you remember Mr. Landers, the credit investigator. He is one of us, of course. From San Diego. They do dress so peculiarly out there. Anyway, we knew you were growing more and more puzzled and upset about the Barnetts' disappearance, so we wanted to reassure you. We thought Mr. Landers could make some sense out of it for you. Landers had wanted to act when he was young. But the last time he was on stage was as an undergraduate at Stanford. Considering the hiatus, I think he did a fine job."

Jackie spoke with an effort. "What about the McDonalds? And Francie's parents?"

"You mean the automobile accident in Ohio? That also was concocted for your benefit. Francie's parents *did* die in a car accident, but that happened when Francie was a sophomore in high school. We were positive she hadn't told you about it. So when we needed to explain their disappearance, we brought her parents back to life."

A wave of rage swept through Jackie. She thought it would overwhelm her and that she would pass out again.

"Actually," continued Arnold, "that wasn't Jerry who called Pete in California. It was a tape of his voice that we'd made earlier. We had to give you some warning that the McDonalds weren't going to be around when you returned. And we knew that by then Jerry would no longer be here to help us himself. So we called on the talents of our own Richard Kelly. Electronics is a little hobby of his.

"You know, that's what's so wonderful, Jackie. All of us contribute to the general well-being. Each and every one. It's teamwork all the way. We rely on Eileen Cole for the initial screening. Because of those years she spent at CCNY, she has access to all sorts of state and city records. Dozens of information/data banks are available to us. Once we find a pair of potential candidates for one of our apartments, we bring in Richard's real estate agency. That questionnaire you were asked to fill in was, of course, a plant. It always amazes me, in this computerized society of ours, the extent to which an individual's personal life still remains personal. The computers don't turn up everything. Then we have to make a direct appeal to the person in question. Just as we did with you. We can't be too thorough in checking out our candidates. Once by mistake we got a couple in here who broke up after three months. What a mess. We'd already invested a lot of time in training them, and we really had to scramble to replace them."

"Why couples?"

"We need two people at a time, and couples with stable relationships are easiest to deal with. We *could* recruit two single people, I suppose, but the building isn't set up for that. I'd hate to have to divide these lovely apartments into studios."

Jackie was still puzzled by their insistence on couples, and her lack of comprehension must have been apparent.

"The *volume*, Jackie," he said. "One person isn't enough. We need two people to give us the correct volume."

Of course, thought Jackie bitterly. She closed her eyes, and began to laugh softly.

"There, there," said Arnold, touching her shoulder. "It's difficult, you know, finding appropriate couples. Especially when we throw in extra specifications, as we did this last time with the Santos. We wanted a couple who didn't speak English. We thought all you young people were becoming a little too . . . what shall I say? Cozy. We want everyone here to be friendly. But not too friendly. It's a fine line.

"Once we've selected a couple, the rest is easy. The building has never let us down. An apartment here is an irresistible lure. We usually approach our couples indirectly. With the Santos, we put the word out via a Latin American society whose board I'm a member of. We'd already run a complete check on them, so it was just a matter of letting them know about the apartment.

"And then there's the stolen jacket routine. We've used that one many times. It's a very effective way of making it seem as if a new couple arrives here totally by chance. And it gets everything off to such a happy start, too, with the new couple thrilled by their stroke of great, good fortune.

"Buddy's got the whole business down pat. At first, he didn't want to come in with us here at Number Twelve, but we made him a great offer. He was exactly right for us in so many ways, and we liked the idea of a black super for its cliché value: It's the expected thing in this neighborhood and goes virtually unnoticed. Don't underrate Buddy, by the way. Sometimes it suits him to play the slow black, but he's a smart man. Most of the time. And versatile, too. It was Buddy, of course, who took care of Allan Anderson. We couldn't let you and

Pete break training for a trip to Europe, and an *eating* trip at that!

"The thing that most grieved me—I should say all of us—was the miscarriage. We all love children, so it was very hard for us to face. But, you see, we had to. A fetus is such a drain on the resources that we need. As it turned out, it proved more difficult to accomplish than we imagined. We were certain that the episode in the garden would do it. Why, when Ben tested the loose step, even while holding the railing, he almost took a bad tumble. But we didn't calculate on the reflexes of true youth. We were lucky with the park incident. We had followed you on your bicycle route many times before. It was a crude plan, but it worked. By the way, I was the man in the deerstalker hat. I knew that the singularity of the hat at a calculated distance would produce the right effect. Panic.

"Then there was that untidy business with Francie's bracelet. It was Buddy's one mistake in all these years. When I confronted him with it, he told me he had needed some extra money and he was sure we'd never miss the piece. So he decided to pawn it. Then, imagine, he got confused and ended up in a thrift shop instead. At that point, he got scared and left the bracelet anyway. Which brings us to where we are now. The normal training period is nine months. Odd that it should be that, isn't it? We're ahead of schedule by almost one month, but, even so, you and Pete are in the peak of physical condition. You have achieved 'the glow.' And for that we have Ben to thank.

"He's an incomparable trainer, remarkably attuned to the potentials of all our young couples. He's able to select exactly the right mix of exercises for each one of you. When we were first starting out, he followed the lead given him by our subjects themselves. If someone was a weekend skier, Ben brought him to the point where he could negotiate the Nosedive at Stowe with ease. If they liked to get out on the tennis court, he made them into A players. But we soon found that that approach wasted too much time and energy. Now Ben almost always chooses a combination of swimming and running as the fulcrum of his training programs. Swimming for the all-around workout it provides the entire body. Running for something a little more spiritual, for the attitude it fosters of perseverance, of never giving up. Ben's able to gauge the exact level of stress at which each individual's body begins to metamorphose, and he knows precisely when to move a subject from one plateau of achievement to the next. And he has one more very special quality. He's a wizard at reading the psyche. It was his idea to ask Allison to be such a flirt with Pete. Not for his sake. For *yours.* He reasoned that a little sexual jealousy would motivate you to start your training, and he was so right, wasn't he? And imagine, you were jealous of a woman of sixty-three! That's Allison's true age. ·

"Yes, we all do our best to help. Phoebe and Miriam's cooking makes dieting a pleasure. And Sylvia's genius as a handwriting expert is critical. In your case, I don't know what we would have done without her. We had to call on her on at least three different occasions. And, naturally, Richard wired your apartment for sound. After all, we had to monitor you on a regular basis to see how faithfully you were following your regimen. Some things we were forewarned of, other things we were able to prevent outright. Such as your indulgence in marijuana. Really, I thought that was passé by now. Such a destructive habit!

"You see, Jackie, how much we care for you? For you, and for future mankind. You and Pete are pioneers in turning the world into a golden age and someday, in the not-too-distant future, your names will be enshrined in textbooks."

Arnold paused and let his glance linger long and tenderly on Jackie and then on the sleeping form of Pete. Jackie stared fixedly at the older man. His words sounded muffled, and she was afraid she might pass out again. She knew that if she did, she'd never wake again. She bit her lower lip in an effort to keep herself alert.

"As I mentioned before, Jackie, we are no longer alone. Over the years we have carefully nurtured contact with others, and now our research is being duplicated, even amplified, by them. There *are* problems yet to be resolved. The injections are beginning to lose their potency and that worries us greatly. Perhaps you noticed yourselves the extreme fluctuations in our well-being, from the vigor of 'the glow' to . . . near collapse. Thank goodness the revitalizing power of the injections is almost immediate!

"Do you recall the day you surprised me coming out of this very room? I was in such buoyant good health that I felt sure you'd notice it and surmise what was happening. Then we would have had to sacrifice both of you. But I realized right away that I simply was projecting my own fears. There was no way you could have guessed that the Barnetts were making their first contribution. The fluid is strongest when it is freshly drawn. Just as it was that day. In between tapping the resources of new couples, we make do with injections of frozen material, and this is where our procedures are less than perfect. Something in the freezing process robs the fluid of much of its . . . punch, but I'm confident that soon we'll have conquered that problem too. Mended our fences, and gone on. On and on, for that is the essence of our effort."

"Excuse me," said Arnold, responding to a sudden ring from the telephone that sat on the table where the Scrabble game had been underway earlier. "That must be Victor. I'm expecting him any minute."

As Jackie watched, Arnold's face darkened. He seemed shocked. He held the receiver away from his ear, inadvertently letting Jackie hear the thin reverberation of what must have been a loud shout. Then he crashed the receiver down.

"That degenerate black friend of yours is back!" he sneered. "How dare he bother us at this hour! It's almost ten o'clock. This time, he's got some effete pals with him. They're demanding to see your apartment. They're saying if we don't admit it's available for rental, they'll report us to the city. For discrimination against homosexuals. Christ! But he'll see."

Arnold panted, as if he couldn't get the words

out fast enough. His emotions seemed to have taken him over.

"He knows too much. He's been a little too chummy with you in that cute little cubicle of yours at Bendel's. Maybe we'll have to deal with him the way we did with your friends, the Andersons. Yes, that's right, Jackie. Mr. and Mrs. Anderson and child-to-be died last night in a mysterious fire that swept their apartment. CBS News reported this morning that the fire department is puzzled. I can personally guarantee that they'll stay puzzled. Now, I've got to go upstairs to help the others get rid of that . . . that loathsome creature. Don't worry, I'll be right back."

It took Jackie a moment to realize, after Arnold had slammed the door, that she and Pete were alone—and that Arnold had not locked the door behind him. Immediately she began to struggle with the adhesives binding her to the IVs. From somewhere inside herself, she found the strength to pull off the tapes, and then slowly she began to ease herself off the stretcher. An inch at a time. She threw a quick glance at Pete. It was up to her, her alone, and she knew it. Now she was ready to try to stand. She grabbed the edge of the stretcher to steady herself, but she was up; she didn't fall. Then, with her heart pounding and dizziness spinning her like a carousel out of control, she reached the door. Then the far wall of the basement. Then a window. This was the way out. Could she pull herself up high enough to get through it? She had to break the glass first. As if in a dream, she swung her elbow against it and shattered it. Her sleeve caught on a

jagged shard of glass that held the fabric for a moment before she was able to free it. Then, before
she could make a move to get through the window,
she heard Arnold coming down the stairs. She
dropped to a low crouch and, with one last burst of
energy, hid herself behind some trash cans on the
opposite side of the wall. She was surprisingly calm.
And then a wave of blackness washed over her, and
she was again floating on a dreamless sea.

54

Jackie was running. Faster than she had ever run before. But why was everyone passing her? The harder she pushed, the more people sped by. It was almost as if she were on a treadmill. Sweat poured off her like rain sheeting down a windshield. Come on, kid. Pick it up! And then she heard Arnold's laugh. It was right behind her. That horrible dry laugh, like walking through leaves. The laugh came closer. And closer. And then she woke.

For a moment she didn't know where she was. And then it all flooded back. She didn't know how long she had been crouching here behind the cans. Minutes? Hours? She knew only that she had lost enough blood to have made her almost helpless. The memory of dragging herself out of that room came back with frightening clarity. And to have to leave Pete there! Easy girl, she thought, you're not bleached white yet. You're going to find a way out. For yourself. And for Pete. You must.

The light at the top of the stairs snapped on. Jackie willed herself not to move.

"We have no problem as long as we stay calm. In her condition she can't have gotten very far."

It was Ben.

"How can you be certain she got out?"

Eileen's voice was tight as a hacksaw blade.

"There you go again, Eileen. Can't you for once trust the evidence of your senses? You saw the fabric caught on the glass. What more do you need?"

That was Victor.

"Victor's right. Panic will get you nowhere. Buddy and Arnold are out searching now. They'll find her."

That was Ben again.

"We should *all* be out there looking for her."

"Don't be ridiculous, Eileen," said Victor irritably. "Have you forgotten the little matter of the consulate across the street? The cop who stands out front may not be the smartest, but even he would get suspicious if we all poured out on the street in the middle of the night. But they'll find her. She probably passed out within a hundred feet of here."

Victor stopped talking and rapped the laboratory door sharply. Jackie heard the twirl of the combination lock and, a moment later, the sharp retort of the bolt opening. And then, as the door opened, that incredibly harsh, flat, white light illuminated the basement. Jackie knew they had to see her now. She tightened herself into a smaller ball.

"Victor, has Arnold—"

And then the door closed behind them, and Jackie was once again submerged in the warm folds of darkness.

She knew she had to get out fast. She wouldn't have a chance of escaping in the daytime. And if she stayed where she was, it was only a matter of time before they searched the basement thoroughly and found her. She thought how nice it would be to sleep just for five or ten minutes. A little nap. For only a delicious few minutes. No! Get that out of your head! What had Victor said? Something about Arnold and Buddy. Yes. Arnold and Buddy were out there looking for her. Okay, girl, very quietly let's get up and out of here. But which way? The back door? No. If one of them were nearby and heard her, there would be no place to hide. The window? She didn't think she had the strength to get through that. That left the front entrance. But wouldn't they surely be waiting right there? Let's face that when we get there. She slowly raised herself up. Her joints were stiff and cracked with what sounded to her like explosions. They had to hear that. She stood there with the stillness of a wading bird. Nothing. She took a first step, and her head started to spin like a child's toy. Hold it. You *can't* pass out. They'll hear you fall. Then they'll find you and they'll put you back in there. Back with Pete. Side by side. Drop by drop, dying. You're going to faint. No way. Her head cleared, and she walked slowly, achingly, toward the stairs. Thank you, Ben. Thank you all for putting me in such great shape. I'm strong. Stronger than any of you realize. You've bled me, but I have more left than you could ever imagine. I'm going to get out of here. Yes, damn it. I'm going to escape. And I'll be back to get Pete. And then I'll see every one of you rot before my eyes.

Whatever pain and agony she had experienced in running was like nursery school compared with what she was going through now. She had to will herself to take each step. And then she was at the foot of the stairs. Her eyes, adjusted now to the darkness, peered up at the towering stairs in front of her. She remembered a drawing of the main tunnel that led to the Pharaoh's vault in the Great Pyramid. How that tunnel, canted at an unnaturally steep angle, seemed to stretch into infinity. It had nothing on these stairs. Come on, kid. You have to move. She counted each step as if it were a lash against her back. She reached the top, and she knew that she mustn't look back. Now, open the door to the front hall. Just a little way. Easy. The door was well-oiled and opened silently. She had to stop here for a little rest.

The hall on the other side of the door was dark, except for the light cast by a small lamp on the mahogany table. You *are* going to get out of here. Out of this hell. But what do you do now?

The question was answered by the front door's opening. Into the foyer walked Arnold Jensen and Buddy.

Jackie hugged the wall by the stairs, and tried to fade back into the darkness of the corner.

"She's here, Mr. Jensen."

"I think you're right. But first I want to check

the garden again. If she's not there, we'll know she's in the building."

Arnold's voice radiated confidence, and he stepped forward and closed the door to the basement. Then he and Buddy headed for the garden. The back door closed behind them.

Now, Jackie. Move.

She crossed the foyer and tugged the front door open. The cold night air hit her with the slap of a paddle. As she began to shiver, she became aware for the first time of her appearance. She must look pretty freaky in her short hospital gown, with her arms and legs hanging out, naked. Pretty bizarre. But that should help, shouldn't it? Nobody would be able to ignore her.

The street was dark and deserted, but a faint hint of the coming dawn produced a pearl-gray line on the horizon. She edged her way down the front steps and walked as fast as she could toward Madison Avenue. She knew she was lurching like a drunk, but she couldn't stop herself. She stumbled as she neared the corner. Where was everybody? Not a car or a person to be seen. Why hadn't she gone the other way? Past the cop by the consulate. Well, it was too late now. She pulled herself up with the kind of effort climbers reserve for very high mountains. Don't look back, just keep moving. Just turn the corner and you'll be safe. Safe. What a delicious-sounding word.

Jackie rounded the corner and immediately fell into a doorway. You've done it, babe. You got away. You deserve a little rest. A taxi whipped by. And then a police car. You should be out there stopping one of them, kid. But no sweat. Somebody's bound to come along soon, on the way home from a disco or walking the dog. A good person who will stop to help. Break into the basement and save Pete. You really did it, kid. You escaped. Just close your eyes and after a few minutes you'll feel fine. Wake up strong and fresh.

Wait a sec.

Somebody *was* trying to help her stand up. She tried to focus. It was a woman. An older woman. She smelled good. Opium. The new St. Laurent perfume. Now that was class. You flop for the first time ever and end up on Madison Avenue being rescued by an old dame wearing Opium. She was strong as hell, too. She propped Jackie against her side and began to carry her. She must be taking her to a hospital. Bless you, sweet-smelling old lady. And then Jackie was walking up steps. Where are we going now? But it was too tiring to talk. Hard enough to see straight. And then Jackie was sitting down in a nice, comfortable chair. For Jackie, that was always the most important thing in a chair. Comfort. And this chair was like a cloud. Just perfect for a little snooze. Why was the old lady staring at her so closely? Why did she look so familiar? It was only at the moment when she felt the cloth pressed into her face that she remembered who the sweet-smelling old woman looked like. She looked just like Allison.

After

==

Death is an imposition on the human race,
and no longer acceptable.
—Alan Harrington
The Immortalist

At first Vinnie thought the black guy was getting ready to flash. He stood between the trees, almost frozen, his hands deep in his jacket pocket, his eyes locked onto something off to his left. He wore a ridiculous copper-colored Afro wig. Strictly the kind that comes from Forty-second Street. As he got closer, Vinnie almost laughed out loud. But something immediately cut that off. He was about forty feet away and he could see quite clearly that the cat wearing the fright wig was now crouched like a predator. You didn't have to be Kojak to know this weirdo was up to no good. Vinnie carefully put his rake on the ground and started to back off. Real easy, he told himself. This guy's probably carrying a knife the size of a machete. He retreated a bit more and just watched. The guy was like a statue. He didn't even blink. He just stared at the bridge

that spanned the bridle path below the reservoi
He was definitely waiting to rip someone off. An
as a young couple rounded the turn down from th
pump house, the dude very quietly eased himse
erect.

The couple stopped just before the bridge. Th
girl, probably in her late twenties, had long red ha
that wasn't dyed. A sweatband circled her head lik
a cigar band. Even with sweat pants on you coul
see she had a great ass. Her boyfriend seeme
about the same age, and though his face was we
with perspiration, he didn't look particular
winded. They slowly walked toward the bridge. Th
instant he took his jogging jacket off and swung
casually over his shoulder, the dude took off. H
covered the distance so quickly that at the sam
moment Vinnie shouted "Hey, watch out," the dud
snatched the jacket. He turned and ran right bac
toward Vinnie. With an instinct Vinnie didn't thin
he had, he grabbed the rake as the guy raced pa
him, and threw it like a javelin at his legs. Incred
bly, the rake caught him midstride and he tumble
hard to the ground. The jacket flew from his gras
Change, keys, and credit cards burst out of th
pockets like the finale of a magician's trick. Th
man got quickly to his feet, looked at the jack
and its scattered contents for a moment, as if co
sidering whether to stop and try to pick the stu
up, and then, thinking better of it, took off towar
Central Park West.

Vinnie went over to the jacket. As he picked u
a silver key ring crammed with keys, he hear
someone say, "Let me help you."

It was one of those old farts in the powder-blue
gging outfits. He bent down with Vinnie and
lped gather up the credit cards and change.

"That was very courageous of you, young man,"
id a woman's voice behind him. Vinnie looked
und. Another powder-blue. A woman with silly
ngs.

"It was nothing, lady."

"You shouldn't be so modest. If everyone reacted
e way you just did, New York would be as safe as
ndon."

Vinnie grinned shyly and kept picking coins off
e ground.

"Here comes the couple now," said the woman.
Vhy don't you give me those keys. I'm sure they'll
relieved to get them back."

Vinnie handed the keys to the woman as the cou-
e approached. They were with two more of the
wder-blues. Both men.

"You should really thank this park attendant,
ung man," said the woman. "If it weren't for him,
ur jacket and everything in it would be long gone
now."

"Absolutely," said the young guy, energetically
mping Vinnie's hand. "You don't know how
uch I appreciate what you did. Jesus, every damn
edit card and piece of identification I own was in
at jacket. I'd really like to reward you."

"That's okay," said Vinnie, immediately regret-
ng his words. The guy was probably prepared to
y at least a twenty on him.

"Well, then, all I can say is, thanks again. I real-
mean it."

Vinnie, feeling like a fool, stood up and hand
over the change and cards to the young man.

As they all walked off, Vinnie heard one of t
powder-blues say to the couple, "You can call fr
our place."

About a week later, while Vinnie was cleani
the same area with his paper spike, he found a k
ring. It was under a Mounds wrapper. He knew
once that it was the one he'd given to the old la
with bangs. He looked at it closely. There was 1
name on the silver tag. Just the initial 'R.' Hot do
He turned it over and saw the name *Tiffany* in ti
letters. Not bad, Mr. Romano. And, since he
turned down the reward, he felt nothing wrong
stripping the keys off the silver ring and putting t
ring into his jacket pocket. Later he threw the ke
away in a trash barrel near the children's zoo.